# THE HOUSE BY THE SEA

# THE HOUSE
# BY THE SEA

Nicola Thorne

This title first published in Great Britain 2003 by
SEVERN HOUSE PUBLISHERS LTD of
9–15 High Street, Sutton, Surrey SM1 1DF.
Originally published in 1978 in Great Britain
under the title *Rose, Rose, Where Are You?*
and under the name *Rosemary Ellerbeck.*
This title first published in the USA 2004 by
SEVERN HOUSE PUBLISHERS INC of
595 Madison Avenue, New York, N.Y. 10022.

British Library Cataloguing in Publication Data

Thorne, Nicola
  The house by the sea
  1.   Romantic suspense novels
  I.   Title
  823.9'14 [F]


ISBN 0-7278-6023-2

Printed and bound in Great Britain by
MPG Books Ltd., Bodmin, Cornwall.

## Author's Preface

*The House by the Sea* was one of three gothic novels I wrote under a different name in the mid seventies which really marked the start of my career as a full time novelist. I had already had three novels published, but for four years abandoned my career while I ran a small publishing company. Through no fault of mine it ran into difficulties, whereupon I decided to become a writer again and to make, if I could, a profession of it.

Being nothing if not a pragmatist, I looked around to see what people were reading and alighted with enthusiasm upon the idea of the gothic, which was then very much in vogue. This I have defined elsewhere as 'a novel of suspense with supernatural overtones'. The other two, *Haunted Landscape* and *Coppitts Green* (both now published by Severn House), were set in the Yorkshire Dales and preceded *The House by the Sea*, which was inspired by a holiday in France in 1975 in the French port of Le Crotoy on the Bay of the Somme. I found this place fascinating on account of its beautiful setting, its antiquity and also because Joan of Arc had been briefly imprisoned there on her way to Rouen, where she was burned at the stake in 1431.

I can't remember now exactly when I planned the novel because my heroine, Clare Trafford, is a historian and I have always been very interested in history, and was in fact to go on and write a number of historical novels. It could have been an idea that had been germinating since I first stumbled upon the town the previous year.

I took a pretty house for a month, accompanied by my young son, Stefan, and two children of a friend who lived in Ostend, plus a rather difficult *au pair* who was to cause me a lot of grief. So it was a holiday fraught with all kinds of tensions which would probably have made a book in itself.

However, reference to my diary for the period shows that on the whole it was a fascinating and enjoyable holiday, though very hot, and I made copious notes for a possible novel set in and around the town to which I gave another name – Port St Pierre – and in particular on a rather striking chateau which stood by the side of the bay. My diary for August 5 for that year records: 'Began today taking pictures and getting ideas for my book. These two houses on the bay definitely inspire ideas. One is huge, pink-stoned with twin turrets. The other more plain and decrepit but is set among pines. I thought I would set the pink house among the pines.'

If memory serves me correctly, I later found out that the majestic pink chateau was a holiday home for members of trade unions and have only recently discovered it is now a hotel!

Every day I would travel round the countryside with my little brood and make notes for my book while the children played around me. Le Crotoy is very tidal and swimming was not always possible. It also has rather unusual and spectacular flood gates which are opened at certain times and which furnish a dramatic climax to the climax to the novel.

The Somme is also of course very well known as the scene for some of the most horrendous battles in both world wars of the last century and my son recalls, somewhat ruefully, my dragging him and his companions around the battlefields of the Somme, the memorials, cemeteries and trenches in the mistaken belief that it would interest the children as much as it interested me.

Across the bay was the beautiful old town of St Valery which played an important part in the last war. To this and other places I have been given fictional names.

The story of the book is about Clare Trafford, an academic who takes a house for a year to consider certain personal problems and to write a book about Joan of Arc. She becomes fascinated by the noble family living in the chateau, which has three children, not unlike the little flock that I shepherded about with me. She is particularly intrigued by the mysterious, slightly sinister housekeeper Jeanne who may have been a reincarnation of Joan of Arc, or may not . . .

My fascination with the beautiful countryside is evident and, rereading the book after such a long time, I am impressed with all the research I did, not only into the story of Joan of Arc but the ancient dukes of Burgundy and the legend associated with them which forms an important part of the story.

Despite the years which have passed since the book was written I still found it surprisingly modern in outlook and altogether quite engrossing . . . But then I would say that wouldn't I?

There follows the original preface to the book which was published in 1978.

*© Nicola Thorne, Chideock, Dorset October 2003*

### Author's Note

Those who are in any way familiar with the beautiful Bay of the Somme in northern France will immediately be able to identify the towns of Port St Pierre and Port Guillaume, which, in their picturesque settings, face each other across the Bay. They might even think they recognise the château, with its striking position high on the cliff.

They will, however, know that in a work of the imagination an author has to take all kinds of liberties and adapts places to suit his or her purpose; thus the towns exist more in my mind, though I got the idea from reality. So it was with the château. There was this beautiful pink house with twin turrets which I admired from the outside. I turned it round and gave it large grounds, and of course I never went inside, except in the imagination.

Joan of Arc really did lodge in the original château in the town I have called Port St Pierre. Now only a tiny little bit of wall remains and a plaque to say that all those centuries ago she was there. She did cross the bay on her way to her death in Rouen, and I dare say it is pretty much now as it was then.

Finally, although this is not a work of scholarship, I feel I must record my gratitude to Professor Richard Vaughan, whose marvellous series of books on the Valois dukes of Burgundy made me so interested in the subject, though, of course, the de Frigecourt family is pure invention. I consulted a number of works on Joan of Arc but found particularly helpful: *St. Joan of Arc* by Victoria Sackville-West and *Jeanne D'Arc* by W. S. Scott.

In the Tower . . . it is as if one lived
in many centuries simultaneously. The
place will outlive me, and in its location
and style it points backwards to things
of long ago. There is very little about it
to suggest the present . . . It is as if a silent,
greater family, stretching down the centuries,
were peopling the house. There I live in my
second personality and see life in the round,
as something forever coming into being
and passing on.
  —C. G. Jung  *Memories, Dreams, Reflections*


Que voici un bon peuple
Pleut à dieu que je fuisse si heureuse
Lorsque je finirai mes jours, que je
puisse estre enterrée en ce pays . . .
   —Saying attributed to Joan of Arc, 1430

This story is dedicated to my
son Stefan Alexis as a memento
of the wonderful
summer we spent
on the Bay of the Somme.

# A LONG TIME BEFORE . . .

The château, surrounded by its moat, dominated the walled town which served as a major port for the River Somme. Three towers of the château faced the bay, but the windows of the fourth looked in towards the town, and tradition says it is in this tower that she was imprisoned.

Yet she must have seen the sea, her first view of it by all accounts, and the sight of the beautiful bay would have cheered her in the cold and bleak winter days of her imprisonment.

From her window, or the slat that served for a window in that cold medieval castle, she could see the great windmill that stood on a promontory high above the bay, its huge sails turning in the constant winds that buffeted the coast. Beyond it set the sun, when there was sun, and at certain angles the sails of the windmill resembled a cross.

She was there only a month, but during that time she came to love the town and the sight of the windmill. The people of the town were kind to her and became her friends, for she was scarcely out of childhood. Perhaps it was the last happiness she knew before she was sold to her enemies and taken across the bay for the last time. Legend has it that she left a message praising their goodness and saying that when she died it was her wish to be buried among them.

## CHAPTER 1

I first saw the house when I walked round the bay one afternoon early in September, a few days after I'd arrived in Port St Pierre. It was so breathtaking a sight in the mellow afternoon sun—a hazy gold that made the coastline seem incandescent—that I stopped, aware of my bare feet squelching in the wet sand and the tiny crabs and sea insects scurrying to get out of my way. The tide had just gone out, leaving rivulets and expanses of water and the delightful debris of flotsam and jetsam that made the bay a treasure trove for beachcombers and those who dabbled in the pools searching for the crustacean delicacies which were such a well-known feature of the French coast.

Yes, it was a blissful sight—the wide expanse of the bay curving out to the Channel and the huge house standing like a sentinel, its slender twin turrets sharply

13

outlined against the azure blue of the sky. It reminded me of a medieval fairy castle perched on the cliff, with a path winding up to it, just as in children's picture books. It was no grim French *donjon*, however; it was built of warm pink stone, and there was nothing forbidding about it. The conical roofs of the turrets were grey, and all the windows had grey shutters, open now because the sun was low in the sky. A delicate latticework balcony linked the turrets which sat oddly astride the house, one in the back and one in the front, rather than side by side.

In contrast, the grand portico was of white stone with Doric columns, and a gracious double staircase splayed like a fan towards the well-kept formal lawn. Set in the wall was a crest, moulded of the pink stone but highlighted here and there in white. It was too far away for me to decipher.

The garden was formal and heavily wooded; it sloped gently towards the sea wall. The slope enabled one to have a clear view of the magnificent house from the bay, to appreciate the fine details of its architecture, the delicacy of its stonework. It was beautifully proportioned, yet not too regular, with sloping roofs and tiny Gothic spires. It seemed a hybrid of centuries, but mainly eighteenth.

As the sun sank lower in the sky, the house was suffused with a roseate glow, and I knew I had fallen in love with it. Just at that moment, my reverie was interrupted by a dog barking and the screams of small children. The wide front door burst open, disgorging a large black Labrador and three children who tumbled down the princely staircase and romped about on the lawn. I smiled. It was not make-believe after all, but a normal family house.

I was about to continue on my walk, smiling with pleasure at the scene I'd witnessed, when a movement in one of the windows of the turret nearest the sea caught my eye. Someone was standing very still just to one side of the window, looking down on the playful scene below, the three children scampering about, teasing the dog with a ball. A shiver went up my spine—the silent watcher seemed so out of place, almost sinister, in the bright sunlit scene. I felt certain it was a woman, as there was something feline about the shape, but it seemed so strange for her to stand there silently staring instead of leaning over the sill and laughing or talking with the bubbly children playing below. Then the watcher revealed herself, stepping right up to the window in order to look more closely—at me? Her eyes did seem levelled in my direction. I was unaccountably disturbed and quickly resumed my walk, not caring to look back lest that silent predatory figure should think I was prying.

The beauty of the bay was lost to me on that carefree afternoon, as I gazed at patterns in the sand, preoccupied by thoughts of the house and its inhabitants. I decided I was overly concerned, and I turned off the beach, pausing to put on my shoes, after dusting my sandy feet with my hands.

The path from the beach led to the road which I knew would pass the back of the house. I was compelled to follow the road and pleased that I could view the house once again and savour my memory of it when I got home. On either side of the narrow street the small terraced houses clustered together—then the grey turrets were in sight again. I was soon to discover how these dominated the town and formed a landmark for many miles around.

Great walls lined with trees surrounded the back and sides of the house, almost obscuring it, but the upper portion of the house soared skywards, its beauty enhanced by the filigree shadows made by the trees outlining dark niches and tiny roofs with crenellated edges. The large double gate, wooden backed, had a wooden letter box and a small brass plaque beside it. "Château des Moulins," it said. Windmill House.

"Château des Moulins," Madame Gilbert said. "Oh la, la, la, la." And she threw up her hands in her gallic way, gesturing to the sky for all to witness, the hosts of heavenly angels and the rest of them for all one knew. For as I'd found in the few days since I'd arrived in the port, Madame Gilbert couldn't resist making a drama of everything from a simple enquiry about the plumbing or the rent to more worldly issues. She was lost to the Comédie Française, a woman with mobile, expressive features, a gold pince-nez, which I judged an affectation, and a white smock covering her neat black dress. A large gold cameo brooch adorned her throat and a string of glittering beads softened her rather severe appearance. Black stockings and old-fashioned high-heeled black shoes with straps completed her costume.

Madame ran the Agence Gilbert from her salon—poor Monsieur had passed long ago into the oceans of time—she employed a cheerful young woman, Martine, as her assistant. It was Martine with whom I had spoken about renting a house in Port St Pierre for my sabbatical year.

There was nothing at all office-like about Madame's business, but things did get done eventually, and a visit to Madame was an agreeable way to spend part of the day. Her salon had many plants, several glass cases of stuffed animals gazing out with mournful resignation, numerous old family portraits, and a huge roll-top desk at which she did her work.

Madame Gilbert was so enchanted that an English lady, a *professeur*, should choose her modest birthplace in which to spend a year, that she always overwhelmed

16

me with attention. We had taken to each other from that first time a few days ago when I'd stopped to pick up the keys and Martine had climbed into my heaving, exhausted Morris to direct me to 33 Rue du Château. Now it was routine that I stopped by at least twice a day to ask her this thing or that, or some detail about the house I'd rented.

One always had to leave plenty of time for Madame Gilbert. There was no point in being in a hurry to get away, because as she chatted she would stop to instruct Martine in some minor chore, talk on the telephone or speak at length with whoever happened to come into the salon. She had wanted to know all about me, no doubt as a reassurance for Monsieur Giradoux, the proprietor, who lived in Abbeville, but more likely to satisfy her own insatiable curiosity.

Now I waited for the "oh la las" to finish, and for her to rifle among her papers as she always did, and to tell Martine to do something or other, and I sat smiling patiently as I always did.

"Château des Moulins, c'est très beau."

I assured her I thought it was spectacular, elaborating enthusiastically about the architecture, the variety of styles, the colour. She nodded vigorously, but her mouth maintained a downward curve as it did when things were not entirely as they should be. Inevitably bad news was preceded by the expletive "eh."

"Eh!" Madame Gilbert shrugged. "It's a sad story."

Sad? A frisson of fear chilled me as I thought of the beautiful house, the gay sunlit scene as the three children and their dog played on the lawn, and then of that sinister figure as it gazed unsmilingly at them and at me.

"Château des Moulins belongs to the very old family of de Frigecourt. It is only part of their estates, the main house being in Paris and additional properties farther

17

north and in the south. But this was a favourite residence, used in the summer and often in the winter for La Chasse. What a lovely family—of course, I've known them all my life— so talented, handsome. Naturally there used to be a lot of money, but it doesn't make for happiness, as we know."

Madame's mouth drooped, and I felt that the joyful "oh, la las" would not be forthcoming for some time.

"Like all large families of the nobility, they have experienced good times and bad, but the terrible tragedies that befell the de Frigecourts have all been within living memory. In the last war, of the father and mother and three handsome brothers, only two survived."

"Two?"

"Members of the family. The father and two eldest brothers were shot by the Germans for their activities with the Maquis, and only poor Laurent and his mother were left unharmed."

"How awful." I was appalled. "How was the youngest saved?"

"He was too small, only a boy, though the others were not much older, certainly not yet men, except in spirit. Then, poor Laurent, his troubles were not over. Soon after the war, his mother, never strong, died of grief, and he was left on his own in that large house. Then his uncle, who was with de Gaulle in England, had him spirited out of France to safety, to school, so as to be near him.

"When Laurent grew up, it seemed he couldn't bear to return home because of the sad memories, for visits yes, but seldom to Port St Pierre and only for a short time to the Paris house. He joined the wine trade, lived in England, and married an English girl, a young society girl of good connections like himself. He was very happy."

"But what happened to the château?"

"Attendez. I'm coming to that."

Though the story was sad, Madame was a marvellous storyteller and was relishing the opportunity to tell it.

"When his wife saw the château she fell in love with it, and together they opened it and had it restored, beautifully, as you will have seen. No money was spared in making it as perfect as it once was. When it was opened again, only a few short years ago, we were all very happy for Laurent and his lovely young wife, Elizabeth. They had three children—two born in England, the youngest in France—and everything was idyllic. It seemed nothing would touch their happiness, and then . . ."

Then. I'd known there would be a "then."

"Then there was a car crash outside Paris, and Elizabeth was so badly injured she has never spoken since."

"When was this?"

"Well over a year ago, maybe more. She has been in a clinic ever since, barely conscious. Perhaps it would have been better if she had died."

I turned away, my eyes smarting with tears.

"How cruel," I whispered, seeing the children playing on the lawn.

"Sometimes one wonders about the mercy of Providence," Madame Gilbert said, wiping away a tear. "Laurent sent the children permanently to the château, and he works hard, very hard, to forget."

"Will she ever recover?"

"It seems the younger the person, the greater chance of recovery. Still, it has been a long time."

"How old are the children?"

Madame gestured vaguely into the recesses of her salon. "Martine! How old are the de Frigecourt children?"

They were ten, eight, and six respectively, and their names were the eldest, Noelle, Philippe and Fabrice. When they were old enough they would go to boarding school, maybe in England, the two boys to Winchester, their father's old school. Meanwhile there was a nanny and a governess.

"Governess?" The word made me shudder. Shades of Jane Eyre. I thought of the still, silent figure by the window.

"Mademoiselle Jeanne." Madame Gilbert shrugged. "She is supposed to be very clever, but we see nothing of her. We see more of Rose, the young English nursemaid, who is quite gay and likes to help with the shopping. Jeanne is rather reserved, a loner. She spends a lot of time on her own when she is not teaching."

And looking out of windows? I wondered. Then perhaps the situation at the château wasn't so sinister. I had a vision of clever, plain, solitary Jeanne gazing mournfully to sea. Did she have some sad secret in her life? Governesses in books always did.

"It's sad but . . . rather romantic," I said.

"Romantic, yes. Madame is a romantic, n'est-ce pas, Martine?" Madame smiled at me fondly.

"I fell in love with the house too, like Madame de Frigecourt. Do you think I could ever see the inside of it?"

Madame spread her hands expressively. "Oh, la la la, Madame. You are here for a whole year. I think in that time you would perhaps have the chance, although with Laurent not here and the place run by servants, it is not easy."

"The children . . . I saw them today. I love kids . . . Perhaps if they speak English?"

"Ah, les enfants." This was definitely an idea. Madame smiled tenderly at me. I knew that once again she'd endeavoured in her cunning French way to open up part of me that was meant to be kept private. She had managed to learn, for instance, that I was married but had left my husband in England for a *year*. And no, there were no plans for us to meet.

20

I wagged a finger at her. "Madame Gilbert," I reproached her mockingly. "No, we never had children. We were too busy with our careers."

"Maybe later, when you have finished your book." Madame's eyes widened innocently, but already in the hopeful anticipation of some delicious secret.

"All right, Madame, you might as well know, we're thinking of a divorce. We're having a year apart to see how we feel."

"Ah." Great satisfaction on her part to have confirmed what she'd undoubtedly suspected. I always wanted, once the truth was out, to explain to everyone why Tom and I didn't get on. It was my sense of personal failure that made me want to tell all, to clarify it for myself as much as for anyone else.

Madame grimaced in sympathy and touched my arm.

"We're quite happy," I said ridiculously, as though anyone could be quite happy not knowing what he was going to do with his life. "And we're being quite grown-up about it," I said, gathering up my shopping bag. We were grown-up, in years if nothing else.

"Pauvre petite." Madame insisted on seeing me to the door.

It was quite a day for the violins. Madame was loving every moment, in a mournful sort of way.

## CHAPTER 2

I seemed to fall instantly in love with everything at the end of that beautiful hot summer we all enjoyed. Maybe it was to compensate for the lack of love in my personal life. I loved the château, I loved Madame Gilbert, and Port St Pierre had been a *coup de foudre* the day I drove in in my vintage Morris Minor, steam coming out of all vents, baggage piled on the seats, on the floor, and on the roof.

Tom always said I kept the Morris as an affectation, so that people would notice me, which was a typically Tom-like thing to say and, unfortunately, as with a lot of what he said, partly true.

"Here comes Clare Trafford in her funny old Morris; isn't she a scream?" people said, and I knew it. It was the same with the large, black bag full of holes and tied with string in which I carried my books and papers and the oversized spectacles that were poised on the brink of my nose when I lectured. I guess I did have a streak of exhibitionism in me; my dear mother was French and I attributed all these affectations to her influence.

Of course, I'd also fallen in love with number 33 Rue du Château, although it was a far cry from the pink house on the cliff. It was white with green shutters; the front door led straight on to the pavement. The salon ("bien confortable, très propre," Madame Gilbert had assured me) had a marble chequerboard floor, functional furniture, and a large stove to heat both the water and the house with a chimney that disappeared out of sight into the ceiling. To the left as one entered the front door were the kitchen, bathroom, and a small room which I converted into a study. A wooden staircase led straight from the salon to a wide upstairs hall lined with cupboards, three good-sized bedrooms, and a lavatory with washbasin. Not, indeed, so plush as the château, but spacious by the standards of our two-room flat off Lamb's Conduit Street in London.

I unpacked my shopping. I ate sparingly during the day but always had a fish and meat course at night and about two-thirds of a bottle of wine. Tonight I had some pelourdes, a type of shellfish, which I stuffed with garlic butter and breadcrumbs and did in the oven, and an entrecôte. It was funny that Tom always criticised my cooking, because when I was on my own I adored it. Everything I made for Tom was either raw or burnt.

I worked every morning—though a sloppy housewife I was a disciplined scholar—and revised after dinner at night for an hour. Then I went to bed and read. It was a perfect life. I couldn't think, looking at my present wellbeing, why I'd so long endured Tom's painful presence, with his superior stares and sneers. No wonder I'd spoiled the cooking.

As I washed up I felt happy, free. Yes, free. I was in my chosen town in my chosen part of France—Picardy— home of the battles of Agincourt, Crécy, and others, not to mention the agonies of the Somme in two world wars.

But more than that, Port St Pierre was built on the very spot where my girl Joan had been handed over to the English in 1430 by the Burgundian troops. It was her last and longest place of imprisonment before her journey to Rouen and her trial. She said she'd been happy here.

Everyone said it was very quaint that I, a liberated twentieth-century female academic, should specialise in a medieval woman many considered spurious in intent. What fascinated me were the paradoxes of her nature, about which much conflicting testimony had been written.

She'd been the subject of my doctoral thesis in medieval history, and I was about to add my own to the many tomes which had been written about her, having persuaded a publisher to commission such a book on the strength of my thesis, and to pay me an advance. I was studying Joan from the point of view of an emancipated young woman, who, if not exactly of the bra-burning variety, had strong views about the rights of women.

That was really the basis of the trouble with Tom. He didn't want a partner and he didn't want a servant; he *did* want a homey, fecund, domestic admirer who could also engage in conversation, cook a good meal, clean, type, and excite him in bed. Unfortunately, I was not she. Perhaps I fulfilled some of these roles, but I was inconsistent and on the whole inadequate.

Tom and I had quarrelled for five years over these issues, and when I was due for my sabbatical from University College and had selected the subject of my book, I chose to separate from Tom while I wrote it. I moved to

Port St Pierre on the beautiful Bay of the Somme, a town far from Tom but not too inconvenient, and situated in countryside with history enough to thrill the heart of any medievalist.

Tom was taken by surprise when I just upped and went. Did I hope to shock him into what a friend of ours called "my form of submission"? In other words, did I want from Tom the same thing that he wanted from me? Of course not. So why couldn't Tom see that I am the most tolerant soul alive?

As I prepared for bed, ran my bath, and soaked in the warm suds that night, I thought about the story of the young owner of the Château des Moulins and his tragic life. One didn't know exactly how far along in the war the sad events had happened, but if his brothers had been old enough to be in the Resistance it was reasonable to assume the present Marquis was forty or forty-five years old. I wondered how old Elizabeth was. What a happy scene it had been this very day with the black dog. How I wished I could get to know the children!

I went to bed, my head teeming with schemes for contrived meetings, and when I dreamt it was of the pink château overlooking the bay.

In the end, I got to know the family quite easily. I'd established a daily routine—work in the morning, a late lunch of a sandwich and a cup of coffee, then a walk round the bay or through the town, shopping on the way home for my evening meal or stopping for a chat with Madame Gilbert. I'd taken a beach hut because the days were still balmy and many of them hot, and with a deck-chair placed out of the continuous wind I could sit and read, sunbathe, or just enjoy the many splendid beauties of the Bay of the Somme, from the tiny point of Le Hour-

25

del almost opposite, round to Port Guillaume, from which William the Conqueror had sailed to conquer England, to the mouth of the canal and the flat marshlands with their beautiful variety of dried flowers, to Port St Pierre itself. The tide varied every day, and if I had time and it was warm enough I took a quick dip and then exercised on the beach.

There were those who would not have recognised, in the new athletic Clare, the jaded academic who only weeks before had drifted round London smoking too much, staying up too late, and complaining that her husband didn't understand her.

For a week I had no contact with the château, except for my droning on about it to Madame Gilbert, no sight of the children, nothing. Then one day I was reading on the beach, sprawled half awake in my chair, my large hat flopping over my face, when something hurled itself at me almost knocking me to the sand. For a minute I was terrified, until a furry black head caressed my arm and a large pink tongue licked my hand. I began to laugh in joyous recognition, and then there was a confusion of childish voices, and the three appeared running hard from the direction of the château.

"Goofy, Gooooofffie!" shrilled a young voice. "Viens ici, *viens*, Goofy!"

Casting a disdainful glance in their direction, Goofy continued to do homage to my hand, obviously having a way with women.

I was excited and eagerly watched the approach of the children. First came Noelle, then the elder brother, and the youngest last. The two eldest were dark, the younger boy very fair. The girl had an open gamin face, a slightly turned-up nose, and straight brown hair. Her smile and the light in her clear blue eyes gave her a bright, bubbly appearance. The boy next to her had identical features and an impudent smile. The third had the brown complexion and blue eyes of the others but he had straw-colored hair and more aquiline, regular features—a beautiful child, sturdy and well-built.

Then they were in front of me, in a variety of postures, expressing alarm, apologising all at the same time for the outrageous behaviour of Goofy.

"Goofy!" I addressed them in French, though I was sure they must speak English. "What an outrageous name for this beautiful dog."

"Oh, Madame, his name is Le Prince d'Argenteuil; he has a pedigree this long"—the elder boy gestured exaggeratedly with his arms—"but he is so silly and sweet that we call him Goofy after the dog in the cartoon."

"He's gorgeous," I said, determined to please and to make friends with them all. I tickled Goofy gently under the ears.

"My name is Clare Trafford," I murmured without looking at the children. "I've come to live here for a year."

"Tiens!" the girl spoke. She was a tomboy, I could see, with faded jeans and a denim shirt; her nose was attractively freckled. "Who wants to live in Port St Pierre?"

"Don't you live here too?"

"We have to." She looked suddenly wistful. "We used to live in Paris and just come here for the summer. Now it is all year round."

I pretended to know nothing about them.

"Don't you go to school?"

"We have a teacher, Mademoiselle Jeanne. When we are older we shall go to boarding school. Our mother is very ill."

They all looked solemn now.

"Tell me your names," I encouraged.

"I am Noelle, this is Philippe my big brother, and Fabrice the baby."

"I am *not* a baby," Fabrice called angrily in his gruff little voice.

"Baby, baby," chimed the other two, and little Fabrice, who was indeed almost as tall as Philippe, turned in a rage and pummelled Philippe's chest with his fists.

Then a shadow came between us and the sun, which I thought had for a moment been obscured by a cloud. I looked up, and the slight dark figure I'd seen at the window gazed down at us.

"Children," she said quietly but with authority, "what are you doing here?"

The effect on the children was startling. They had been clustering round me and Goofy, squatting on the sand. Now they jumped to their feet and stood almost at attention, their heads hanging abjectly. I thought their behaviour curious, as they had not been doing anything terribly wrong. I turned to look at the governess because I knew it was she.

In her appearance Jeanne seemed harmless enough, unsmiling, though, and obviously perplexed by the unexpected situation. She was of medium height and slender, with smooth black hair and an olive complexion, which suggested she came from the south of France. She had a rather short nose, a narrow mouth, and luminous eyes of that dark velvet brown that is almost black. They were large and slanted attractively at the corners; they seemed to be concealing her secrets even as they bore into the eyes of others.

I could understand that the children would treat her with respect, maybe even with fear. I can't remember now what she wore that first day I saw her, because

Jeanne's clothes were always completely anonymous, toneless; they were mostly brown or black or dark green in colour and all with a little collar and small pearl buttons leading down to a neat belted waist. Unfashionable, a reminder of the turn of the century when poor girls of genteel birth became governesses as the only way of earning a living.

I go into Jeanne here in great detail because she was to become such an important part of the story I have to tell; but even though I later saw her often, I never got to know her at all and never understood her well. Or rather, when I did get to know her better it was in the context of St Joan, the subject of my own study, and that came about in a most extraordinary and unexpected way . . .

The children went on mumbling about the dog and me and goodness knows what, and I went on looking at Jeanne; it was left to Goofy to bound away and relieve the uncomfortable moment.

"Mademoiselle is reading, can't you see?" Jeanne chided gently. "It is rude to disturb her. Apologise for the behaviour of the dog and come now; your play time is over and we have work to do before tea."

"Oh, they have apologised," I said quickly, trying to soothe her with the well-known Trafford charm. "They were charming and I enjoyed talking to them. I was telling them I've come to live here for a year, so it's nice for me to meet people."

"*Live* here?" Mademoiselle Jeanne reacted with the same startled disbelief as had her charges.

"Just to write a book. I'm English."

For a moment Jeanne's impersonal mask dropped and she looked genuinely interested.

"English? But you speak perfect French. You have no accent at all."

29

"My mother was French but has lived in England since she married my father when she was very young. My name is Clare Trafford."

I paused invitingly, but Mademoiselle didn't volunteer her own name. One by one the children had slipped away, with polite nods, and were running after Goofy in the direction they had come. Mademoiselle's eyes followed them.

"We must get back to class, Mademoiselle. The children have a normal school day. Au revoir."

She bowed to me and walked away and I sank back dejectedly in my chair. It *had* been a start; but I saw I would have to make a great effort if I were ever to penetrate the defences of the pink house.

Certainly everyone was friendly enough, especially the children, but was there a reason for their apparent reluctance to receive new people—even Madame Gilbert had appeared to think it would be a hopeless task—or was I being fanciful?

## CHAPTER 3

Though it was no business of mine, all that summer I pondered over the affairs of the de Frigecourt family and wove little fantasies about them in my mind. Except for my work, I hadn't much else to do. Tom and I had agreed not to correspond except on essential matters; I didn't have a television, and there was only one cinema in Port St Pierre, which seemed to specialise in lurid films of little appeal to me. I did a lot of walking and some driving to research background material for the book. Quite a few local places had been associated with Joan as she made her way from her capture at Compiègne to Rouen, a journey that took seven months. There were Arras and Beaurevoir, Drugy, St-Riquier, Cambrai, and numerous small shrines and places where she'd stayed.

Joan's life was extraordinarily well documented, and some devoted historians had discovered where she was, what she was doing, what she wore, and what she was saying almost every hour of every day. It amazed me when one considered that we had no clear idea of what she looked like, and the few representations of her that have come down to us are of doubtful authenticity.

By November 1430 Joan had reached Port St Pierre and had been imprisoned in the castle here almost a month. The castle was built almost on the spot where the Château des Moulins now stood, only it occupied more land than the Château. The topography of the town, too, had changed a great deal since the fifteenth century. In those days the sea had made inroads as far as Rue, and over the centuries the land had silted up so that now the two ports of St Pierre and Guillaume on opposite sides of the bay guarded the approach to the Somme canal.

Joan had crossed from St Pierre to Port Guillaume where she'd spent the night, and historians still debated whether she'd gone by boat, by horse, or on foot across the bay, citing tide tables for the year 1430 as evidence. What particularly interested me was Joan of Arc's personality. Was she a madwoman or a saint, an hysteric, a witch, a satanist, a political pawn, or a victim of the Church which she loved so much and which served her so badly? What really motivated her? Joan was a puzzling phenomenon, and as I carefully sorted out the details of her short life and cruel death I tried to make my account relevant and comprehensible to the people of today.

I now knew for certain that the Château des Moulins stood on the spot of Joan's castle, and I couldn't wait to inspect the house and grounds in detail. The château seemed to beckon and call me, to entice me with its mysteries. And indeed it was fascinating to speculate how much, if anything, of the old fortress remained and was enclosed within the walls of the current house.

An historian like myself, who is completely absorbed

in her subject, looked for any item or clue that would connect the past with the present and provide further insight into the people and events of those far-off days—a piece of stone, a fragment of timber. Could it be that there was something in the château to connect it with Joan? I couldn't wait to get in and find out. Almost every day, depending upon the tide, I wandered hopefully past the house, but I didn't see the children or their governess again, or even their dog, until I decided to take matters into my own hands and invite them to tea.

The person I spoke to was Rose. She answered the phone and sounded a pleasant, uncomplicated girl, delighted to hear an English voice, her own French being poor. I asked them *all* to tea, Rose included, but she said she'd have to ask Mademoiselle Jeanne, for the children were directly under her care.

I'd had to phone from the post office on the main street because my own house didn't have a phone, and as I waited I could hear a whispered conversation. When she came back to me, Rose sounded flustered.

"I'm sorry," she whispered. "It is not convenient. The children are expecting their father." She paused, and I could feel her reluctance to ring off.

"Well, could we leave it open?" I ventured. "After their father's gone? I mean there's no urgency."

But to my surprise and consternation Rose put down the phone. Or someone put the phone down for her.

I was so unnerved by the unexpected conclusion to my initiative that I immediately went and called on Madame Gilbert.

"It was such a strange ending," I concluded. "She sounded so happy and keen. It almost seems as though they want to discourage visitors."

"Very strange and sad." Madame Gilbert nodded sagely, fiddling with her pince-nez.

"What is wrong with that house, or rather that family?"

I wondered. "I can't say why or how, but I know something is wrong."

Madame Gilbert gave me a look of mild disapproval. "Wrong? Nothing is wrong."

"They don't want visitors, yet there are three normal young children on their own. I can't believe their father would want it like that."

"But they didn't say they didn't want visitors," Madame replied gently. "Did they?"

I looked at Madame Gilbert and recognised that same gallic obduracy I myself possessed. I was, after all, a stranger and there was a close community bond and a loyalty to the de Frigecourt family that no newcomer could penetrate.

The following morning I was at work in my study, considering the position of Jean de Luxembourg, who sold the Maid to the English—at the instigation of the Burgundians—when there was a knock at the front door.

I couldn't think who would want to visit me at eleven in the morning and wondered if it was the post. I half wanted to hear from Tom, which was silly of me, I knew, but it was a bit hard to accept the fact that he'd taken my desertion so calmly. I took off my glasses and went to the door. A perfect stranger stood there, a young girl of about twenty-three. She had a direct, open face and was looking rather ill at ease.

"Mrs Trafford?"

How did she know my name? "Yes?"

"I'm Rose, from the château, the nanny. I'm sorry to call on you like this, it must seem rude, but I wanted to explain . . ." She was nervous and tumbled over her words.

"Come in, come in," I reassured her. "I was just about to make coffee."

As Rose stepped nervously in, I was both excited and

34

intrigued by her manner. The whole thing looked very suspicious.

I left her standing by the stove—autumn was setting in and the day was cool—and went into the kitchen, where the percolator was kept more or less permanently on the boil while I was working.

"There." I gave her a steaming cup and put the milk and sugar on the table between us. "This is a pleasant surprise. I was beginning to think the people at the château were trying to cold-shoulder me."

Rose gave me a startled look.

"It's not the people," she said, gulping the coffee. "It's *her*—Jeanne. I wanted to see you to explain about yesterday. She's very odd."

The staccato sentences punctuated by intermittent gulps of scalding coffee made me realise that Rose was very ill at ease indeed. Then to my utter consternation she thumped her cup on the table and dissolved into tears.

"Rose, here, take this tissue. Why, Rose . . ." What could I say? She blew hard.

"Sorry, I'm a fool. But it's the children. I don't think they're safe. I'm frightened."

Goodness, even in my most exotic fantasies I hadn't anticipated anything like this. I sat down abruptly beside the tearful girl.

Rose was a pretty girl, even with her face distorted by tears. She was above average in height with a good figure and an alert, intelligent face that made one suspect more went on in Rose's mind than one could discern from the outside. She was no run-of-the-mill English nanny, but a girl of considerable intelligence, with a well-defined character and a strong will for one in her early twenties. Now she wasn't acting at all in accord with the first impression she'd made upon me. She hadn't seemed like

35

someone who would be afraid or would break down easily.

"Why don't you have a spot of brandy with your coffee?" I suggested.

"Oh, no thank you! *She'd* smell it on my breath. I don't want *her* to know I've been here."

"Jeanne?"

"You've met her?"

"I met her briefly on the beach. I can't say she gave me long enough to get to know her."

"She wouldn't. She doesn't like people. She's frightened they'll find out about *her*."

"*What* about her?"

"She's evil. She's trying to put a spell on those children. They were perfectly all right until she came. Now they're becoming horrible."

Shades of Henry James. Good heavens. I began to feel in need of brandy myself.

"They seemed like awfully nice children to me," I reflected, "though their behaviour did change when Jeanne appeared . . ."

"There!" Rose looked at me triumphantly.

"But it's quite natural, isn't it, for children to react to those in charge of them? Rose, why don't you start at the beginning? Tell me how you got there and what exactly is worrying you?"

Rose nodded. Her tears had dried and colour had come into her cheeks. Yes, she was a girl of pronounced character. She had a firm chin and a determined light in her eyes.

"I got the job when the children's mother had her accident. The father, the Marquis, liked an English nanny, as his others had been English, and the last one had left just before the accident—to get married I think. The kids were very upset, of course, but you know how it is with young children, they quickly readapt, and they liked coming to Port St Pierre.

"Of course I didn't think the Marquis would leave us here. I wanted to work in Paris, and I understood it was just for the summer holiday—last summer, that was. But then the mother didn't get better and they knew how ill she was and before I knew what had happened he'd decided to get a governess and Jeanne turned up. He's like that, the Marquis, just makes up his mind without asking anybody. Didn't ask me what *I* thought or what *I* wanted to do. I didn't want to live permanently in a place like this with no shops or cinemas. But I couldn't leave the children. I'd grown fond of them. So I stayed."

Rose looked at me and I quickly nodded my head in encouragement, for I didn't want her to stop. However, in retrospect, it *did* seem odd to me that a young girl just looking for a summer holiday job could become so attached to the family for whom she worked. There were to be many doubts in my mind about Rose until the truth was finally revealed. I was wondering about her now— her earnest talk, her obvious desire to impress me.

"After she came," Rose went on, "the children began to change towards me. It was so slow I didn't realise it at first. They got secretive and started telling lies. I couldn't put it down to anything I'd said or done. I couldn't even put it down to Jeanne because she likes to keep to herself and stays in her room when she is not teaching."

"Doesn't she ever go out?"

"She goes out sometimes but I don't know where. I can't drive, but she can and uses the car the Marquis has here. It's a small Renault. I don't know where she goes. In all the time I've been closeted together with her, I feel I've never got to know her at all, and except for discussions about the children, we never talk about anything. She never joins me to watch television and never comes with us on outings."

"It must be a lonely life."

"It is. My boyfriend wanted me to leave it, but I said, 'No, not until I'm happy about the children.' And I'm not."

"In what way aren't you, besides their behaviour? I mean, why don't you think they're safe?"

Rose hesitated. For the first time, I wondered how much of this was genuine? Her tears had dried up awfully quickly. And why did she hesitate? Was it simply that she didn't like Jeanne?

"Well, I don't mean she would actually *harm* them, at least I don't think so, but she seems to have a sinister effect on the children."

"I think you should talk to their father," I counselled. "He's coming soon, isn't he? Did she actually tell you to put me off?"

"Oh, yes. She was very firm about it. Said she couldn't meet strange people without the Marquis knowing. I think he's coming on the weekend."

"Then you should tell him your fears. He's the only one who can do something about it, Rose. I can't."

"Oh, I could never tell the Marquis."

"Why not?"

"He thinks a lot of Jeanne. I know he does. He's told me she's excellent for the children. Disciplines them."

Ah, perhaps this was it. A case of jealousy. Young girlish Rose was too free with the children. Let them run wild. Jeanne had introduced a bit of discipline. But then, why was she telling me all this?

"I must go." Rose looked at her watch. "Lunch is at twelve-thirty. I'm sorry I came now. I think I've upset you."

"Oh no, Rose, you haven't upset me. I just don't think I've been able to help much. You've given me so little to go on."

"I just needed to talk," Rose said, shrugging and giving me a helpless look. "You sounded nice on the phone." But she surprised me anew with her next remark.

"Do you think we could meet secretly with the children? You can see if you think she has affected them, if they're all right."

Her words troubled and excited me. This would be my chance, perhaps, to see inside the château. I was reluctant to become involved in the family's troubles, and above all to agree to secret assignations. I was also exceedingly curious.

"Well, I *do* teach older people, Rose. I am not at all an expert in child psychology. However, I daresay I know enough to see if they are *disturbed*. Anyway, I like kids and they usually like me. I've got some doubts about doing this secretly, though, but—this one time . . ."

"Oh thank you!" Rose's gratitude appeared genuine. "Can we make it for tomorrow? It's Wednesday and they have the afternoon off."

"That's fine then. I'll take my car along the Cayeux Road and you can walk on the beach toward the dunes. At about three?"

"But we mustn't let anyone know we planned it."

Rose had become furtive again.

"No, I promise you it will look accidental."

I saw Rose to the door and stood watching her until she disappeared around the corner at the end of the street.

Rose mystified me, even more than Jeanne, and I wondered now if there really was something about that château, or at least the staff in it, that could make one genuinely afraid for the children who lived there?

## CHAPTER 4

After Rose left I was too restless to work and instead
drove into Abbeville to see a film. Autumn was approaching and I felt the cool winds blowing in over the bay. The
last few days had been cloudy, not suitable for walking. I
hoped that by the next day when I was due to meet the
children it wouldn't have turned to rain.

Situated along a strategic route, the ancient town of
Abbeville was razed to the ground in the two world wars
and a few before that, including the Hundred Years War,
when Burgundians and Armagnacs had skirmished and
battled round the counties of Picardy and Artois. But the
citizens of Abbeville had been kind to Joan, and some of
them had gone upriver to visit her in Port St Pierre.

In the late afternoon I shopped for groceries and then
went to an American film poorly dubbed into French. On
impulse I decided to treat myself to dinner and relaxed

over a perfectly cooked meal—snails, blanquette de veau, and half a bottle of Pouilly-Fumé. It was quite late when I took the quiet, narrow road back to the Somme estuary, dawdling along with the Morris. As I chugged into Port St Pierre shortly before midnight, an ambulance came speeding out of the town in the other direction. I wondered whether its destination was Abbeville or Rue, but apart from that gave it no thought and enjoyed a sound night's sleep. It was well I did, because my nights were far from sound for some time afterwards.

The next day the town was humming with the news that Rose had been found half-drowned on the seashore and was in critical condition. The postwoman told me when she delivered a parcel of second-hand books sent from Oxford, and I almost dropped them in shock.

"She was caught by the tide," the postwoman explained. "If one is stranded it can happen; the water forks and you are left on a sandbank in the middle of the bay. It seems as though she'd been crossing the bay, maybe walking from Port Guillaume at low tide when the bay was all dry, but she was caught. At least that is what one assumes."

"She walked across the bay when high tide was expected," I wondered aloud. "What an extraordinary thing to do."

The postwoman shrugged and bade me good day. I dumped my parcel and hurried over to see Madame Gilbert.

"She couldn't swim," she explained. "Everything is so tragic for that family. Maybe she will recover."

From the look on Madame's face it seemed doubtful.

"She couldn't *swim?*" I echoed. "In that case, surely she would never have attempted to walk across the bay, tide due or not."

"And in the dark," Madame said, with her characteristic shrug. "C'est *extraordinaire!*"

"I don't think she'd do it," I said. "I don't think anyone would."

Madame Gilbert looked at me with her shrewd eyes, her pince-nez shining in the light. "What are you trying to say? That someone *drowned* her?"

"Madame, I'm not saying anything like that. I just say that I don't understand how she drowned, or almost drowned. When did it happen?"

"No one knows. They missed her at dinner and Jeanne was angry at having to take her place."

"The tide last night was about nine o'clock, so it would have been almost dark. I saw the ambulance when I returned from Abbeville just before midnight; then Rose's accident must have happened during the late evening or night, which is singularly odd."

"I will find out what I can from the gendarmerie," Madame Gilbert said. "They will have made a full investigation. Leave it to me, and then if the girl recovers we will know what happened."

I didn't mention to Madame Gilbert that Rose had been to see me. I don't know why I felt secretive about it, but I did. If I told Madame Gilbert, the whole town would know, and people would want to know why she'd come.

I wanted to see Rose, yet I had no reason for going; I was not even supposed to know her. Already I was becoming involved in a web which, all things considered, was really of my own making.

But I need not have tortured myself, for Rose never recovered from her coma and within two days she was dead.

The terrible tragedy that had afflicted the de Frigecourt

42

family, or rather someone connected with it, cast a cloud over the entire town. No one could talk of anything else, but few appeared to have known Rose well, if at all. Although Laurent de Frigecourt had come almost immediately, the huge gates of the château remained firmly closed, and I felt helpless to penetrate that strange house dominated by the enigmatic Jeanne. Was it coincidence, or could Rose have been right that there was something sinister about the silent governess who stared blankly out of her window?

Rose had been found unconscious at about eleven p.m. by a fisherman looking for bait. Her body was washed up on the shore. The tide was going out by then and no one knew how long she'd lain there. I thought it strange that Jeanne had not thought to search for her, but maybe she had.

I was consumed with curiosity and felt a definite involvement in Rose's death. Usually a sound sleeper, for the past two nights I had tossed and turned in my bed, unable to dismiss it from my mind. Had her visit to me endangered her? What mystery was the house concealing? I owed it to Rose to find out, both as a fellow countrywoman and one to whom she had entrusted her last confidence.

In the end I wrote the Marquis a letter. It was the obvious thing to do. I said I was shocked to learn of Rose's death, I had slight acquaintance with his children, and was there anything I could do to help?

I expected a refusal, but what I got was an invitation. He sent a note round by hand asking me for a drink that very evening. I was both exultant and strangely afraid, as though I were on the brink of an exciting but rather terrifying journey, which indeed it proved to be.

I immediately cast about for something suitable to

wear. What was appropriate for a marquis? I was a jeans and tee shirt type at work, and a caftan and beads type while haunting the groves of Academe.

One nice thing Tom had managed to say about me was that I had a good figure and since then I tried to take advantage of this asset. Being tall and dark I went for exotic colours, and that evening I got out my best Thai print, decked myself with an assortment of beads, carefully applied my eye makeup, and completed my toilette with a touch of Javanese perfume.

My appointment was at six sharp. It is almost longer to drive to the château than to walk because of the one-way system; but I didn't dare be observed on the streets of Port St Pierre in this attire. They would think the Witches' Sabbath had arrived in person.

I was indeed expected. The gates of the château were open, the lights of the interior warm and inviting. At the sound of my car a man appeared at the top of the steps, and then suddenly the children swarmed round him and bounded down the steps, preceded by Goofy, as they had been that very day I first saw them. They stopped shyly by the car, and I felt shy too until I saw the wonder in Philippe's expression as he gazed at the ancient vehicle.

"It's at least as old as I," I volunteered. "Maybe older."

"Tiens, alors . . ." He gestured excitedly to the others, and they took turns sitting in the driver's seat, jumping up and down.

"Children," their father said to them in English, "you must take care with Madame's car."

"I don't think anyone *could* take care of it," I said, and held out my hand.

"In its way it must be an antique," Laurent de Frigecourt said with amusement, and as we shook hands I could see he was as charming as his children and as I knew he would be. "Come inside. The night is so cold.

44

Children, go to your playroom. Cécile will give you your tea this evening. Come, Madame."

The children rushed ahead of me, and Laurent de Frigecourt followed me as I sashayed up the stairs in my trailing gown. If I closed my eyes I could almost imagine I was Madame de Pompadour, and this Versailles.

The first thing one saw was a grand hall with a double staircase, which seemed to follow the contours of the outside steps and sweep grandly upwards. In the hall was a huge chandelier and, off the hall, doors to the other parts of the house stood invitingly open. My first thought was that despite its grandeur the château had the simplicity of a family home; there were children's boots, fishing nets and other paraphernalia cluttering the hall. The Marquis shooed the children upstairs and invited me into a large salon, a long, elegant room with bay windows. The walls were hung in striped silk and the furniture was mainly Louis Quinze. The room was more formal than the hallway yet still comfortable, with low modern sofas facing the sea view and scattered tables piled with books and magazines and vases of flowers. I guessed the children would be on their best behaviour in this room.

"It was most kind of you to write," the Marquis began, gesturing towards one of the sofas. "Please sit down while I get you a drink. Will you have whisky, gin or sherry? You see, for several years I was brought up in England."

"Gin and tonic would be nice. May I smoke?"

"Please." In an instant he was offering me a silver cigarette box, and I selected an English cigarette, which he lit for me. I could see he was appraising me and, I think, liking what he saw. One is really quite bruised by a failed marriage, and the attentions of someone of the opposite sex become especially important. Although I knew I hadn't failed Tom sexually, I still felt rejected as a wom-

45

an, which was why I suppose I'd gone to such trouble with my appearance this evening. I knew I looked good, and that helped me to relax.

Laurent de Frigecourt was a tall man with dark brown hair and a healthy, tanned complexion, as though he spent a lot of time outdoors. I was surprised by his obvious youth and, for all his troubles, his air of calm serenity. Like the children, he had blue eyes that were almost violet. I assumed Fabrice's blond hair came from his mother.

"I adore your château," I said, sipping my drink and observing his lithe figure as he lit a cigarette and sat down opposite me.

"It is beautiful," he said wistfully. "Unfortunately, the circumstances for the children being here are not the happiest, and now . . ."

"It was awful about Rose," I said quickly. "What a terrible shock."

"Oh, it was awful. An accident, but how, no one knows. She couldn't swim."

"What was she doing by the water at night when she should have been with the children?"

The Marquis took a drink and shrugged. "That is a complete mystery. Usually after school is finished—I do insist on a proper school day, and as you know they are long in France—Rose takes over. This particular day she was not at tea and no one had seen her except Cécile, our maid, who saw her go out about two. Normally she did take a walk at some point during the day, or go shopping, but she couldn't drive and never used the car that I leave for the senior staff. She wasn't seen again after that by anyone except the fisherman who stumbled upon her on the beach just after eleven at night. She'd been there some time according to the doctors, otherwise she might have been saved. She died as much from exposure as from anything."

"How dreadful."

"Well"—the Marquis shrugged—"these things are dreadful. God knows why they seem to happen such a lot in our family. I suppose you've heard my wife is very ill following a car accident over a year ago. She will probably never recover but could live for years. However," he said, looking at me, "in these situations one develops certain inner strengths, and this helps one to cope."

"I'm glad you've found the strength," I said quietly. "The children must be a great comfort to you."

"Oh, they are; I wish I could see more of them. It's a great anxiety for me, but Jeanne is a most capable woman and they seem very devoted to her."

"And Rose?"

"Well, Rose . . ." He screwed up his face. "I don't know how to explain about Rose. They never seemed quite so attached to her as they have been to other nannies or to Jeanne. I think Rose was a bit jealous of Jeanne and resented her. Of course, Rose was a young girl and you know what they're like, always wanting to be out and having a good time. Jeanne is very devoted to the children, altogether a different type. I don't think Rose liked having Jeanne over her, because she came later, after my wife's accident. But I felt I had to have an older woman in charge."

I sat silently taking all this in. I longed to tell him about Rose's visit to me, but I knew it would sound strange and would involve me with the family in a way I didn't want.

No, if I was to play the detective, I felt I would do better to keep what I knew to myself and see what I could find out about Rose's death and about Jeanne and the children. Surely no one would bar my visits now, after I'd been entertained by the father. And what was the truth of that? Had Jeanne really stopped my coming before?

"As for your offer of help, Mrs. Trafford, I can only say thank you and do feel free to come visit whenever you like. The children took to you right away and talked to me about you." He wrinkled his eyes. "It seems there is a fun-loving quality about you they detected immediately. I must say, if you don't think it rude, I admire your outfit enormously."

Under that steely male gaze I had the grace to feel myself blushing. My caftan was of heavy Thai silk and glittered with all the colours of a peacock.

"Is Mr. Trafford not with you?"

"He's in London."

"I don't know how he can be so restrained with a wife like you."

I'd decided at the beginning not to be coy about our separation, and even though I felt most susceptible to Laurent de Frigecourt's male charm, neither of us was either free or in a position to flirt, however mildly, without some statement of fact, on my part at least. As for him, I assumed from the tender way he spoke about her that he was still very much in love with his young wife.

"My husband and I have agreed on a year's separation. We're both on the staff of colleges that are part of London University, and we found that our work and personal lives didn't gell, as they say."

Laurent de Frigecourt looked embarrassed. "I'm terribly sorry. I hope . . ."

"You didn't upset me at all. I've come here to write a book and I love it."

"It is lovely. Port St Pierre reminds me of my childhood. For me as a boy it had everything—the sea, adven-

48

ture, exploration, the hunt—we adored our summers here. We sailed and swam and then, well, I suppose you can hardly not have heard about the disaster to my father and brothers."

"I was terribly sorry to hear about it," I murmured.

The Marquis got up and walked over to the window, brooding into the dark.

"I was eleven at the time, my brothers fifteen and seventeen. I couldn't talk about it for years, but in time that, too . . . It seems there was a traitor who betrayed all my father's Resistance group, which was centred on Rue. There were ten of them, all caught one night in 1943 and taken away. We never saw them again and only heard after the war that they'd been shot."

"All ten of them?"

"Almost all. Two were killed when they were captured and one got away, but we never found out who had betrayed them."

"Are you sure they were betrayed? Couldn't the Germans just have known?"

"There is no doubt about it. They were crawling up to a bridge at midnight, a prearranged spot for sabotage, and suddenly the whole area was illuminated and they were surrounded. They'd been one of the most effective Maquis groups in the area. The German officer who directed the operation said they were brave men but they should have been aware of the Judas among them."

"Was it the man who got away?"

"Well, we think not, because it was he who told us the story. Had he been guilty, I don't think he would have come forward. But I did hear that he lived the rest of his life a very sad, lonely man because certain people resented that he'd escaped. My family knew him—he was a local fisherman—and we never thought he was guilty."

The Marquis got up to freshen my drink and lit cigarettes for us both. I could see he was in a mood to share confidences, and I supposed that despite the glamour of his life he might still be a lonely man, deprived maybe any close relationship with a woman. Whether or not he had close male friends I couldn't know. He now wore an anguished expression as he nervously puffed at his cigarette and then stubbed it out half-smoked.

"Oh, you know what terrible things happen in wartime. You never know the truth about anything. Long afterwards a rumour came back to us that one or both of my brothers had escaped from the concentration camp. A man who'd been a prisoner of war returned home and swore he'd seen one or both of them after the war was over. They were very similar in appearance. But nothing was ever proved and, although I got in touch with an agency that tracks down wartime refugees, the quest was fruitless. And if the story were true, why should my brother not have come home? It didn't make sense, but it did cause us a lot of grief. It is so much better to be sure of something, however unpleasant, than not to *know*. Don't you agree? Now, of course, we do know. The war has been over for thirty years."

Laurent lit another cigarette; talking to me had seemed to calm him. "As a family we've had a lot of tragedy. It isn't amusing to be the only one left. To a small boy, one's older brothers are heroes, and mine even more so because of what happened to them. I idolise their memory."

He stopped speaking abruptly, close to tears, and got up on the pretext of fetching a clean ash tray. When he looked at me again he was in control, but his eyes were bright. He was certainly a man of acute sensitivity whose family's misfortunes must have caused him great pain. He looked at his watch and suddenly the mood changed.

"My goodness, it's nearly time for dinner!"

"Then it's time for me to go."

"No, please join us. There is always food enough for an army."

"Oh, but I couldn't . . ."

"Oh, but you could, and you shall. Besides, I want you to get to know my family better if you are to keep an eye on them while I'm away."

What could I say to *that*?

## CHAPTER 5

I was shown round the château before dinner, and Laurent—over our second gin we'd agreed to exchange Christian names—gave me the guided tour. He explained that the original château *had* stood on this site, and next to it the ancient windmill which one could still see in old representations of the town. In the early days the house had been merely a shooting box, being so near to the dunes and La Chasse, but in the eighteenth century, as wealth spread from Paris to the seaports, the recently created marquis—the earlier Frigecourts had been vicomtes—decided to make it into a *grande maison*.

A great deal of reconstruction had gone on since the house had first been built. As in many old houses, one room led into another, so that separate corridors and doorways had had to be made. The tiled hall was one vast coat of arms. I meant to ask Laurent about this, but at that moment the children came decorously downstairs—up to then I'd never seen them merely walk—followed by Mademoiselle Jeanne, who gave me a friendly smile.

The children were dressed for dinner, the boys in dark shorts, white shirts and ties, and Noelle in a long frilly dress. I was glad I'd put on the silk caftan. Assembled in the dining room the children nodded at me gravely and then bowed their heads for grace, which Laurent said in Latin! The table was beautifully set with silver candelabra, Sèvres plates and cruets, and crystal glass for the adults; the meal was simple and excellently cooked: soup, mussels in a green garlic sauce, roast chicken with *pommes de terres* and green beans, cheese, and ice cream. The children ate heartily, Fabrice being occasionally reprimanded for his manners, but the other two were the embodiment of the best upbringing. Mademoiselle Jeanne ate sparingly, I noticed, and seemed always to have her eyes on one or another of her charges. I *did* think the children's behavior unduly restricted—there was an almost uneasy feeling about the meal, as though everyone were on unnaturally good behaviour.

When Laurent made his remark, it produced the same impact as a boulder heaved into a mill pond.

"So tell us, Mrs. Trafford, about your book on Jeanne d'Arc."

I looked at him, my mouth falling foolishly open. "You know I'm writing a book about Joan of Arc?"

"But yes"—he looked about him, surprised. "Didn't you tell me your book was about Joan of Arc?"

"No, I don't think I did."

"Well, someone did; I don't think it's important." He waved his arms about airily. "I'd like to know what new things you have to say about her. You know she was connected with the old château that used to stand here?"

"Yes, I know; she was imprisoned there for a month.

53

There were four turrets, and she was imprisoned in the tour du roi." I proceeded smoothly with my history lesson, to which all listened attentively, but mentally I was churning over in my mind this apparently trivial remark of Laurent's. It so happens that I'm very secretive about my work and what books I'm writing. One reason is that academics are the most awful thieves and won't hesitate to snitch an idea from someone who has already done all the research. The only people whom I'd told about my book were my supervisor and Tom, and neither, I knew, would ever have breathed a word to another soul, certainly not so far as Port St Pierre, Picardy. Madame Gilbert had been keen to know the subject, but all I told her was that it was about medieval France and I muttered something about Edward III and John of Luxemburg, who fought at Crécy nearby.

Now that it was out, of course, one had to make the best of it. But how had he known? How could he *possibly* have known? The only one from the château who'd been inside my house had been Rose. Even supposing she'd had time to nose about my study—and I couldn't believe it possible while I'd been in the kitchen—she'd never seen Laurent again before her death.

Then, given this as a reasonable hypothesis—that I'd left something around that Rose had seen—whom had she told? The children? Jeanne? But if I started questioning them, they would know that Rose had been to my house, and if they did, wouldn't they think it odd I hadn't mentioned it already?

Suddenly my food tasted like sawdust, and I wondered if I were under inspection, if they all wanted to know why I'd concealed the truth?

But looking at them nodding intelligently, eating, drinking, it was hard to think they could be other than

54

what they seemed, even Jeanne. They appeared to be friendly, agreeable people who liked each other and liked me.

"Yes, it is a bad chapter in our history," Laurent observed when I'd finished my little treatise. "Joan sold to the English by the French, very shameful."

"But Monsieur," Jeanne said quietly, in a subdued voice that nevertheless seemed to vibrate with emotion, "Jeanne d'Arc was not sold to the English by the French, but by the Burgundians. It is not the same thing."

"Oh, yes, it is," Laurent replied. "They were French."

"They were *not* French, Monsieur le Marquis. They were traitors!"

"But..." Laurent began, then seeing Jeanne's face seemed to reconsider. I must say her expression amazed me. It was as though someone had said something either obscene or offensive about her or a close member of her family. She kept her voice very low, but I thought that if he pursued the subject, she would either start screaming or leave the room.

I think he thought so too, and he turned to me to help him.

"The history of the Valois dukes of Burgundy *is* complicated," I said smoothly. "They were always at odds with the French crown and indeed sided with the English almost throughout the Hundred Years War."

"They were not French at all," Jeanne hissed.

"Mademoiselle, they were *related* to the French king, but in the sense that they created their own state and perpetually sought a crown from the Holy Roman Emperor, perhaps you are right," I said, and Laurent gave me a grateful smile. The subject was dropped and the rest of the meal consumed while we talked about other things.

Immediately after dinner the children were taken upstairs by Jeanne, kissing their father and politely shaking hands with me. Cécile came in with coffee and then said that if that was all she would be going.

Laurent nodded and smiled, and Cécile curtseyed awkwardly and retired.

"You have only daily staff?" I asked him, "except for those who look after the children?"

"Well, we never spent more than a few months a year here at the most. Madame Barbou cooks for us when we're here and helps at one of the hotels when we're away; the same with Cécile. We're very lucky they've been able to stay with us this year. May I give you a brandy with your coffee?"

I declined his offer and he got a whisky for himself, settling back in the sofa with a deep sigh. "So, what do you think of Mademoiselle Jeanne this evening?"

"You mean her outburst about the Burgundians?"

He nodded, puffing at a cigar, his eyes narrowed, watching me. Had his faith in Jeanne been shaken?

"It was awfully strange," I began. "I must say her reaction surprised me. But if she is an historian..."

"It seemed almost personal to me." Laurent went on puffing. "She appeared to resent something very deeply."

"Interestingly enough, I had the same feeling," I said, "as though something offensive had been said about *her*."

"Exactly. It worries me a bit."

"I shouldn't worry," I said, longing again to tell him about Rose, "if you are otherwise satisfied with her."

"It worries me that she is solely in charge of the children. Alone here with them."

The children aren't *safe*, Rose had said. I felt myself go cold, despite the warm room.

"You see," Laurent went on, "my family is descended

from a branch of the royal Burgundian line. Jeanne must know that."

I felt excited, apprehensive.

"Why must she know?"

"It's often talked about. Our coat of arms ..."

"Of course, I'd meant to ask you about that."

"You must have seen it in the hall, the Burgundian lion and the bar sinister. We are directly descended from John the Fearless, second of the four Valois dukes of Burgundy."

"Yes, they did get around, didn't they," I murmured. "Especially Philip the Good; he had at least twenty-three natural children."

"Oh, at least." Laurent laughed. "Well, his father, John, who murdered the Duke of Orleans, wasn't much better, progeny-wise. One of his favourite mistresses was Isabeau of Ponthieu, a girl of noble stock whose father was one of John's councillors. It was apparently a real love affair, and she bore him three children. But all the Valois Burgundian duchesses were women of some account in their own right; they frequently looked after their husbands' property while they were fighting, and John's wife Margaret of Bavaria was no exception. She was quite happy to turn a blind eye to John's many affairs, but Isabeau, especially after three children, was turning into a problem and Margaret seems to have seen her as a threat. Accordingly, Isabeau was married off to one of the knights in John's court, the Sire de Frigecourt and the family ennobled.

"Her eldest son by the Duke of Burgundy was also named John, or Jehan after his father, and he became a considerable soldier, fighting for Philip the Good, who succeeded his father after he had been murdered by the Orleanist faction at Montereau ..."

"This is just my period!" I exclaimed delightedly. "Philip the Good defeated Joan at Compiègne."

"Of course. I'd forgotten you were an expert."

"They definitely met," I said, "though few knew what transpired between them except that Philip was mighty pleased with his captive."

"Well, his bastard brother, Jehan de Frigecourt, made a lot of enemies, too, because he was warlike and aggressive, but after becoming a considerable landowner he prospered and lived to a ripe old age. Ever since his time, we've been able to trace our line quite clearly, and in the eighteenth century Louis XIV made the then Vicomte de Frigecourt a marquis, as we know how he liked to flatter his courtiers and keep them about him and out of harm's way at Versailles.

"The de Frigecourt family first lived at Hesdin where the Valois dukes had a castle, now long since vanished. When the ancient château that was on this spot was no longer used as a prison, it was taken over by another seventeenth-century de Frigecourt—Hesdin being not so far away—who wanted a house by the sea. He tore most of that existing structure down and built what is the present château.

"Incidentally, Clare, seeing that you *are* so interested in this period, you will have heard of the famous booty of the last Valois duke, Charles the Bold."

"Oh, the *Burgunderbeute!*" I exclaimed, "the fabulous jewels and treasures he carried about with him, as they did in those days."

"Exactly, even onto the field of battle! Well, after he was slain at Nancy by the Swiss, most of the Burgunderbeute disappeared and was never seen again. *But*"—here Laurent gave me his disarming smile—"legend has it that another de Frigecourt, also on the same battlefield, made off with the treasure when he saw his Lord Charles was dead and fed it slyly into the family coffers. Both my mother and grandmother used to refer to it wistfully; they believed that it still existed somewhere, and they yearned to see and wear the fabled jewels."

"*Here*?" I said excitedly. "Buried treasure?"

Laurent laughed. "Hardly. The château has been knocked about so much since the sixteenth century, I should have thought it would have been found before now. No, he probably sold it—*if* the story is true—and used the money to increase his temporal possessions."

"It's a fascinating story," I said. "I'm very interested in your relationship to the Valois dukes and the connection with St Joan. Especially considering that the place where she was subsequently imprisoned became de Frigecourt property. That *is* an extraordinary coincidence! It alone makes my trip worthwhile. It also makes Jeanne more mysterious; her outburst was odd, almost vindictive."

"Maybe she's a royalist spy!" Laurent joked. "The only one left. No, I'm not worried about Jeanne; she is honest and reliable, of good peasant stock, the backbone of France."

"A bit like her namesake," I said, struck by the comparison.

"Pardon?"

"St Joan of Arc. Good peasant stock; come to think of it, she may even resemble her, though we have no clear idea what Joan looked like despite all that has been written about her. It's just a notion."

And one that continued to intrigue me as, after our farewells and my promise to keep an eye on the family, I drove myself slowly home. Jeanne *did* intrigue me. It seemed farfetched, but could there, *possibly*, be a connection between her and St Joan and the ancient de Frigecourts?

I brooded about the de Frigecourts and Jeanne, but on

the whole I managed to get on with my work. Then two days later I had a letter from Tom, which I'd wanted, but then resented. That unsettled me, so I gave up work for the day and decided on a long walk with perhaps a swim at the end of it, if the tide was right.

I walked briskly into the country, with the aim of exercising my mind and body. Both were tired. I'd only been a month in Port St Pierre and already I was up to my neck in the affairs of a strange family. Now Tom wrote saying he thought we had made a mistake and should get together again. He was having a sabbatical too, and when it had been planned last year we'd thought we'd take it together, maybe go to America, where Tom, as a research psychologist, could catch up with the latest American work.

"I think we should give it another go," Tom wrote in his scrawling hand. "I can't bear the thought of what has happened and that it may be irreversible."

I had assumed it was irreversible. Goodness, five years of marriage, and neither of us getting any younger, especially me. After all, the female breeding mechanism did have a shorter life span than that of a male, and for very good reasons, too. But if my marriage to Tom was a failure, then I might want to try again and have a family. I did like children and didn't want to confine this to other people's. When we were first married, we decided to postpone a family in order to pursue our demanding careers; then as we started to bicker and disagree we knew it was unwise to try and make children mend a bad marriage.

What worried me, as I walked along on that glorious day, the colours turning to browns, coppers, and reds, was that I *had* missed Tom, but I couldn't decide whether it was the strangeness of separation, the absence of sex, or a real feeling of loss.

My road was leading to the bay—all roads round here

led to the bay—and I could see the tip of Le Hourdel as I came round a bend and saw the dunes that were between me and the sea. I'd come well round the bay, and Port St Pierre was only a remote gleam in the sunshine. Here it was wild and desolate—the venue for La Chasse. Every now and then I heard the phut-phut of a gun. The French were wild about La Chasse; the de Frigecourt ancestors certainly were. Philip the Bold, father of John the Fearless, had caused two great works on hunting to be written especially for him—Gace de la Buigne's *Delight of the Chase*, in verse, and *Book of the Chase* by Gaston Phoebus. I started to walk across the dunes, taking care to be on the right side of the notice which warned of the awful things which would happen to those who didn't take heed of the hunters.

The truth was that Tom and I were two emotionally immature academics in their early thirties who'd been married five years. I always admired people who could make up their minds and stick with it. Tom and I both came to a firm decision one day and changed it the next. In the end, I'd been the one to break up the marital nest, and now I was regretting it. I remembered that morning with our flat in a tip and a crestfallen Tom reluctantly carrying my things down to the car. I'd had to harden my heart.

A sudden sharp gust of air and a sting made me stagger, and ahead of me the sand spattered. Dazed, I stopped and held my hand to my cheek, starting to tremble when I found it wet. Slowly lowering my hand, I knew what I would see. Blood. I'd just missed being shot. The horror of it had me sitting on the sand, shaking violently, not even trying to take cover. A stray shot, but from where? Except for the birds, the air was very still. Surely *someone* must have known a shot had misfired and they'd nearly killed me! But the phut-phut of the guns was very far away and all around me was silence. I suddenly leaned forward and was violently sick; then I lay on the sand for a few minutes until my heart rhythm and my breathing returned to normal. I think my face was only scratched because the blood flow soon stopped. Still, no one came. I couldn't believe that anyone would be so callous as not to offer help.

It was despicable, but it was human. I rose unsteadily to my feet, glanced round apprehensively, and set off toward Port St Pierre feeling uneasy and far from the security of home.

I called first upon Madame Gilbert, who was most concerned. She made me sit down and thrust brandy to my lips, though I had recovered somewhat during the hour-long walk. Then, despite my protests, she despatched me across the road to Dr Bourdin to seek a dressing.

Dr Bourdin had obviously been awakened from his siesta—it being just after three—and grumbled about it not being surgery hours. However, when he learned the reason and saw my face, he became more solicitous.

"Tiens, Madame, you were lucky the shot was not higher." He went to his steriliser for his instruments.

"You mean I could have been killed?"

"Of course. A bullet is a bullet." He was looking closely at the wound, cleansing it with an iodine pad he held with forceps. "You should have been more careful."

"I was careful!" I protested, wincing at the sting. "I was on the beach and well away from the notices."

"Eh"—he shrugged—"then someone was careless—that is rare, here, anyway. Now I will give you a tetanus injection, just to be sure."

He gave me a kindly smile—the smile of a comforting, ageless family doctor, a bit slow, but capable and honest.

"You must be more careful next time, Madame, and keep *well* away from the notices."

When I returned, Madame Gilbert nodded her approv-

62

al of the large piece of gauze which almost obscured my cheek.

"Ah, bon. Doctor Bourdin is very skilled; he is from the faculty at Amiens. Now, ma chérie, I will get Martine to escort you to your house. You must rest; it has been a shock."

"Not at all, Madame." But I was trembling again; a delayed reaction. How sweet of her to be so perceptive.

"We must take care of you; after the accident to Rose, someone will think the people of Port St Pierre do not like the English."

I looked at her, and the idea gave me another shock. Perhaps she was right.

I gave in and allowed Martine to come home with me, and then after she had gone I lay on the couch and dozed off. I had really had a terrible fright.

But my adventures were not over for the day. Just before dark there was a knock on the door, which I always left open, as people do in the country. Thinking Martine had been sent to look in on me, I called out to come in without getting up. I felt silly when Laurent de Frigecourt put his head round the door and seemed surprised and embarrassed to see me à la Récamier.

Indeed, I don't know which of us was more confused, especially as he held a large bunch of flowers in his hand. My goodness, was I being courted? No, he'd heard about the accident, of course.

But he hadn't. He stared at my face, and his concern was gratifying.

"Clare! What have you done?"

"I've been shot," I said proudly. "I was nearly a victim of La Chasse and would have appeared, stuffed, on Madame Gilbert's wall, as a warning to all future tenants."

He stopped me, laughing, and I had to explain what had happened.

"But this is serious," he said.

"Of course it is, or was."

"And no one appeared?"

"Not a soul."

Laurent sat down next to me on the sofa.

"That I can't understand. Anyone who was near enough to hit you *must* have known."

That uneasy feeling was with me again. "Don't say that," I said. "It makes it sound . . . deliberate."

Laurent spoke with concern. "Oh, I didn't mean they *intended* to shoot you, but they must have known there had been an accident. Why they didn't come forward I don't understand."

"I do. I mean, people do become cowards about accidents. Maybe when they saw I was all right, they thought they wouldn't bother."

"That isn't very gallant," Laurent protested.

"Oh, it's certainly not gallant, but it is understandable. That is"—I paused—"unless, as Madame Gilbert suggested, someone doesn't like the English."

"You mean, after Rose; but that is absurd."

If he thought it was absurd, he still wasn't smiling. I realized that Madame Gilbert's remark had struck a chord. Someone who didn't like the English, who didn't like the Burgundians, who seemed to hate them in fact . . . but it was all such a long time ago. The Hundred Years War finished in the fifteenth century, five hundred years ago; the English and the Burgundians were then allies against the French monarchy, and both were equally culpable for Joan's death.

Did Jeanne, for some extraordinary reason, have a fixation about the subject of my study? About her namesake? We knew she had intense feelings about the Burgundians. I was suggesting that Jeanne had something to do with Rose's death and my accident. But we knew on both occasions she had been in the house.

"What are you thinking?" Laurent asked. It had been a long silence.

"Oh, nothing." I smiled vaguely. "Why are you here, and with flowers?"

Laurent rose and began to pace back and forth, frowning.

"I've come to ask a great favour."

"Of me? Well, anything I can do . . ." I felt nonetheless apprehensive. I knew I'd been a hit with him personally last night, but these flowers and the letter from Tom were complicating things. It was flattering, but no man had fallen *so* fast.

"It's that Cécile had an accident on the stairs yesterday and twisted her ankle. The sprain is so bad, she can't move."

I almost laughed with relief. Really I had too exalted an opinion of myself. Here I was thinking he was about to make some sort of intimate suggestion, and all he wanted was a new kitchen maid. But me?

"You want me to help in the house?" I must have sounded slightly incredulous.

"No, no, not at all! It's simply that without Cécile, Jeanne has even more to do. Just at the moment Cécile is hard to replace; it's the end of the holiday season and the hotels are still fairly full. I only wondered—as you like the children and the château—if you would consider moving in for a few days, just to keep an eye on things until I have a new nanny. I'm going to Paris tomorrow to find one."

Was Laurent still unhappy about Jeanne? I found the whole thing very puzzling. I was also reluctant to fall in with his suggestion. Something seemed to tell me that I was becoming too involved with the de Frigecourt family.

But how could I refuse? Laurent was looking at me

anxiously. A man one could not help liking, even admiring. And, yes, it would be exciting to live in the château for a while, to explore it, to have the library and that enchanting view of the bay.

"May I let you know tomorrow? I can't say yes now. I must think about it and see how I feel."

"Please couldn't you . . ."

"No, tomorrow," I said firmly. "Or not at all. The chances are that I will agree, but I have my work."

He could see I meant what I'd said. He moved to go.

"Will you have a drink before you leave?"

"No, I must go. Jeanne has had the afternoon off."

"Jeanne wasn't in the château this afternoon?"

"No. As I see so little of the children, I like to have them to myself sometimes, to give them lessons about their family history."

"When would Jeanne have left the château?" I asked idly.

"When?" Laurent screwed up his eyes. Obviously he hadn't a clue as to what I was getting at. "Just after twelve. I saw her take the Renault out just before we had lunch, and we ate early."

I'd been shot at about half-past one.

## CHAPTER 6

There was no question now that I had to go to the château. I felt I owed it to Rose, and I owed it to myself as well. There had been two accidents, one fatal, within a week of one another. And I wondered, how did Cécile come to fall down the stairs? I thought Rose was the link, Rose who had been at my house—she had talked to somebody and thus linked me with the de Frigecourt family.

I drove myself up to the château and found Laurent waiting impatiently for me. He looked tense and ill at ease, and I wondered what else had happened, but he smiled when he saw me and showed me where to leave the car.

"You don't want this old crock to spoil the reputation of the château," I said, noticing it was well out of sight.

"On the contrary, I think it would enhance it. The children are very excited about seeing you."

"I thought you looked worried."

"Well"—he hesitated—"it's Jeanne. I don't think she's very pleased."

"That doesn't surprise me. But I shall be very discreet and not interfere with her authority."

"That's what I told her. I said you really wanted to stay in the château for pleasure, but you would give her any help she needed."

"And?"

"She said *she* didn't need any help; it was a housemaid that was wanted and could you clean?"

At this piece of impertinence I laughed aloud. "I would, but according to my husband, that's one of the many things I'm no good at."

"He's hurt you, hasn't he?" We were climbing the stairs.

"Tom? I'm a bit fragile emotionally, yes. I suppose I've hurt him, too. I was actually the one who moved out."

"The children are in the schoolroom. I'll take you up and show you your bedroom."

I had never been upstairs. The grand staircase curved at the top so that one could approach the first floor from either the right or the left. The corridor was wide, with a thick carpet, and hung with scenes of La Chasse, prints, lithographs, and one or two oils.

"The children are on this floor, and so are you. The schoolroom and their playroom is on the next floor as well as my bedroom and some guest rooms. Jeanne took a fancy to the tower, so she has a room in the front turret."

The one I saw her looking down from, I thought.

"The back of the house we keep closed. In fact, it's far too big a house altogether; it should be a hotel or something. But Elizabeth loved it as soon as she saw it, and. . . ."

"Maybe she'll see it again soon," I said.

"Somehow I don't think she will," Laurent said quietly.

"Oh, Laurent, was that why you were looking so anxious?"

"In part. The news is not good. She's in a coma again, and I must hurry off to Paris today. I'm so grateful to you, Clare. Here, this is your room." He flung open the door of a large, sunny room. "Rose's room."

"Rose's room," I breathed, entering.

There were two windows looking directly over the bay. One could see Le Hourdel from one, from the other Port Guillaume. The windows were covered with gay chintz curtains and the floor with a simple pink carpet. There was a huge comfortable-looking double bed, a big old-fashioned wardrobe and a tallboy, a dressing-table, a chair, and a small table set by the window. The walls were painted white, and on them were hung a long gilt mirror and one or two pictures. It was an attractive room and very French-looking.

"It's charming," I said.

"You don't mind it being Rose's room?"

"Of course I don't! Just put the case on the floor, Laurent, and I'll unpack later on."

"It's one of the prettiest rooms on this floor," he said. "Jeanne thought you would like it."

"How kind of her," I said, wondering why Jeanne should be so concerned about me.

Rose's room. Did I mind? Of course I didn't.


Laurent left before lunch to go to Paris. He'd said goodbye to the children at breakfast and stayed only to see me installed. I saw him off and then wandered back into the house feeling strangely lonely, wondering what I'd done. It was all unfamiliar, and I wasn't really wanted. The house seemed to echo hollowly as I went slowly

69

through the hall and upstairs. Tucked away in the school-room, the children were remote, and the large rooms and corridors seemed deserted. In the kitchen Madame Barbou would be preparing lunch. I hadn't met her yet.

I finished unpacking, putting a few personal things round the room, and then shut the shutters against the hot noonday sun. With the light suddenly gone, Rose's room looked like a tomb, I thought irrationally, as I left and went down to lunch.

Jeanne was in very good form during the meal, and the atmosphere was relaxed. The children were chatty, and Fabrice even fell off his chair with excitement. He was immediately reproved by Jeanne. She did have a strong influence on them, there was no doubt about that. If she laughed, they laughed, and if she was grave they were grave. When she smiled, I saw that she had attractive teeth, very white, and she looked almost pretty.

After lunch the children went into the garden to play, and we had coffee in the salon by the bay window, where we could keep our eyes on them. It looked almost like summer; the trees in the garden were still green, the tide was high, and the bay sparkled with a summer-like haze. I suddenly felt happy and optimistic; I was going to enjoy my stay here, all would be well.

"Milk with your coffee, Madame?" Jeanne stood at the side table where Madame Barbou had put the tray.

"Please call me Clare, if we are to live together. Yes, milk please, Jeanne. Thank you." I took the cup from her, looking into her eyes, and went on, "I think Monsieur de Frigecourt was only thinking of you when he asked me to stay. I shan't interfere, only to give you moral support."

Jeanne's expression was inscrutable. "It was very kind of the Marquis to be so thoughtful. You must let me know if there is anything you want."

"I don't want to be any trouble, especially with the shortage of staff!"

"You will be no trouble, Madame . . . Clare."

"Do you find it a strain teaching children of different ages?"

"No, we have a big schoolroom. Philippe is quite a scholar, though Noelle has natural brilliance. Fabrice is good with his hands; he will be an engineer or a soldier."

"Where were you before, Jeanne?"

"I taught at a school," she said and got up, putting her half-empty cup on the table beside her. "Oh dear, I *told* the boys not to climb trees."

I had the feeling she had deliberately interrupted the conversation, perhaps because it was too personal. I joined her at the window and saw Philippe slithering down a tree and jumping to the ground. But there was no sign of Fabrice.

"I hope Fabrice isn't up in that tree," I said in alarm. "It is much too high for him; the trunk is too smooth."

We both hurried to the door, possessed with a single thought, and when we arrived at the terrace we saw that Fabrice had appeared, clinging to the tree and looking fearfully down at the ground. When he saw us he began to cry, like a frightened kitten that has lost its nerve. I rushed down the steps calling words of encouragement.

It was only as I stood underneath the tree that I realised the very real danger Fabrice was in. He was very high up indeed. How he'd got there in that short a time I had no idea. He wailed loudly and uncontrollably.

"Fabrice, it's all right," I called. "Don't worry, don't panic." Philippe, white-faced, stood by my side. "Philippe, how did Fabrice get up there?"

"On my shoulder, Madame."

"It was very naughty of you. Hurry and find a ladder."

As he turned and ran back to the house, I looked at Jeanne, who remained where she was on the small terrace at the top of the steps. Maybe it was a trick of the sun, which was shining directly on her, or of my eyes—I don't know—but she was staring at Fabrice with an intensity of expression which frightened me, as though she was somehow willing him . . .

God! There was a crash and a scream, a branch hurtled down past me, and acting instinctively I held out my arms and braced myself to receive the shock of Fabrice's falling body. It was over in a second as I grabbed his waist and fell with him to the ground, cushioning his head in my arms. We lay still, Fabrice screaming at the top of his lungs, but I knew he was all right. Both our bodies seemed to tremble in unison.

We were surrounded then by Jeanne and two others, Madame Barbou, who had come running from the kitchen, and a man who I suppose was the gardener, clutching a ladder. Hands reached out for us, and everyone spoke at once. Madame Barbou took Fabrice in her motherly arms and cradled him like a baby, murmuring soothing endearments.

"He's all right," I stammered. "I knew I'd held him close." I felt sick, and I was winded. Fabrice had fallen like a stone, his body heavier than he looked. The gardener gave me his arm and we all walked slowly towards the house. Once inside we were again inspected for cuts and bruises, but there was nothing.

"You saved Fabrice's life," Noelle gasped, beginning to cry.

"Nonsense," Jeanne said, rather sharply. "Madame broke his fall, that is all. He was too near to the ground to be seriously hurt."

"He was halfway up the tree!" Philippe said in his grave voice. "I would not like to have fallen from that height."

I would not like to have fallen from it either and privately considered it a miracle that we were both unharmed. I was confused and disturbed; the incident seemed ordinary, yet it was unnerving. A boy falling from a tree—that happens every day. Again I thought of the light shining upon Jeanne's face and the look in Jeanne's eyes as she gazed steadfastly at Fabrice.

I shivered suddenly, and Madame Barbou suggested I go to bed and she would bring me a hot drink "pour vos nerfs, Madame." The dear French; what a useful word "nerf" was. Unlike "nerves" in English, it could mean many things—shock, remorse, anger, any physical or mental disturbance. Madame Gilbert's "nerfs" were most agile.

"And Fabrice will go to bed, too," Madame Barbou continued, "and I will bring him some nice hot milk."

"I don't *want* to go to bed!" Fabrice stormed, still sobbing.

I sat down with him and took him on my lap rubbing his tousled blond head. "There. If Mademoiselle Jeanne permits, neither of us will go to bed. We shall just sit here and have our nice hot drinks and perhaps play something together. That will make us forget better, won't it?"

"Play soldiers?" Fabrice inquired, visibly brightening.

My heart sank. I had planned to do some reading; my work had been neglected. However, I looked at his sturdy body and his tear-stained face, and I was so grateful he was whole and unbroken that I would have done anything for him.

"We'll do anything you like," I said. "But first we shall sit here quietly, while Madame Barbou brings us our drinks and the others go off to the schoolroom."

If Jeanne resented my assumption of authority she didn't show it. She looked much paler than usual, and she seemed to smile gratefully at me as she ushered the other children out of the room, speaking in the hushed tones one reserves for the sick.

"Venez, leave Madame and Fabrice to rest; they have had a shock."

Fabrice gave a deep sigh—maybe seeing the others

73

shooed off to the schoolroom had a soporific effect—and sank back against my chest. I hugged his legs and held him close, looking out over the bay; the tide had turned and the ships anchored there were leaning over on their keels. His little blond head sank, his breathing became regular, and I knew he was asleep. He was such a trusting, loving child. The line between life and death, happiness and tragedy, was so fragile. Thank God he was safe.

By the time Madame Barbou came in with the drinks, I was drowsy too.

"Le pauvre," she said bustling up to us, her kind face creased with concern.

"I'll stay with him," I said. "Let's put him on the sofa and cover him up." We carried him gently between us.

"Do you think he *could* have been killed?" I asked her, sipping a brew of hot milk and brandy with sugar.

Madame Barbou shrugged, her large body quivering slightly. "After all, it was a heavy fall, who knows?"

And I thought yes, a fall is like a bullet; if correctly placed, both can kill. But no one had pushed Fabrice; that I knew for sure.

"There have been too many accidents in this house." Madame shook her head mournfully. "It is terrible, Madame; they say the house has a curse."

I hastily took a draught of my toddy. "Who says the house has a curse?"

"It is a legend, Madame, ever since I was a child. The de Frigecourts have not been a fortunate family."

"You mean the family is cursed, or the house?" I asked impatiently, as though we were talking about something entirely normal.

Madame Barbou looked puzzled. "It is the family, Madame, though it goes with the house. It is called the Burgundian curse. The curse of Burgundy. Monsieur Laurent will tell you more about it."

74

"The curse of Burgundy," I repeated. "Of course. Burgundy and the de Frigecourts."

Someone who hated Burgundians and de Frigecourts. And who else would that be but Joan of Arc? But I didn't dare share my thoughts with this good simple lady who went on speaking:

"As children we were not allowed to play near the house or its grounds. In those days the château was neglected and surrounded by trees. This goes back to the Twenties, Madame, when I was a girl and the Marquis had been killed in the war, fighting on the Somme. Oh, how we all suffered in that terrible war. We could hear the guns from Abbeville, and the refugees streamed here from the front at Albert and Arras."

"So Monsieur Laurent's father *and* grandfather were killed in the two world wars?"

Madame Barbou nodded.

"Tragic, but heroic, Madame. It is a family of heroes."

Fabrice stirred and whimpered in his sleep.

"Tell me more later," I whispered, my finger to my lips. "I don't want to wake him up."

She crept out of the room, but I sat still for a long time looking out of the window until the bay was a vast expanse of sand again, thinking.

Fabrice didn't wake until four, and I had dozed as well. Refreshed by our rest, we went up to the playroom and he marshalled his soldiers for the French versus the English, of whom I was in command. Of course, the English would lose. He had a very well ordered mind for such a young child, and a determined idea of what he wanted to do and how to do it. I felt my age as he rushed about the room giving orders and firing numerous cannons at my scattered remnant (which was about half his army anyway).

I was in full flight, with hardly a man standing, when the door opened and Philippe came in, followed by Noelle. Philippe immediately joined the fray on his brother's side and began bombarding me with small objects while Fabrice shrieked encouragement.

"Aux armes, Philippe, the French are winning!"

"It's hopeless," I said, sitting on the floor and laughing, and when I looked up Jeanne was in the doorway looking at the disorder. I thought she was about to reprimand them, or me, or all of us, but instead she said quietly, "Please clear up, it is time for tea."

"Five minutes," Fabrice pleaded. "Clare is losing."

Jeanne's eyes swept the floor and took in the cavalcades of blue- and red-coated soldiers camped on artificial mountains, drawn up in ragged lines of battle.

"Where are the Burgundians?" she said quietly. "Madame, you should have the Burgundians to help your English soldiers; then maybe you would win."

I looked at her rather stupidly, but she had turned and was directing the children in putting the soldiers back into their various drawers and boxes.

After tea I decided to have it out with Jeanne. Was I not newly resolved to be firm and more positive in my approach to things, so that there would be no more situations such as I had with Tom?

The children were watching television in a small room across the hall next to the library. Jeanne seemed inclined to linger over the tea things, and I accepted her offer of another cup.

"Are you quite recovered now, Clare?"

"Oh, completely. It was just a shock."

"And I heard you were shot at the other day?"

I looked sharply up at her, but her head was bent over the tea.

76

"I'm unlucky, aren't I?"

"Some people seem prone to mishap," Jeanne went on. "Look at poor Rose."

"Did things often happen to Rose?" I said curiously.

"Rose was never where she should be," Jeanne said, looking at me. "She was always somewhere else. She had no sense of responsibility at all."

"How unsuitable for a children's nursemaid."

"It was unfortunate, in these circumstances. Oh, she was very good with children, of that there is no doubt; but she had to be supervised, and of course it was not my job to do that. She needed a strong woman in the house, a mother. Rose resented me because I tried to exercise some control over her."

"So you and Rose didn't get on too well?"

Jeanne stirred her tea and looked at me thoughtfully. I could quite like Jeanne if only some of this mystery were cleared up, if only I weren't so suspicious of her. She had an interesting face, rather wistful-looking, as though she had a story to tell that would be worth hearing.

"Rose and I had nothing in common. She wasn't interested in anything to do with the intellect; she was restless here and wanted Paris, while I love the beauty and tranquillity of Port St Pierre. She only wanted to enjoy herself and to chase men."

"Men, here?" I said with interest.

"Oh yes. Rose had a lover."

She waited for the impact this would make on me, but I didn't react too strongly. After all, this was the twentieth century and I'd had a few lovers myself before Tom. But the way Jeanne said, "Rose had a lover" made it sound like a sin.

"I don't find that surprising. Rose was a pretty girl."

We both knew at once what I'd said, and Jeanne looked at me, a slight smile playing on her lips. It wasn't either a triumphant or a malicious smile. She seemed simply to be calling my bluff.

"Why didn't you tell anyone Rose had been to see you?" Jeanne said quietly. "I thought it was strange you never mentioned it."

I blushed hotly, trying to hide my embarrassment by turning my face to one side. She made me feel so foolish.

"I don't know why I should have," I said defensively.

"Because of her death?"

"Goodness no!"

I was horrified. Any minute I'd be accused of having done Rose in; but in fact, it did look incriminating.

"I wondered what you had to hide?" Jeanne went on, in the same gentle voice.

"I didn't hide anything," I protested. "I simply thought it was irrelevant."

"Did you know Rose in England?"

"No."

"You knew her only from ringing her here?"

"I rang *you* here to ask you to tea, and spoke to Rose."

"And that was the very first time you'd spoken to her?"

"Yes."

"And did you ask her round to tea by herself?"

"No . . . no." I had the feeling I must be careful of a trap.

"She came round to talk about me, didn't she?"

I didn't reply. I was desperately trying to think how I should play this, how I should fend off Jeanne's insinuations.

"No," I said at last, "she came to apologise for her abruptness on the phone."

"And to say that it was my fault."

"She implied that it was your fault, yes."

"Rose was trying to have me sacked," Jeanne said flatly, looking at me. "She was trying to build up some

78

horrible picture of me, and I never knew why. She was very anxious to see the Marquis so that she could fill his ears full of poison against me. I simply murmured that day that you were a complete stranger—you were after all—and that as the father was due back soon I should like to ask him. She hurled down the phone deliberately, so as to make you think it was my fault. Was my attitude not reasonable?"

I floundered; it was all so entirely plausible. "Yes, yes, I suppose it was."

"Yet Rose hurried round to you to tell you how nasty I am, how difficult." She held up her hand to stop my protests. "Don't say she didn't. Rose did it with everyone. With Cécile, Madame Barbou, the doctor and his daughter, with everyone we ever met. She would get to know them and then start whispering about me. I know, because sooner or later it all came back to me.

"You see, Clare, I know what she said, but . . ." Something about her forced me to look into her eyes. "It was not I who was evil, it was Rose."

# CHAPTER 7

At that moment, the children came into the room saying that the television was boring. Jeanne said it was near bedtime anyway, and I offered to help give them their baths. I felt certain the charged atmosphere in the room must have been obvious to the children, but they seemed unaware of what had transpired between Jeanne and myself. After a romp in the hall with Goofy, who was never allowed on the upper floors, they streaked upstairs followed by the two of us, breathless and laughing.

After our extraordinary conversation I felt an intimacy with Jeanne that was wholly unexpected. She had convinced me that somehow Rose had wronged her; that she was a gentle misunderstood person, a victim of Rose's mischievousness. I hadn't then asked myself all the questions that so badly needed to be answered, but as we splashed with the children, rubbing them down, getting them into warm pyjamas, and taking turns reading them stories, I felt a rapport with Jeanne that would have seemed incredible a few short hours before.

I was looking forward to continuing our talk and went downstairs to wait for her after kissing the children and leaving her to tuck them in. I didn't want to encroach upon her territory.

I waited in vain, however. When Madame Barbou announced dinner, she said I should be on my own, as she had taken a tray up to Mademoiselle Jeanne in her room.

"She sends her apologies," she told me, showing me to my solitary seat at the head of the long dining room table.

"She has a migraine, she suspects brought on by the events of the day. Poor Mademoiselle is not a healthy person, you know. Now I can see you are a sturdy robust woman, but Mademoiselle is—" Madame Barbou fluttered her hands, "nerveuse, if you understand what I mean." She hovered over me, and I knew that she wanted to gossip. I took up my spoon and began my soup.

"Madame, if I am to eat alone please do not lay this table especially for me; a small table in the salon . . ."

"Ah, bien sur, Madame, but tonight I did expect Mademoiselle Jeanne. Is Madame going to stay long?"

"Oh, no, just a short stay until you get more help."

"And Madame didn't know the family before?"

"No."

"Nor poor Rose, I suppose." Madame Barbou didn't seem to expect an answer. "She was a funny girl. She and Jeanne didn't get on at all, of course."

"It must have been difficult in the house," I murmured over my soup.

"No, it was not difficult. They were discreet and kept it from the children; they each did their own tasks well, I must say. But Mademoiselle Jeanne was always having to take over from Rose; Rose had a habit of disappearing."

"A boyfriend?"

"Ah." Madame was gratified I'd guessed so quickly.

"Not exactly a *boyfriend*, Madame, an *older* man, much older."

"Really? Did he ever come here?"

"Oh, no, indeed. Rose was *most* secretive about it, but my daughter Agnes goes to the market in Port Guillaume and she saw Rose with this older man at least twice."

"Rose went to Port Guillaume to meet him?"

"Evidently."

"But it's a long way without a car."

"There is a bus."

"Or I suppose she could have crossed the bay if the tide was right."

It was a fascinating thought. Rose trysting with a lover by boat.

"Did she ever talk about her friend?"

"Never. That was the strange part. She was very secretive."

"Do you think she went to see him the day she had her accident?"

"*Accident*, Madame?" Madame Barbou's voice was scornful.

I put down my spoon and stared at her. "You don't think she had an accident?"

"No one would walk across the bay when the tide was due, Madame."

"But then, why didn't anyone say anything to the police?"

Madame Barbou looked taken aback. "What can anyone say, Madame? What can anyone prove? Besides, what is the point of stirring up trouble? The de Frigecourt family has had enough trouble already. She was a funny girl, a stranger really. Why should we care how she died and upset our own family again after the wars and

82

the killings and the accident to Madame la Marquise . . ."

Now I was beginning to understand. Justice was justice, but the love of this small community for its land-
owning family seemed to transcend all that.

This thought left me in a sombre frame of mind as I
went up to my room, Rose's room. It was not unusual for
communities to close up against a stranger. What Madame Barbou had admitted shed new light on the circumstances surrounding Rose's death. I had always thought
the investigation into the nanny's death a cursory affair—
and this had surprised me. But now the reason was quite
obvious—to protect the de Frigecourt family at all costs,
they've had such an awful time.

Or was that the only reason? I stopped abruptly on the
stairs when I thought of the pretty Rose and the attractive
Marquis. Perhaps they were having an affair. Maybe
darker deeds had been done in this house more recently
than I had contemplated.

It was dark on the staircase, a light shining obliquely
from the corridor. The house was perfectly still, and
again I felt that same quiet joy from just being in it as I
had had looking at it that very first time from the beach.
To me, it was a friendly house. How many people had
been born, lived, and died here from the days when it
was merely a shooting box for the noble de Frigecourts
trapped at Versailles? The milestones of life imprinted an
atmosphere on a house as much as they formed the character and expressions of people. The Château des Moulins was grand enough to absorb all that had happened
within its walls, bad things as well as good.

I went into the children's rooms to be sure they were
all right. Philippe was already asleep, one leg dangling
out of bed, so I tucked him in, kissed his dark face, and
covered him with his blanket. I lingered over Fabrice to

make sure he was all right, but he was breathing gently, his arms clasped around his pillows—fast asleep. Noelle was still awake; she raised herself to greet me and I could sense she wanted to chat, but I tucked her firmly in, and as I bent to kiss her she put her arms up and wrapped them firmly round my neck.

Surprised, I knelt on the floor, enfolded her in my arms, and hugged her. Her body was trembling, and I saw that she was weeping.

"Noelle, darling . . ." Her thin shoulders shook with the violence of her sobbing and I sat with her until she quieted down, stroking her cheeks and making soothing noises.

"I . . . i . . . it's F . . . F . . . Fabrice." She shuddered. "He could have been killed."

"Darling, don't think about it. All little boys fall off trees at one time or another. *I* don't think he could have been killed," I lied.

"Yes, he could have. Oh, I can't bear it after Mama."

"There, there . . ." I tried as best I could to comfort the little girl who'd been without her mother so long.

After a while Noelle sat up and rubbed her eyes. Even then, she looked almost beautiful, and as I smoothed her hair back from her damp brow I thought she would tease a lot of men when she grew older. She gazed at me solemnly.

"We are an unlucky family. Madame Barbou says we are cursed."

Curse Madame Barbou! It was typical of these emotional French, I thought, forgetting my own half-French ancestry, which Tom said was the cause of the many upheavals we'd had.

"Madame Barbou is talking nonsense. There is really no such thing as a curse. You are a happy, lovely family, and when Mama is well you will all be together again and live happily ever after. There now, smile?"

84

Knowing what I knew, was I doing the right thing? But wasn't it better to comfort the child than to let her go on weeping?

"I love you," Noelle said and I blushed in the darkness.

"I'm glad. I love you too. Now go to sleep. I'm only two doors away if you want anything."

But I was anxious and full of foreboding as I made my way along the dimly lit corridor to my room. I *was* drawn to the children, I *did* love them, but to have them dependent upon me was a terrible responsibility. I hadn't come to Port St Pierre to become a foster mother for real parents who were unable to discharge their duties.

Rose's room. A soft breeze greeted me as I went in, even though I'd closed the windows before I went down to dinner. I put on the bedside light and thought again how pretty it was; one felt immediately at ease here. I went to the window and looked across the bay—my bay, Laurent's bay. Everyone who looked at the bay seemed to love it. The tide was out now and there was no moon. But far out to the mouth of the bay I could see the ribbon of light that the Channel made on the horizon; over there was England. And Tom.

Opposite me, on the other side, the lights of Port Guillaume highlighted the enchanting old town. I thought of Joan on her last journey to Rouen crossing the bay, with what misgivings? I thought of Rose and her mysterious lover, and then of all the soldiers in both wars who had been killed in this valley of the Somme. How many ghosts were here? For some reason, I recalled those rows of red and blue French and English soldiers and Jeanne's strange remark, "Where are the Burgundians?" And then that odd, almost terrifying expression on Jeanne's face, and Fabrice falling into my arms like a stone.

For a couple of days after that, nothing untoward oc-

curred. I worked well, slept well, and enjoyed enormously the huge meals provided by Madame Barbou and her
daughter Agnès. At this rate, I might sacrifice the trim
Trafford waistline. I saw Jeanne and the children together at mealtimes or after school and spent a lot of time in
my room working. My Joan was making exceedingly
good progress, perhaps, I could not help thinking, because I'd come to a spot where she had once lived. Still, it
was a strange thought.

Wednesday afternoons the children had off and I
offered to relieve Jeanne, who was looking tired, and take
them for a walk.

"Only if you're sure it's no trouble," she said.

"Of course it's no trouble! I've done a lot of work these
past two days. Jeanne," I said on an impulse, "did you
speak to Rose after she'd seen me? Was it Rose who told
you about my work on Joan of Arc?"

Jeanne gazed at me with that mild expression which
seemed so knowing.

"No, Clare. I guessed Rose had been to see you because I heard her asking Madame Barbou if she knew
where you lived. I knew how sly she was and that she
would try to make trouble. She was also late for lunch
that day and by the way she looked at me when she got
back, I knew she'd been up to something."

"You're very perceptive, Jeanne."

"Yes," Jeanne began slowly, wondering whether or not
to go on, "I do have a certain amount of second sight. I
often know things before people tell me, or before I even
see them. That's how I knew you were writing about Joan
of Arc."

"But," I began, and stopped.

"You think it's nonsense, don't you? It's something I
never wanted or asked for but have had since a child. I
know things that are going to happen. As soon as I saw

you, I knew you were going to move into the château, that we were going to know you a lot better. And, when you said you were writing a book, the knowledge sprang to my mind that it was about Joan of Arc."

"Then you told the Marquis?"

She shrugged. "I told him you were an English writer working on a book about La Pucelle; I suppose it slipped out."

"It must be very frightening, a power like that."

"It doesn't bother me. Sometimes I'm wrong, and I never know what is going to happen to me, only whether people will affect me for good or for bad. I . . ." Jeanne hesitated and the expression on her face frightened me. "I . . . as soon as I saw you on the beach talking to the children I was very apprehensive; I felt you were going to bring me harm."

"*You* harm? Me?" I was incredulous.

"Clare, I can't explain it, and I like you, I really do; but I was afraid of you."

"Are you still now?"

"I don't know. I can't think what could happen."

"That's why you didn't want me in the house?"

"Yes. I'm sorry, I see I've upset you."

"Well, it's not a nice feeling to think one might be a psychic force for the bad."

"I have been wrong in the past. I may be wrong now."

"I hope you are, Jeanne. Let's try and forget about it."

But this was easier said than done. My feelings about Jeanne were now in complete disarray. She could be mad, evil, or stupid, or she could simply be telling me the truth. As I'd spent years married to a psychologist—a broad-minded one at that—I knew a little about the paranormal. It was an absorbing subject; and it made my study of Joan fascinating. Did she hear voices or didn't she? Was she hallucinatory? Joan definitely had had second sight. The sword of Fierbois was an example, and so was the secret message she gave the Dauphin Charles at Chinon that convinced him she came from God. She also knew she would be wounded and when, and she undoubtedly knew that she would die, but not how.

My Joan and this Jeanne were rather alike. It was a bizarre thought.

Soon the fun of the afternoon, seeing the children and the dog race about on the sand, seemed to dispel these disturbing ideas from my mind. The afternoon sparkled with the wind blowing over the sea and the waves cresting with foam. The cold of the early October day gave the air a crispness, a hard, diamond-like quality. The children had taken off their shoes and were running in and out of the water throwing sticks for Goofy. I thought it was cold for the sea, but they had heavy sweaters on.

"Be careful," I cautioned. "Fabrice, be careful of the tide; it will soon turn and will take you with it."

Philippe raced up to me, his handsome face eager to reassure me. "Have no fear, Clare. The water is shallow today. You could walk across the bay with the tide."

"Well, don't," I said. "You keep your eyes on your brother who always wants to imitate you."

Philippe laughed and sped off. As the tide began to retreat they followed it, and soon they were far out in the bay; I had kept a straight course and the tide was moving away from me at an angle. We had long passed the town and were approaching the dunes where I'd been shot. My hand flew to my cheek, and I was filled with a urgent, irrational fear. The force of the wind made me bend my body to strive against it, and to my alarm the children were moving farther and farther away as they followed the sea. Philippe had taken no notice at all of what I'd said. I started to pant as I ran after them, filled with dread. I was furious with them for giving me such a

88

fright and that made my task harder; the wind blew and buffeted me and the sand swirled up, making each step more difficult than the last.

I stopped, rubbing the sand from my eyes, cursing the wind. Ahead of me, slightly to the right obscured by the dunes, a figure was gazing intently at the children, who were the only figures on the beach. He bent down, and when he straightened up, he held something in his hand which he raised to his shoulder.

A gun! Someone was aiming a gun at the children. I called out and started to run, tripped and came crashing to the ground. I raised my head, but the wind blew my hair across my face into my eyes. I beat the sand struggling to get up, but the wind roared in my ears, and I felt helpless and confused.

Then there was a firm hand on my shoulder and a man's voice saying into my ear, "Madame, are you hurt?"

I grasped at the hand offered me, a firm, brown, masculine hand, and was pulled up onto my feet.

"I saw you fall. Did you twist your ankle?"

The gun was resting casually in the crook of his left arm as he helped me up with his right hand. I looked ahead of me and the children were only specks on the horizon.

The children!" I exclaimed angrily. "Look where they are!"

"They seem perfectly safe to me, Madame. True, I thought they were a bit far out, and I was examining them with my telescope to see how near the sea they were."

"Your telescope!"

"I have a telescopic sight on my gun."

He gave me such a charming, friendly smile I felt almost dizzy with relief. And I'd thought he was going to shoot them! What a disordered imagination I had. I leaned heavily on my protector.

"Ah, you saw me; you thought I was pointing the *gun* at them?"

I nodded, too weak and ashamed to reply.

"But Madame, why should I point a gun at your children? Still, it was a perfectly natural fear. I'm sorry."

"Someone took a shot at me the other day," I said by way of explanation. "Maniacs, you know, one never can be sure. I must go and get the children. They're much too far out. They'll be in the Channel before they're finished." I tried to go forward but my ankle collapsed under me; the pain was intense.

"Oh hell, I've sprained my ankle!"

"That is too bad. Here, let me go after them and then you will feel less anxious."

As he left, he put his gun down and started to run with long vigorous strides. He was about fifty, a good-looking man of athletic build, a full set beard clipped close to his face, which was deeply tanned as though he spent a lot of time outdoors. His hair was thick and curly, mostly grey but streaked with black. He had on a duffle coat and high boots over his trousers. I looked curiously at his gun and saw the telescope over the barrel. I lifted it. It was heavy, but by squinting along the sights I could see four figures on the waterline chatting animatedly. Philippe called to Goofy, who was wet and dripping, and the four began to walk back. My kind saviour had Fabrice by the hand. What luck!

But when I saw them close up I was less pleased. Fabrice was soaked to the skin, turning blue with cold, and the other two were very wet. My relief turned again to indignation, and I began to scold them almost before they were within earshot.

"Philippe, you should be ashamed. After all I *told* you. Noelle, you as the eldest . . ."

90

The man laughed and took my arm, helping me along. "Madame, you are upset. The children are none the worse for wear and have had a very good time. Let me drive you in my car."

The children eyed me warily and kept close to their protector as we trudged to the car parked by the side of the dunes. He had a large white Mercedes with a German number plate. He opened the boot for the dog and the back door for the children.

"I'm afraid they'll ruin your car," I said apologetically.

"That's no problem. I'll put a rug on the seat."

The children shuffled in, glancing guiltily at me while the man helped me into the front.

"How's your foot?"

"I'll have to hobble for a day or two, but I think I'll live, thanks to you."

"Where to, Madame?"

"The château, the big pink château on the bay."

"Ah, the Château des Moulins. I know it. My name is Gustav Schroeder, Madame."

"I'm Clare Trafford."

"You're English?" He looked at me with surprise. "Your French is excellent!"

"I'm half-French, but England is my home. Your French is very good too."

"Ah, but I'm half-French too; my mother came from Alsace."

"What a coincidence. I mean our both being half-French." Schroeder was driving expertly along the road towards the town.

"You're familiar with this area?"

"Very familiar."

"Did you know the de Frigecourt family?"

"Yes, before the children were born. It was a long time ago. Here is the lane, I think, and there is your château."

He looked lingeringly at it before he stopped by the gate.

It seemed that everyone who saw the château was impressed by it.

"Won't you come in?" He was helping me out of the car.

"Thank you, not today. I have an appointment. A lucky chance made me see you as I was on my way to the car."

"I'm very grateful."

"Not at all, Madame. I hope we have the pleasure of meeting again another time." He patted the children on their heads as they tumbled out of the car, then released a rather indignant dog from the boot; Goofy wasn't used to that kind of treatment and shook himself vigorously, showering us with water.

"Philippe," I commanded, "give me your arm. Thanks to you I can hardly walk. Au revoir, Monsieur, merci."

"Rien de tout, Madame, rien de tout." He gave a little Germanic bow, waved and got into the car.

"What a nice man," Noelle remarked as he drove off, but I was too busy hanging onto Philippe, wincing with pain at every step, to reply.

## CHAPTER 8

Rose's room. Something had awakened me, and I lay in the dark room with those words forming and reforming themselves in my brain. Rose's room, Rose's room, Rose . . . Why had I woken up? I felt a twinge of pain in my ankle; maybe I'd moved and disturbed it. We'd bathed it and bandaged it and I'd sat with it on a stool all evening, doing my best to look both disapproving and martyr-like. I was furious with the children for the shock they'd given me more than for the pain of my injury; after Rose the thought of their being swept out to sea was terrifying. However, to make up for their behaviour, they'd been angelic, doing everything they could to help and please me, long cuddles before going to bed.

Jeanne, also helpful and sympathetic, had nevertheless been rather amused by the whole incident.

I lay in the dark room thinking; my eyes began to close,

heavy with sleep again. Suddenly there was a sharp and terrible scream. Without a thought of ankle or anything else, I hurled myself out of bed and flung open the door. The corridor was in darkness, but I had no doubt the scream had come from Noelle's room, two doors away. I hobbled toward her door, flinging it open just as she was about to scream again. Her room was brightly lit by the moonlight streaming in through the window.

"Noelle . . ." I rushed to her side and gathered her in my arms; she was trembling violently, and as I held her she began sobbing against my chest. I recalled the other night when the same thing had happened. Despite her tomboy air, Noelle was a very nervous child.

"Shhh . . . there . . . did you have a nightmare?"

It was some time before she could talk, and seeing that the moonlight made the room look eerie, I drew the curtains and put on the light.

"There. Was it the moonlight playing tricks?"

Noelle looked puzzled; she was staring at a corner of the room, the far corner from her bed, near the door.

"I was restless," she began. "I kept waking and thinking how much we'd upset you, and then, then I saw . . ." She pointed towards the corner of the room and dissolved into tears again. "Over there."

I held her tightly, strangely fearful myself. "And saw, Noelle?" I was trying hard to keep my voice steady.

"Something in white, like a ghost." She started trembling again.

"Darling, it was the moonlight. I swear it was; you should draw your curtains when there is a full moon. It plays tricks, especially with sensitive people like you."

"But I saw it so clearly in the moonlight. It was a girl, like me."

"A little girl?"

"Well, a bit older maybe."

94

She seemed very sure. I went to the corner just to look round; but it was bare of furniture or anything that could have appeared ghost-like in the moonlight.

"Did you ever see anything like that before?"

"No."

"Then it was a dream. Shall I stay with you until you fall asleep?"

"Please, can I come and sleep with you?"

"I don't see why not." The bed was plenty big, I was too tired to sit up, and my ankle was throbbing. I nodded and she climbed out of bed and ran to my room. I hobbled after her, first putting out the light and opening the curtains. I looked about me, studying the room as she had seen it in the moonlight. Almost any place could look spooky with the moon like that. Perhaps a cloud had caused some shadow? But the sky was clear, a still autumn night.

Noelle was already in my bed when, after taking a couple of painkillers, I got in beside her. She reached for my hand and held it tightly, and I talked softly to her, saying that she shouldn't be afraid.

"What about the curse?"

"There really are no such things; they are all make-believe."

"And ghosts?"

"Ghosts don't exist either."

Gradually the hold on my hand relaxed and she was asleep. But I lay awake a good while longer. It was strange that I had woken up thinking of Rose *before* Noelle screamed. Her scream didn't wake me. Noelle was considerably younger than Rose, who had looked younger than she was. But why would Rose haunt a room two doors away? I shivered involuntarily and held Noelle's thin body close to mine. I needed comfort too.

❁    ❁    ❁

Both Noelle and I slept late, and so we looked tired and wan at breakfast, but everyone else was cheerful, especially Jeanne. She was most intrigued about Noelle's story and questioned her closely. I watched Jeanne carefully. What was she up to now?

"Run along," she told them after they'd finished their bowls of coffee, hot bread, which Madame Barbou brought from the boulangerie on her way to the château, and apricot jam.

"Get out your books and I will be with you soon."

Generally she went up with them and I finished my coffee in a pleasant stupor, usually with a cigarette while I had a look at *Le Monde*.

"Well?"

"Well, Jeanne?"

"Do you think she did see something?"

"Of course I don't. Do you?"

"I don't know." Jeanne sat back tapping her fingers on the table. Her normally impassive face seemed alive with some secret excitement.

"A young girl, she said."

"Yes?"

"Have you thought who it might be?"

"Rose?"

"*Rose?*" Jeanne repeated in genuine astonishment. "Rose was not a young girl. She was twenty-three."

"That seems young enough to me."

"But it is not a *young* girl." She was breathless now. "Jeanne d'Arc was a young girl."

"*Joan of Arc?*" I almost fell off my chair in surprise.

"She was nineteen when they killed her, seventeen when she started her career, *eighteen* when she was imprisoned in the château at Port St Pierre."

"You honestly think it was Joan of Arc?"

"Don't you?"

"No, I don't. I think Noelle was having some sort of emotional disturbance."

"But Joan wore white—remember her white armour? I have thought for a long time there was a presence in this château. I told you I had second sight. I really believe that the spirit of Jeanne d'Arc dwells here, and that is how I knew about you."

I took a lungful of smoke and gave the morning smoker's hearty hacking cough.

"You don't believe me at all, do you?" Jeanne went on accusingly. "You think I'm mad."

"Of course I don't think you're mad. I just don't believe in ghostly manifestations of people, especially saints, long dead. If we are to believe the church, *your* church incidentally, Joan is in heaven among the blessed."

"Ah,"—Jeanne twined her hands together—"but spirits have many ways of manifesting themselves; look at the saints who have appeared to many people. St Martin de Porres was seen in several places at the same time."

"Are you particularly interested in St Joan, Jeanne?"

"Yes," she breathed. "I feel sometimes that I am possessed by her. I was restless and disturbed until I came to Port St Pierre, and I think now that she sent me."

"Why?" I tried to keep my voice perfectly calm during this extraordinary conversation. One is not married to a psychologist for five years for nothing.

Jeanne's luminosity had gone and she looked strangely haggard, as though her vision had taken its toll. "I don't know. It has not been revealed to me yet. God works through his creatures."

I remembered what she'd said about me. "Do you still think I'm a danger to you?"

"That may be part of the plan," she said, quietly pushing back her chair. "We shall see."

"Well, I shan't be here long," I said, but I don't think Jeanne heard me.

I smoked another cigarette and accepted Madame Barbou's offer of fresh coffee.

"Jeanne is strange, n'est-ce pas?" she said in her cheerful way as she cleared away the breakfast dishes.

"Did you hear what she said?"

Madame Barbou looked at once defensive and apologetic. "Eh, one could not help . . ."

She had been eavesdropping, no doubt on her way into the dining room.

"Did anyone ever see a ghost here before?" I asked.

"Oh, *yes*, Madame. Before the first world war, the Marquise would not come here because she had a vision before the death of one of her children. And then before the Marquis and his two sons were taken, Madame la Marquise had a premonition and said she saw the spirit of a young girl in white."

"Then Noelle must have heard the story," I said, rationalizing the little girl's vision last night, but I was vaguely uncomfortable.

"It is always so before deaths, Madame."

"How unpleasant," I said, getting up. If I encouraged her in this sort of chat she'd think I believed it and it would be all over town. "I'm going into the library to wait for the doctor, Madame Barbou. Jeanne was kind enough to phone before breakfast. My ankle is twice its normal size today."

"Ah, pauvre Madame Trafford; let me help you." She gave me her arm as we crossed the hall.

The library was a long middle room overlooking the wall guarding the right side of the château. As it was a fairly dark room, with no view of the bay, it was necessary to have the light on even during the daytime. Laurent had told me it was the one room that had never needed to be restored, shielded as it was from the storms. It was indeed a delightful room, panelled and lined with books, all carefully catalogued and numbered—essays, belles-lettres, geography, topography, classics, the great French works of fiction, Balzac, Molière, and a whole section devoted to history. There were some beautifully bound volumes among them, and in the middle of the room was a case containing some very rare manuscripts of the fifteenth-century Valois dukes, which Laurent had casually remarked were priceless and ought to be under lock and key, only no one knew about them! This made them safe, he said.

There were two tables in the room, both old and covered with scarred, faded leather. I got a volume of Burgundian history and settled down to wait for the doctor.

The last Valois duke, Charles the Bold, the one with the treasure allegedly "rescued" by an overzealous de Frigecourt, had a passion for hats and I was reading an account of his *trésor* when I looked up. A young woman stood at the door smiling. For one ghastly moment I wondered if she were another emanation of the supernatural, but she looked perfectly modern and normal and carried a black bag in her hand.

"Madame Trafford?"

I nodded and got to my feet.

"Please sit down. I know your ankle is bad. I am Doctor Bourdin's daughter, also a doctor. My father has an attack of the mal de foie—he is overfond of his food you know—and I have come in his place."

"How kind. Would you like to go into the salon where the light is better?"

"No, why not here? If you would just take off your sock and pull up your trouser leg, I'll look at the ankle."

I did as I was told, and the dark-haired young woman bent over me and began manipulating my ankle while I groaned and ground my teeth until my forehead was covered with sweat. I wondered if she'd just qualified.

"Sorry, did I hurt? I wondered if you'd broken a bone, but I see now that it's simply a sprain."

"Simply," I muttered. "Thanks."

I watched her as she bandaged the ankle, a girl of about twenty-six, of medium height and with a nice neat figure and a capable face. She was plain rather than pretty— what the French call *jolie-laide*—attractive in an odd sort of way.

"There. Keep off it for two days and I will come and see you again."

"Won't you have some coffee? I don't want to stay here, so if you will give me your arm we can go into the salon."

"Weren't you working?"

"Only desultorily. I was waiting for you. I usually work in my room."

"Are you going to stay here long?"

"I hope not."

"You don't like it?"

"On the contrary, I love it, but I've come here to write a book, and what with one thing or another I don't seem to be making much progress. Last night we had a ghost!"

"Really?" Dr Bourdin helped me to the sofa and tucked a cushion under my ankle.

"Have you heard of ghosts here before?"

"Only vague rumours. You know, every large Gothic house has a ghost. But during much of my life the family has not been here and the house was closed. I was born after the war when the tragedy happened."

"Did you ever meet Elizabeth?"

"The mother? Oh, yes. They had a big party when the château was opened, and they invited everybody. Then we were also asked to dinner with the mayor and other local worthies. It is tragic about the mother, yet they say—

my father keeps a careful eye on them—that the children do not appear too much affected. I am studying to be a pediatrician, so this kind of thing interests me."

"Noelle said she saw the ghost last night."

"Did she?"

I thought Dr Bourdin seemed to attach a lot of weight to this announcement, and she looked unusually thoughtful. I questioned her about it.

"Well, it's silly. It's part of the rumour and supersition, of course, but they say that someone in the family always sees a ghost here before a death. That's just because . . ."

"I know, Madame Barbou told me. Do you believe in phenomena like this?"

"Ghosts? Not really, but I do believe in some kind of paranormal manifestation of subconscious mechanisms and desires. I would think the children are inevitably disturbed in some way, even though Mademoiselle Jeanne is thought to be very good with them. Then there was also Rose . . ."

She looked at me and I looked at her. She was an uncomplicated, straightforward young woman, so why not?

"Did you know Rose?" I asked.

"I met her, yes, here and at the surgery, but to say *know* . . ."

"Do you think her death was accidental?"

"Really, Madame Trafford, I wasn't even here at the time. I am studying at Amiens."

"Yes, but you must know what everyone else thinks, what your father thinks. You must know."

"It seems they think it is unusual, but the police were satisfied and . . ."

"And no one wanted to further disturb the de Frigecourts."

"Oh, I don't think that . . ."

"I do." I wriggled my foot with annoyance. "I think that was the most important factor. They've had so much trouble already, that sort of thing."

"That evidence was suppressed?"

The young Dr Bourdin was no longer smiling. She had the tight secretive look of one citizen of a community protecting the rest.

"I didn't say anything about suppressing evidence. I don't think anyone wanted to look into the death very carefully."

"The French police are very thorough. Besides, it was done from Abbeville, not from here. They were quite satisfied. This seems to have become an interrogation, Madame."

"No, it's *not* an interrogation, but Rose came to see me the day she died and told me she thought all was not well here."

"So *that's* why you're here?"

"Partly, a sort of female Hercule Poirot. What we have here are accidents and ghosts, and the governess—the one in charge of three helpless children—claims to have second sight and to be possessed by the spirit of Joan of Arc. And you call everything here normal?"

I was becoming very heated indeed; Dr Bourdin would be prescribing tranquillisers next. But instead she sat down next to me and looked at me thoughtfully.

"You really are worried aren't you?"

"Yes, I am. Jeanne worries me and the dead Rose worries me also. Jeanne is very much alive, but she has some connection—or thinks she has—with a long dead saint. Rose is recently dead, and we don't really know why she died. I said why, not how. Then we have the ghost of a young girl—Noelle was very clear that it was a young girl. Jeanne thinks it's Joan of Arc; I think it's Rose."

"Why should it be either?" Dr Bourdin said quietly.

"You are both thinking what you want to think without being objective at all."

"My husband would be appalled," I said with a smile, "even to imagine me thinking such a thought. We are all for scientific empiricism where I come from. I admit the idea of Rose does haunt me, personally, but I suppose if the apparition has been seen before it is more likely to be Joan, though why she should warn the family about impending deaths I can't imagine. Strictly speaking, as descendants of the hated Burgundians, she should be at permanent enmity with them. That's a thought," I said stopping abruptly to give myself time to think. "What about the curse?"

"What curse?"

"The Burgundian curse. Madame Barbou told me about it, though she had little to say. I linked it in my mind with Joan and the de Frigecourts. Joan hated them; maybe she cursed them and came back to haunt them. Yet what did they actually *do* to her apart from being remote offshoots of the dukes of Burgundy? It's unlikely she'd be so vicious just for that."

"You've lost me, I'm afraid, Madame Trafford," Dr Bourdin said pointedly. "And I think all this talk about ghosts and curses is *very* fanciful. Such stories we dismissed even as children."

I was being gently reprimanded. I who called myself an empiricist had strayed into wild and romantic regions. I suddenly felt ashamed.

"I'm sorry," I said contritely. "I'm being absurd. It must be the pain causing my imagination to wander. But I've had no one to talk to, so you must forgive me."

"Oh, I do. You must not be afraid to confide in me. We regard the family as our family and will do anything for them."

"I know. Even protect the Marquis."

"Monsieur Laurent!" She was clearly astonished. "You think he had something to do with Rose's death?"

"Not for a moment; he wasn't even here at the time. But assuming he and Rose were emotionally involved, might not the town want to hide that?"

"Perhaps they would, except that I know for sure there has never been the slightest suggestion of Monsieur Laurent's involvement with Rose or anyone other than Elizabeth. I would know if there were. My father knows everything, and he would tell me."

Well, that seemed that.

"But Jeanne is more worrisome," she continued. "If she talks like this to the children . . . "

"No, I don't say she does, and her behaviour with them is exemplary; she's kind yet firm, and they respond positively to her. But the way she talks to me is weird." I told Dr Bourdin about Jeanne's knowledge of my work and her premonitions about me. Then, very reluctantly, I recounted the circumstances of Fabrice's fall and the expression on Jeanne's face. All in all, it sounded rather lame and fanciful, but Dr Bourdin's eyes studied my face.

"You think she has a sort of evil eye? That she can cause things to happen?"

"I didn't until this moment," I said, "but perhaps that's exactly what I do mean. That would explain Rose, Cécile, Fabrice, the children going too far out to sea, and even my gunshot she could have done herself."

"But why would she? Why would she shoot you?"

"Because Rose had been to see me."

"She killed Rose for going to see you?"

Now the whole edifice began to crumble. Frankly, it did sound rather absurd.

"It doesn't work, does it?" I said at last. "It's all too

fanciful. Besides, Joan was a *saint*, after all. Saints don't have the evil eye, do they?"

Dr Bourdin got up, carefully ignoring my question. "I must get back to my father's surgery. But let's keep in touch."

"Come for tea," I said suddenly. "See the children. Judge the atmosphere for yourself."

"I'd love to, I'll come tomorrow," she said.

But before tea time the following day the meaning of Noelle's apparition had all too sadly been realised.

## CHAPTER 9

Elizabeth, the children's mother, died during the night. She had never regained consciousness and had died peacefully and painlessly in her sleep. Laurent brought us the news in the morning, coming to the house while the children were at lessons and I was working in the library.

He told me first, and all formal condolences were useless. I could see that; he bore the look of a man whom tragedy had aged ten years.

"Even though it has been like this for over a year, I can't get used to her death."

"Go and see the children," I said. "Talking to them will help you."

It was an awful day. Noelle was the most upset, but they all cried, and their father cried, and Madame Barbou cried so much that the lunch was ruined. Even Jeanne cried, but I was dry-eyed. I had never known her, and you can't cry for someone you've never seen, however sad the circumstances. So I did what I could, trying to be helpful. Jeanne and Madame Barbou packed for the children and I helped get them into their best clothes. By mid-afternoon they had gone with their father back to Paris to stay with an aunt until the funeral.

Jeanne offered to go with them, but Laurent was firm about her need for a rest and the ability of his aunt and her staff to look after the children. He suggested she go home, because he wanted to give Madame Barbou a rest and close the château for the week or so they would be away. But Jeanne seemed reluctant to accept the offer of a free holiday and said that if she did stay here she would be no trouble, taking her meals out.

For me to return to 33 Rue du Château was a mixed joy—yes, I wanted to get back, and no, I didn't—but whatever happened, I realised that the death of the children's mother would make a difference in everyone's life.

I cleared up my things in the library, returned borrowed volumes to their shelves, and went upstairs to pack. The silent house had a deserted feeling as though the children's presence alone gave it life. I wondered if Jeanne would stay on here by herself. Would I? Yes, why not? What was eerie about a place simply because it was large?

And had a ghost, I thought, opening my door and nearly fainting with shock as a shadowy figure moved away from the window and came towards me. I flicked on the light:

"Jeanne! You gave me an awful shock."

"Clare, I'm so sorry. I thought you'd gone."

"How could you think I'd gone? All my things are still here."

"Well, I mean before I came in I thought you'd gone. I

came to look for a book I'd lent Rose. Did you see it? It's called *The Last Journey of the Maid,* a funny little book I found in a shop in Amiens. It might interest you."

"There was nothing here when I moved in." I still felt shocked and annoyed. The book thing seemed awfully flimsy to me. "The room had been cleaned out."

"That's what I thought," Jeanne said looking round distractedly. "Sorry to have given you such a fright. Will you be coming back here?"

"I don't know. I wasn't much help to you with my ankle, was I?"

"Still, it was nice to have company and nice for the children, too."

I smiled at her and sat down, taking a cigarette from the bedside table.

"And what about your premonition?"

"Oh, that." Jeanne's expression was serious as she dropped into a chair by the window. "I told you I wasn't always right, but this time I was right that there was going to be a death. I had a premonition of disaster, about the Marquise. Your aura is different now, Clare."

"My aura?"

"We all have an aura. Sometimes I can see them quite clearly. Rose had no aura, and that meant she was hostile to me, or that she was a ghost. I don't think that, do you?"

"It seems unlikely." I smiled as I flicked the ashes in the ash tray. My conversations with Jeanne were quite extraordinary.

"I think things will be better now," Jeanne continued chattily. "The death of the mother was the menace. I feel these things before they happen."

"Aren't you going to see your own mother, Jeanne?"

"I don't think I will make the journey. France is a big country, you know, and we come from a small village in the Rhône valley, miles from anywhere. I have to go to Paris and change, and Dijon and change . . ."

"Why, *you're* a Burgundian!" I said beginning to laugh. But Jeanne didn't find it amusing; her figure visibly straightened and her mouth puckered.

"I'm a Frenchwoman, Clare; it's not funny at all."

"But you said the dukes of Burgundy were not French."

"The Valois dukes, as you know, wanted to make a separate kingdom of Burgundy. They did not regard themselves as French but as a sovereign state."

"That's true. I read only yesterday in one of the books in the library that Charles the Bold said the French kings had usurped the kingdom of Burgundy by turning it into a duchy."

"It was the great King Louis XI who helped the Swiss kill Charles, the last of the Valois dukes, and thus restored Burgundy to France."

She certainly knew her history.

"Jeanne, why does it matter to you so much—because of Joan?"

"Of course. I told you that her spirit possesses me. Joan *hated* the Burgundians, traitors to the true kings of France. She has never forgiven them."

*Has?* The present tense. This must all be very vivid for Jeanne.

"Then why do you work for a family in direct descent from John the Fearless?"

"That I didn't know," Jeanne said quietly, "when I first came. I found out later, of course. I came here because of Joan's association with Port St Pierre and the château. I didn't realise that descendants of her persecutor owned the château."

"Doesn't it make a difference?"

"Difference? How could it? I've grown to love the family and the children. Our church teaches that the sins of the father are not passed on to the children. How could I hate them for something that happened five hundred years ago?"

"Then why does Joan?"

"Joan doesn't hate the family of de Frigecourt, but she has never forgiven the old Burgundians, the Valois dukes."

"But it is a coincidence, isn't it? You don't think it has any connection with your coming here?"

Jeanne's voice suddenly dropped to a whisper. "I don't know," she said. "I really don't know, but you see, Joan did come to warn Noelle there would be a death. She is here."

The room was very cold and suddenly there was that little breeze that just seemed to stir the air, although no doors or windows were open. I felt oddly depressed, and the château seemed a haunted, unwelcome sort of place. For the first time, I didn't want to be there at all; I wanted to be gone.

"I have to pack," I said. "I want to sleep at home tonight. Michelle Bourdin very kindly offered to drive me home; she'll be here in a few minutes. I'd invited her to tea and had to ring and cancel because of what happened. You're sure you'll be all right on your own, Jeanne? You know where I live, don't you?"

"I shall be perfectly all right," Jeanne said. "I shall enjoy the peace; but if I do get lonely, I'll call and see you, Clare. I'd like that, to see you in your little house."

After Jeanne had gone, I packed quickly because I didn't want to keep Dr Bourdin waiting. I put my clothes on my bed and then looked for my suitcase. Curse it, I'd put it on top of the wardrobe. If only I'd remembered in time, I could have asked Jeanne to get it for me. With a sigh I pulled a chair over to the wardrobe, climbed painfully onto it, and groped for the case; as I did, I touched something just in front of the case's handle. A book.

First I got down the small case and then climbed up again for the book. It was a very slim book, poorly bound and rather cheap-looking, the sort of thing one tosses aside without a glance. I wondered why it had been thrown up onto the wardrobe, until I saw its title—*The Last Journey of the Maid,* printed in Amiens in the nineteenth century by someone called Charles Reduc. The name meant absolutely nothing to me. I'd give Jeanne a call on my way down and return it to her.

Then I thought it very *odd* of Rose to have tucked it away on the wardrobe, as though she'd meant to hide it. The wardrobe had a carved ornate ridge on top that made it look higher than it was, so it was necessary to stand on a chair, as I had, to see onto the actual top. Even then it was high, and I, who am quite tall, had had to grope. Very interesting. I decided it was worth taking the book home to have a quick look and returning it to Jeanne when I saw her again after the children were back.

Michelle Bourdin came up to my room for the case and gave me an arm to help me down. She was an extraordinarily kind girl and besides I liked her. She was near my own age, and I thought of her as an ally; she was not just being nosey but was genuinely concerned and interested. I told her on the way home about my most recent interview with Jeanne.

"Don't you think it's a coincidence that you're writing a book on Joan of Arc and Jeanne claims to be possessed by her?"

"Yes, it is a coincidence, but coincidences are part of life, don't you think? They happen all the time. I certainly don't think that it was intended or that I was meant to be here or anything like that. I don't believe in such things. My husband and I like to think that, although we are broad-minded, we have scientific minds, as befits scholars."

Michelle laughed. "Here's your house. I'll carry your case and then I have to run. Someone's broken a leg on the other side of the town. Oh—my mother has asked you to lunch tomorrow."

"But I couldn't."

"Of course you could. She'll be offended if you don't. You can work all morning, and I'll pick you up at about one."

Yes, it was nice to be home. I thought of the Rue du Château as home; the château itself was, well, different. It was comfortable, but it wasn't home-like. On the way, Michelle had stopped at one of the delicatessens in the main street and bought me a ready-made meal—a delicious quiche, salad, and cheese—which I ate early in front of the stove which Martine had kept burning in my absence. It only needed attending to once a day. Then, exhausted, I went early to bed.

I awoke in my nice room, the walls covered with wallpaper of blue cornflowers, the ceiling white. From my window I saw the pinks and reds of the sloping roofs of the nearby houses. Usually there was a saucy black cat who liked to tease the dog tethered in a neighbor's backyard, but this morning it was not there.

Yes, it was comfortable and cosy. I'd slept like a log; all I wanted was someone to bring me morning tea. As it was, I had to hobble downstairs and make it myself. There was another letter from Tom; I hadn't answered the last one and suddenly felt bad about it. He enclosed some mail for me and just added a note with his hope I was enjoying myself and some chat about mutual friends. Tom seemed to be restraining himself from anything intimate. Hell, if only I didn't feel so torn every time I heard from Tom.

112

I had a bath and worked hard all morning, trying to forget about him.

The Bourdins were good bourgeois stock, maintaining a neat home and an ample table. Madame Bourdin was a large, good-natured lady, with that serene expression that a well-filled life seems to bring to people in their late middle age. I was sure I would never achieve it. Dr Bourdin had been the town's sole physician since he'd qualified; they'd lived in the same house all their married life and had brought up their four children there. Besides Michelle there were a brother, Nicolas, who lived at home, and two elder children who were married, one, a son, a doctor in Paris, and the other a daughter who lived in Lille.

The house smelled good as we went inside and Michelle introduced me to her mother and her brother Nicolas, who was a couple of years younger than she—a tall, taciturn type who owned a boat and fished for a living. To my delight, Madame Gilbert had also been invited, and they were all curious, as we sat down, to hear about what had happened at the château. By previous arrangement with Michelle, I was not going to mention the ghost or my conversations with Jeanne.

It was a delicious lunch—soupe de poissons, fillet of veal with vegetables, marvellous cheeses, good wine, and apple pudding.

"I'm going to get so fat," I said, sitting back, "after Madame Barbou's cooking, and now this. No eating for a month."

"Are you going back to the château?"

"I don't expect to. Monsieur Laurent is looking for a new nanny, and I do have my book to write. I think Jeanne has these children well in hand."

"It's tragic about the mother—those poor children." Madame Bourdin was obviously thinking of her own well-cared-for brood.

113

"In a way, it is perhaps the best thing," Madame Gilbert said in a practical tone of voice. "I do *not* mean to say I do not regret *very* much the accident to Madame Elizabeth; but seeing that it happened and that she might never have recovered . . ." She spread her hands in a gesture of resignation. "Monsieur may marry again and the children will have a mother."

"I feel they will leave Port St Pierre," Madame Bourdin murmured. "And the château will become a ruin again."

"From something that Monsieur Laurent said to me, I think that's what he might do," I said. "That is, if he doesn't remarry soon. He says it's too big for a home and would make a better hotel."

"Ah, that would be terribly sad; for generations the de Frigecourts have lived there."

"One must be practical in this age," the doctor said, lighting a cigar. "I don't think the de Frigecourts have the money they once had. No one has; the state has seen to that! To keep up that château, and a house in Paris, and in Provence is not possible. I think he will sell."

"It's too sad to think of," I said. "The very idea makes me shudder."

"But why? Such is the fate of many large homes. Is it not good to make it into a hotel or a holiday home that can be of benefit to many?"

"Yes, in a way, but a hotel is not a home, and that château has belonged to the same family for centuries. I think it would be a shame to see it pass into the hands of strangers. What a pity they can't find the family treasure that has been hidden away for so long."

"Treasure?" Madame Gilbert said with interest. "What treasure?"

"The *Burgunderbeute*, the fabulous treasure of Duke Charles the Bold. According to Laurent, it was stolen by one of his ancestors on the field of battle."

114

"Oh that is a *story!*" Madame Gilbert laughed. "It is like the family ghost—all rubbish. No one believes anything about treasure or ghosts." And she shrugged her practical French shoulders as though to discourage further arguments, an attitude that didn't quite deceive me, like brushing the dust under the carpet to hide something unpleasant. I felt there was a lot she didn't want to talk about in front of a stranger, however much she liked me.

"Besides," she said, "the main thing is that the children will have a family life with their father. He should take them back to Paris and give them a home, mother or not. Both Laurent and his wife, dear charming girl though she was, were always somewhere else other than with their children, who have been brought up by nannies, governesses, and so on. There has been no family life. I myself was bold enough to tell Monsieur Laurent, before his wife had her accident, that they should all settle down in one place or another. I still remember the smile he gave me, more or less telling me to mind my own business, but with such charm—that family, so gifted. Little Fabrice is the image of his uncle Jean, the eldest brother, only seventeen when he was taken away; ah that was terrible."

"Terrible," Madame Bourdin murmured. "Your sister Thérèse was only a baby, but I can remember the awful shock. The whole family was wiped out except for the sad little boy and his Maman in the big château."

"And if you think Laurent has charm, you should have seen Jean. What a boy—excellent in everything, school, games—what a career he would have had."

"What was the other brother called?"

"Henri? Ah, Henri was a very different kind of boy. He had the family charm, of course, they all had; but he was a much quieter type; no one ever knew exactly what was going on in Henri's mind. He was very secretive, always hoarding his things.

"They used to say he would be a banker." Dr Bourdin laughed and put a fresh match to his cigar. "Yes, he was a curious boy."

"How?" I said, intrigued. "How *curious?*"

"I know what my husband means," Madame Bourdin interjected, fidgeting with an item of cutlery on the table. "Henri was not like the others, except in appearance; all three brothers shared a strong facial resemblance, except that Henri had a broken nose, which left him with a pugnacious appearance. I would say that whereas Laurent and Jean and their father were extroverted, Henri was introverted and very aware of himself. And whereas his father and brothers were generous and outgoing, Henri was greedy and self-centred. He always put himself first and got what he wanted because the others didn't mind so much. They were too generous to notice how mean he was, but we outsiders saw it. Hélas." She shrugged and got up. "Who are we to judge? Perhaps he would have got over it, and in his capture and death no doubt he showed the noble nature of the de Frigecourt family."

Madame Bourdin started to clear the table. It seemed a signal for us all to move. I felt tired and in need of a rest. I really was in poor shape and my ankle throbbed.

"Do you mind if Nicolas drives you home?" Michelle asked. "He's going to the port and I would like to do some studying."

"Of course!" I thanked them for the meal, shook hands, kissed Madame Gilbert and joined Nicolas, who had the car ready outside the house.

From the corner of my eye, I inspected his profile. He hadn't said a word during the meal, but had tucked away a prodigious amount of food. I thought it odd how children in families varied. Nicolas was like a peasant, yet his father, sister, and brother were doctors, which was considered a step up in the world, though I myself think

116

the medical profession an overrated one. I studied the brown sturdy hands with dirty nails which gripped the wheel firmly.

"Do you fish every day?" I asked, making conversation.

"With the tide. We come in on one and go out on the next, twelve hours on and twelve hours off."

"It must be a tiring life."

"It's a living."

"You must know a lot about the tides, Nicolas. Do you think Rose could have died accidentally?"

"I think she could have died accidentally—but crossing the bay when the tide is due? Unlikely. Eh, perhaps she did it on purpose."

"You think she killed herself?" I asked incredulously.

"What else?" He looked at me, his eyes intelligent beneath that tough exterior. One should not underestimate this man, I thought, doing what Tom would disapprove of—making a rash judgement solely on the grounds of appearance.

"I never thought of that," I said. "But why should she kill herself?"

"It always seemed obvious to me," Nicolas said, coming to a stop outside my front door. "Rose was stood up in love and she drowned herself. People do it quite often, you know; but she couldn't do it properly because of the low tide, and she froze to death instead."

Then with a cheerful nod and wave he drove off, leaving me deeply in thought. Why not, after all? The one thing we hadn't thought of was that Rose might have done it deliberately. In many ways, it had a terrible sort of logic about it.

## CHAPTER 10

The fifteenth century was a great age for superstition; it both fascinated and repelled me. Sorcery, necromancy, and astrology vied with the fierce dictates, the absolute authority of a church determined to suppress all dealings with the supernatural not approved of by itself. It was thus easy to call Joan a witch, because everyone believed in witchcraft, even the church—most of all the church. If she didn't come from God—and how could she, argued the church—she must have come from the Devil.

In fact, there were many curious things about Joan that could be ascribed either to saintliness or to sorcery. Her childhood was extraordinary; she claimed to have first heard her voices when she was twelve. Once she had started on her mission, nothing could stop her; she had incredible power over people, especially hard-bitten military types. She proved an agile commander in the field of

118

battle, yet we know she had never studied the art of warfare. She had foreknowledge of all kinds of things. When she was captured, she leapt from a high tower and suffered no injury. Her answers at her trial, conducted by learned theologians, were almost as cunning as the questions. Yet she refused to recite the *paternoster*, which made everyone suspicious, because witches were supposed to be unable to recite the Lord's Prayer without stumbling. She also had an odd friendship with a Marshal of France, the Baron Gilles de Rais, a companion in arms who was executed after her death for practicing demonology.

From time to time, history witnesses the birth of a remarkable person, and no one can really say why. Joan was one of those people. In the fifteenth century Joan of Arc could flourish; today, she would be locked up and submitted to a battery of psychological tests.

I thought that I should talk to Jeanne about her namesake. If she was indeed possessed by her spirit, she should be able to unravel a lot of historical mysteries—and that might make my book a best seller.

Thinking about Jeanne reminded me of the little book. Where had I put it?

It was nighttime and I was reading by the stove, my foot comfortably up on the sofa. The single lamp cast a warm glow on the checkered floor; outside the wind was howling and I thought of the storm-tossed trees and the swirling waters of the bay. Would there be a solitary light in the turret of the otherwise darkened château? My house was protected from the wind because it was in the centre of the town, but even so I felt it strong and gusty.

I found the book on my desk, with a pile of reading materials I'd brought back from the château.

It was a curiosity. The paper was coarse and it looked as though it had been privately printed; the type was uneven, as though someone had laboriously set it by hand, and the binding was undistinguished. Maybe the mysterious Charles Reduc had printed it himself—a real labour of love?

It was written in very prosaic French, and so far as I could tell simply went over the well-known facts of Joan's capture at Compiègne in May 1430, her journey to and arrival in Rouen nine months later, and her death there in May 1431.

There was obviously nothing here of interest, I thought as I leafed through it, yawning, and if Jeanne was indeed possessed by the spirit of the Maid she should have found it as boring and as irrelevant as I did. Possessed or not, she was an intelligent woman and obviously knew her history.

Yet she had told me it was interesting, and had thought it of sufficient moment to lend to Rose. Why? I closed the book and as I did I noticed that because it was so badly bound the case was lopsided; it hung limply instead of flush to the spine of the book. I opened it again and two things happened simultaneously—a letter fell out, and I noticed that a section had been detached from the hand-sewn binding, and that this had caused the case to be dislodged.

Before I examined the pages, I picked up the letter and saw that the envelope was new and bore the most recently issued English stamp. The envelope was addressed to Rose in round, immature handwriting.

Should I read it? Had I a right to? I didn't have many scruples, but reading other people's letters was one of them. So I looked at the book. The pages had been hand-sewn in sections of sixteen pages, and eight were missing out of one of the middle sections. They had been torn rather badly and had left jagged edges.

The question was, who had removed the pages?

Jeanne? Rose? Or had they been missing when Jeanne had bought the book? Knowing Jeanne, I was sure she would neither have purchased an imperfect book, nor torn the pages out in such a careless manner. If she had done such a thing, she would have done it neatly, with a knife, and then she would not have lent the mutilated book to anyone.

Pleased with my deductive powers, I decided it was Rose who had despoiled the book and then hidden it; she was going to tell Jeanne she had lost it and then, when a suitable opportunity arose, throw it away.

Now to the letter. It was obviously relevant to my case I said to myself, as I attempted to justify reading it. It was very short and said:

Dear Rose,
Your letter which arrived yesterday really worried me. You shouldn't stay on in that place if you are unhappy, and what do you mean about not being able to leave because something has come up? This is very disturbing to me.

My mum is quite scared at what you have to say about the governess. She doesn't believe in witches and wonders if your nerves are alright. I said you meant "bitch" but my Mum said she didn't think so.

You know, darling Rose, how much I miss you, and I wish you would decide to settle and marry me. We could have our own children and that would be much nicer than looking after other peoples.

If you like, I can try and get leave and come over and fetch you. If you haven't enough money let me know, but please write soon because I was worried about not hearing from you for such a long time.

I love you, Rose
Cliff.

I sat over the letter for a long time, letting it lie in my lap. It spoke volumes. It told me that Rose was unhappy, which I knew, and that she thought Jeanne was evil, witch-like, which I also knew. Although she had mentioned a boyfriend, I hadn't known the relationship was close enough for marriage to be a consideration. Or had it not been mutual? Had Rose been having an affair here with someone else, someone whom she crept out at odd times to meet? Someone who might have killed her, or caused her to kill herself? I thought it odd that the loving Cliff had accepted her death so calmly. No one had heard of him in these parts, and that made me wish I could learn more about Rose.

For the first time, I wished that Tom were here.

He would be very helpful if I put him in the picture; a talk with him would clarify my thoughts. Tom's logical, incisive brain would be able to isolate a few relevant facts from this morass. He also might be able to talk to or see Cliff, whose address in Croydon was on the letter.

The very next day I sat down and wrote a long letter to Tom. I told him the whole story from beginning to end, factually, objectively, leaving out nothing. I read it over very carefully when I had finished and thought how easily open to interpretation the facts were. One could say there was nothing really to point to any mystery, or one could say, yes, there was something odd here. Tom would know. Tom would also enjoy being consulted. I was here fulfilling the role of the little woman, and Tom would like that.

I sent the letter by express post and, that out of the way, got back to work. I remained working all week, seeing nobody except Madame Gilbert. Jeanne didn't call, and Michelle was in Amiens. It was good for me to immerse myself in hard academic work again, and the puzzling de Frigecourt situation seemed to recede to the back of my mind as I wrestled with the problems of interpreting Joan and her mission. My ankle got better; I slept well, ate well, and walked for at least an hour every day. I avoided the bay and the château, though, and discovered more about the hinterland beyond Port St Pierre.

The town was on a peninsula and one could walk quite easily from one side to the other, following the main street from the Place Jeanne d'Arc, which overlooked the fishing boats tied up at the jetty, to the wide beach with its bathing huts on the other side. The beach walk led to the dunes, which I wasn't keen to explore again, so I concentrated on the port side of the town, which formed the rim of the bay.

A curious feature was a pair of great sluice gates containing a huge basin of water, the purpose of which I was never able to discover. They filled each day with the tide, and were then closed; when the tide was out, they were opened again and released, with a considerable amount of force, this huge containment of water into the bay. One could walk along the rampart up to the sluice and then beyond, joining a path that led to the Noyelles road. I explored the marshes and the countryside beyond, and generally came back to the town at dusk, the best part of the day, when the lights were starting up and, if there had been any sun, the horizon beyond was streaked with the pinks, greys, and golds of sunset.

One such day, about a week after the children had gone and I'd almost forgotten about the château and the de Frigecourt family, I returned home to find Laurent sitting in his car waiting for my return. I greeted him warmly and asked him in.

"You look very well, Clare. I think the change from us has done you good."

"I think it has, Laurent, but don't forget I had a bad ankle, too, and that was hardly your fault." I was walking about the house switching on lights, feeling ill at ease. Laurent was standing by the stove watching me, which didn't help. There had been a warmth, an intimacy in his greeting that made me feel like an immature schoolgirl. I didn't quite know how to cope with it.

Yes, I was attracted to Laurent de Frigecourt, but I had just reopened negotiations, as it were, with my husband. I silently poured out two whiskies, added soda water, and passed a glass to him. He looked puzzled.

"Clare!"

"Sorry, is it too early?"

"No, but there's something in your manner. You're strange. I was really looking forward to seeing you; you're a family friend, Clare. Part of us."

"No, I'm not!" I said, with a vehemence that surprised me. "I mean I am a family friend; I love the children, rely on that. But I'm not part of your family, Laurent, I'm not."

"As you like," he said quietly. "I'm sorry, though, I mean that you reacted like that. I think we must have upset you."

"Oh, you didn't upset me at all, Laurent, don't be absurd."

"Then something happened. Was it Jeanne?"

"Jeanne didn't upset me—nothing upset me. I . . . Laurent." I sat on the couch and looked up to where he was still standing by the stove, glass in hand. "I have come here to work, to write a book; to some extent my career depends upon its success. I'm considered bright. I'm a full lecturer. This book could make me a senior lecturer and a Reader within five years. At forty I could be a professor. I just might make it, because I know I'm considered that good.

"My marriage has suffered because of my ambition. I know Tom may be rather old-fashioned, but I definitely didn't put everything into it that I might have. My work came first and my marriage came second, and I think in many ways Tom was a good husband. He was a soul mate."

"You still love him, don't you?" Laurent said. "You're really trying to tell me that if I've got overtures in mind, I should forget them."

"Laurent! I was trying to tell you I can't move back to the château!"

"I've shocked you. My wife was buried only last week. How can I be thinking of someone else?" Laurent sat down beside me and took my hand, or rather he placed his hand on mine.

"Clare, Elizabeth was ill for nearly eighteen months. I loved her terribly; she was my wife; but when someone can't see or talk, can only lie there in a very deep sleep from which she will probably never emerge, she does die a little; she is beyond you in some indefinable way. She is someone you love, but she is no longer that vibrant human being you made love to, with whom you shared so many adventures, joys, and sorrows, who bore your children. And I feel like that about Elizabeth now. I love her, and part of her is always with me, but she is gone and I am here, alive, and I am a normal man and I want a woman. I want to marry again, eventually, maybe have more children, make someone else happy, be happy again myself. I have been sad for such a very long time, Clare."

"I know you have, Laurent." I could think of nothing else to say, yet a deep despair seemed to possess me. Did I know what I wanted, the way Laurent did?

"I liked you immediately, you knew that," he went on. "That night in your caftan with the vibrant blacks and greens you seemed like an astonishing new force that had come into my life—something that one might attain, if the circumstances were right. I knew Elizabeth was dying, and I would have done anything to save her for me, for the children."

"I understand; don't torment yourself. I know you weren't being unfaithful to her. I was attracted to you, too; but I also had a catch, still have. My husband, Tom."

"But you left Tom."

"I left to sort myself out. Tom keeps on writing to me."

"And you've also written to him?"

"I wrote the other day. I think he might come over."

"Did you ask him to come over?"

"No, but he knows I'm worried."

"Worried about what?"

"About Rose, how she died."

Laurent looked at me as though he'd seen a ghost. "About *Rose?* You're worried about Rose?"

"You've almost forgotten about it, haven't you?"

"No, but . . ."

"Yes, you have; yet it was only a month ago or a little more."

"A lot of things have happened since then."

"I know. I didn't tell you before because I thought it would worry you even more, but Rose came to see me the day she had her accident, and she said she was unhappy at the château."

"Did she say why?"

"She thought Jeanne had a bad influence on the children."

Laurent got up with an explosive gesture and began pacing the room. "And you think that had something to do with her death?"

"I don't know, Laurent. I simply don't know."

"But you've seen Jeanne, you've lived in the house. Do you think she has a bad influence on the children?"

"No, I don't."

"Well?" He was losing patience. It was hopeless to go on. He was frustrated and cross and humiliated; what could I tell him that he would believe?

"We've lost the point," I said. "We've mixed our relationship up with other things." I got up and faced him. "I won't know how I feel about you, Laurent, until I've seen Tom again."

"Then you can choose," he said bitterly.

"No, I don't flatter myself that I have that kind of choice. What I've just said would be enough to put any man off."

"It's honest," he said gruffly. "Not a quality a lot of women are noted for. But I always thought you hadn't detached yourself from Tom, just by a few of the things you've said. You mention his name in almost every conversation."

"Do I? I didn't realise that."

"He's so much a part of you."

"I did leave him rather abruptly."

"Then there might still be a chance for us?" He put his hands lightly on my shoulders. I knew he wanted to kiss me, and I wanted to kiss him, but I knew we wouldn't. It would be one of those tantalising things. "I'm not saying this year, even next. I wouldn't dream of remarrying until it was decent to do so. I mean for my own sake as well as propriety, but I wanted to tell you that I'd missed you and thought about you—to be honest with you as you've been honest with me."

"Shall we leave it like that?" I said, smiling and releasing his hands. "I'd love to see the children again. How are they?"

"They took it very well. Kids don't really understand, you know. Only Noelle and Philippe came to the funeral. They were very grave, but they don't talk about Elizabeth much."

"They will," I said, "and you must keep her in their minds, as their mother, whatever happens."

"Oh, and we have a new nanny."

"My goodness, now you tell me."

"That is actually what I did come to tell you; that and to ask you to dinner and see if you want to pick up your things. The other thing was forced on me, by seeing you. I didn't mean to come out with it just yet."

"It did rather shake me," I said, "but these things happen, especially when one pushes them under the surface. But I will come up to the château with you and get my things. I won't stay to dinner. I want you all to settle down. Are you staying for a while?"

"As long as I can. I have to go back to Paris and then to Germany on wine business, but I want to see the new nanny in."

"Is she all right?"

"I think she's good. She's very well qualified, a nurse as well as a trained children's nanny. She's a lot older, which is a good thing after Rose, who was a bit flighty."

"How old?"

"Thirty-five. The snag is that she doesn't speak good French or much English. She's Swedish, but she was all I could get, qualified, and at such short notice."

"How did you get her?"

"Some agency put her on to me. I've given her a month's trial."

"That sounds fair enough, though the language is a problem."

"Yes, the language is a problem; but she is very willing, and the children seem to have taken to her. Her name is Lisa."

"What does Jeanne say?"

"Jeanne hasn't said anything. I don't ask Jeanne's opinion when I engage other staff. I've asked her not to

128

tread on Jeanne's toes, and to be discreet. Anyway, Lisa's job is a nursemaid, to look after the children's bodily needs, their clothes, hair, feeding. She can take them for walks and play with them; she doesn't have to speak French for that."

Indeed, when I met her an hour or so later, Lisa was, at least to my eyes, everything that a sensible children's nanny should be. She was a large, heavy girl with hair plaited above her head. She wore a blue smock with a badge on it, very efficient-looking, and she seemed the sort of dependable, trustworthy person who would keep a calm head in an emergency.

In an otherwise nondescript face, however, she had a surprising feature—the most piercing blue eyes that I have ever seen. They were not warm eyes; they were appraising, and they seemed to be keeping their own judgement about everything they saw.

But then it wasn't up to me to approve of Lisa, and after I'd made polite conversation, greeted Jeanne, kissed and talked to the children, I made my way up to my old room to pack the rest of my things.

Rose's room. Yes, there was an atmosphere here. I could feel it as I closed the door and looked at the neatly made bed, the sparse, heavy furniture with my few things scattered about. There was that gentle unexplained breeze, and I suddenly felt a restlessness of the spirit, an agitation as though I had unfinished business here. Something seemed to pass by me; an invisible presence disturbed the air, and I felt I had only to reach out in order to touch someone, something. The urge was so strong that I stretched out my arm, and then withdrew it, feeling foolish, like a blind person groping in the dark.

I don't know how long the feeling lasted, not long, but I saw myself transfixed in a moment of time, and the eerie sense of apartness sent a chill through me—as though the life of the house pulsed on, leaving me apart. It was then that the possibility occurred to me, for the first time in my life, that I was in the presence of a psychic force, something not subject to rational explanation.

*Was* someone, was Rose trying to get through to me? And if so, what was she trying to say?

## CHAPTER 11

My experience in Rose's room and the long talk with Laurent left me feeling terribly disturbed. Clearly the château was an unhealthy place for me, because I didn't believe in psychic phenomena as intangible as the force that had affected me, and I felt the need to attribute it to mood or emotion. I had packed my things and left the château quickly, with only a cursory farewell, which Laurent seemed to attribute to my desire to put space between himself and me.

For the next few days I kept well away from the château, even in my walks. Laurent and Lisa and all the others had to sort themselves out. I was staging a tactical withdrawal. I thought it odd that I hadn't heard from Tom, and in a strange way I was disappointed. I'd misjudged his mood, that was clear, but if Tom's silence helped me to decide how I really felt about him, perhaps it would turn out to be a good thing.

One day I woke and lay looking out of my window; the cat was teasing the dog and his barking had woken me. It was a glorious day, one of those days when the sky has a delicate blush of pink to its azure blue, the air is warm, and the earth seems alive with subterranean stirrings.

I needed to get away. Take a long drive, maybe stay the night somewhere. Joan needed a good rest. I'd been working at fever pitch the last few days to keep my mind off the other side of my life in Port St Pierre, and the assortment of facts and interpretations I'd unearthed needed a good airing, a long thoughtful drive to help me assimilate them.

I packed the car, took an overnight case, and without telling anyone, drove up the N.1, taking the right turn at Montreuil and following the N.39 along the winding valley of the Canche. At Contes I turned left and followed the tiny river Planquette, only a stream at times. The lush green wooded valley was like a little Switzerland with everything in miniature—the neat houses with their masses of potted plants and the villages which seemed so completely self-contained, so far away from the business of the Channel ports.

Bernanos immortalized this valley in *The Diary of a Country Priest*. Cavron, Fressin, Planques, Agincourt . . . Of course, as an historian I spent a lot of time walking over the battlefield, some distance from the village and marked only by a solitary imposing stone. Joan was three years old when the decisive battle of Agincourt was being fought not so far away from her. It was important as background for Joan's future, because it led to the Treaty of Troyes in 1420, which promised Henry V of England the throne of France by marrying him to Charles VI's daughter, Catherine. The other child of Charles VI, though his mother was at pains to deny it, was the Dauphin, whom Joan caused to be crowned King at Rheims.

132

By nightfall I was in Hesdin, which long ago contained one of the great castles favoured as a home by the Valois dukes and long since destroyed. I found a nice hotel there and spent the night in this ancient town of Artois, burial place of many of the knights, the flower of French chivalry, who had fallen in 1415 at Agincourt.

The next day I got up late and tossed a coin as to whether I should continue on the N.39 I had rejoined at Hesdin and go as far as Arras and south through the battlefields to the Somme valley, or go straight back via Abbeville to Port Guillaume, which I had never properly explored, and at which I was forever gazing from Port St Pierre.

I decided on Port Guillaume and after a leisurely, tranquil drive—the car had taken a new lease on life in France, perhaps under the threat of the scrap heap and the way everyone laughed at it parked outside my door as they passed it in Rue Château—I arrived there in the early afternoon.

In many ways Port Guillaume was more spectacularly situated than Port St Pierre. It was older; the château in which Joan had actually *lived* in Port St Pierre no longer existed, whereas the gate under which she had *passed* in Port Guillaume still stood. The cobbled streets rose gently to a high escarpment, a plateau on which stood the old church, forming a high wall or battlement overlooking the town.

I parked my car outside the walls of the old town and went through that gate. I climbed slowly, pausing to admire this old house or that, this perfectly kept garden or that spectacular view across the bay to Port St Pierre and the château, clearly visible but tiny-looking from this distance, with its grey-roofed twin turrets.

Gazing at it from afar, I felt at peace with myself. I really did love the château; who could help but love that ancient, noble house standing so serenely overlooking the bay? I'd been wise to take this break, to occupy myself with other thoughts. I'd allowed the concerns of the family and Laurent's declaration to overwhelm me. Distance had given me perspective. I saw a light come on in the château and thought of the children in their schoolroom. The light reminded me that it was getting dark and I should go back to the car and head for home.

As I turned down the hill, I glanced into the window of an especially pretty house set in a partly walled garden. A man was lighting a pipe, and as he drew on it and waved out the match he looked up and our eyes met. Recognition was instant, but it wasn't until he opened the window and leaned out that I realised who he was.

"Bonjour, Madame! You are exploring our lovely town."

"Monsieur Schroeder! You *live* here?"

"Come in, come in. I'll open the door."

What a surprise! I looked at my watch. I didn't want to be late, but I couldn't be rude. I shook hands with him at the door and he led me into a small, elegant drawing room furnished with taste and care and dominated by a large desk at which he'd obviously been working.

"I don't know why, Monsieur Schroeder, but I thought you were visiting the area that day we met."

"I said we'd meet again soon. No, I've rented this place just for a year. I live in Heidelberg. I'm a scholar of sorts, an antique dealer, but right now I'm writing a book. This is indeed a lovely part of the world."

I was looking out of his large bay window.

"What a magnificent view! You can see across to Port St Pierre, and as far as Le Hourdel."

"Yes, isn't it?" he said, joining me. "You don't realise how fine a view until you are actually inside. We just manage to avoid being obscured by the trees."

"And the château! You can see that quite clearly too. Look, the lights are beginning to come on."

"Ah yes." He screwed up his eyes as though he had just noticed the château. "So you can. I hope your foot wasn't too badly hurt that day?"

"Well, it was, rather. I was laid up for almost a week."

"I'm sorry to hear it. How are the children?"

"Their mother just died."

"Oh, dear, I'm sorry to hear that. Are you living with them?"

"Oh, no. I was just there as a guest. Thank goodness I've moved back into my own rented house."

"Thank goodness?"

"I'm writing a book, too. I couldn't get on with any work there.

"I can imagine. Three children must be a handful."

"The nanny had died, too. The family has had quite a tragic time."

"It seems so. Can I get you some tea? Please don't say no. I have a store of Jackson's teas which I drink every day myself."

He disappeared into the kitchen, and I longed to go over to his desk and look at his papers—academic curiosity—but I wouldn't have liked anyone to do that to me, so I remained where I was, gazing out of the window. Soon he was back carrying a tray.

"I know the English habits. There's milk for you and lemon for me."

"Do you go to England at all?"

"Very seldom; occasionally for a sale if it's important. I still buy antiques, but not so much as I used to. I enjoy writing. Tell me"—he poured the tea carefully into exquisite China cups—"what is the subject of your book?"

"Joan of Arc. I know it sounds mundane; but I'm a medieval historian and she happens to interest me."

"I'm sure it is most interesting; she anticipated women's lib by about five hundred years, didn't she?"

"In a way, yes," I laughed. "Come to think of it, she

135

did. And tell me," I continued, "have you been shooting lately?"

"No, not this week, not at Port St Pierre. I shoot elsewhere as well, you know, but I have wanted to press on with my book."

"What is its subject, may I ask?"

"Certainly. Jewelry. The history of the court jewels of France."

"What a magnificent subject."

"It will be a magnificent book. A large German publisher has commissioned it, and it will be printed simultaneously in many languages, with plates all in colour. They call it co-edition and that cuts down the cost. I have completed my research and now I have retired here to write it."

"How long have you been here?"

"Only since the spring."

"I must leave you to get on with your book, Mr Schroeder."

"Oh please, another cup of tea?"

"No, I really must go. I've been away for a couple of days. I felt like a little tour—Joan has been getting on top of me." And the family, I nearly added, but much as I liked Mr Schroeder, a fellow historian and a sympathetic person, I didn't know him well enough yet to confide in him.

"You must come again."

"I will." I got up rather awkwardly, pushing back my chair so that it brushed against his desk, causing some papers to fall on the floor.

"Oh, I'm sorry." I bent down to gather them up.

"No, no, let me do it." He pushed past me rather fussily. "They are all in order."

"Oh, I'm *terribly* sorry."

Worriedly he sorted them out, then put them neatly in a

136

pile and turned to smile at me. "That's perfectly all right. No harm done."

He showed me to the door and we made the customary polite farewells.

"Perhaps we could have lunch?" he suggested. "I have no phone, but I'll certainly look you up in a week or two."

We waved and I went slowly down the road to my car. It was now dusk, but I was glad I'd stayed. In retrospect, there was something about Mr Schroeder that left me feeling uneasy; he was too charming, too anxious to please, too eager to make a friend of someone he hardly knew. Why? There was nothing at all sexual in his attitude. Yet he seemed to want to know me better. Why? For my super brain, doubtless. Yes, that was it; in some way he wanted to *use* me. But how could I possibly be useful to Gustav Schroeder?

All these things and more I pondered as I walked towards the car. Because the thing that really bewildered me about Mr Schroeder was this: If he were German, why did he write in French? That much I had managed to see from the papers strewn on the floor.

I was bilingual, but having been born and brought up in England I wrote in English and thought in English. I could write in French if I had to, but I would never write a book in French. It would lack that colloquial quality essential for readability. Surely Mr Schroeder had been brought up in Germany and thought and wrote in German? Well, I'd ask him when I saw him again. It was an interesting point; in fact, I found it profoundly disturbing.

I drove round the bay, especially magical now in the dusk as the lights came on in Port St Pierre and Port Guillaume, and in the far distance the beam from the lighthouse at Le Hourdel began winking on and off. It had been a perfect day, breezy but clear and fine. The two days away had certainly been a tonic for me. In town I stopped outside the butcher's shop, remembering that I had nothing for dinner. I was just about to enter the shop when Martine flew out of Madame Gilbert's opposite, waving her arms at me.

"Madame, Madame, Madame Gilbert wishes to talk to you." She looked alarmed and her face was pale. Thinking at first that Madame Gilbert was ill, I rushed inside to find her sitting at her roll-top desk, ringing her hands, her face drawn in anguish. Now I was thoroughly alarmed.

"Madame, whatever is it?"

"Oh, Madame, pauvre Madame Clare. Sit down, sit down."

"Tom . . ." I had an awful feeling of panic and seized her arm. Of course, that's why he hadn't written. Something was wrong. "Madame Gilbert, what is it? My husband?"

Madame Gilbert's face was buried in her hands, but at my words she looked up.

"Oh, Madame, how stupid of me. I have worried you about your husband. No, Madame, it is not your husband—pardon me for making you so anxious. It is the whole family of de Frigecourt, Madame. They are all dead!"

For a moment I had a feeling of dizziness and thought I was going to faint. What I'd heard was unbelievable. I stared at her, my eyes begging her to tell me that it was not so, that I had misheard.

"Madame Gilbert, what is it you are saying?" I realised I was whispering.

"Dead," she whispered back. "Dead, except for little Fabrice. He stayed behind with the nurse. At the last minute, Laurent decided it was too windy for him. The only one left alive, the youngest, like the last time, in the war."

138

I pulled her arm and we both sat down. "Tell me, for God's sake, tell me all, Madame."

Martine was quietly weeping in the corner. Oh, how I wanted to go back in time, to have this not happen, to know how to have prevented it. All Rose's premonitions had come true. Madame Gilbert tried to compose herself and replaced the gold pince-nez on her nose.

"Well, the father, Monsieur Laurent, is a very keen sailor. He thought that as the weather was so warm and there was a good breeze he would take them all sailing in the bay."

"But this is not the weather for sailing, Madame, it is nearly November."

"Eh. Of course, it isn't. There is a time for sailing as there is a time for hunting, but not for Monsieur Laurent; he decided and that was that. He is a very good sailor, too, and he had apparently not put the boat up for the winter yet. Maybe he was going to do that and decided to have a last sail. Ah, a last sail." She lingered on the words.

Of course, it had been nice; the spring-like quality of the weather had moved me to take a break from my work.

"They were all to go, except for Jeanne, who said she didn't like the water, but after she had got into the boat the new nanny—I don't know her name—decided it was too cold for her and she got out. Then apparently Monsieur Laurent thought it was too cold for Fabrice, too, and ordered him out, not to his liking, as you can imagine. Oh, how he screamed, but it saved his life. Maybe the father had a premonition."

"If he did, he wouldn't have taken any of them," I said shortly.

"Well, off they went, happily round the bay. They were due back for lunch . . . they did not come."

"Perhaps somewhere along the coast . . ."

"Laurent would never have gone into the Channel at

this time of year; he would have stayed in the bay."

"But they just may have; oh, there is hope, Madame Gilbert. I thought they'd found the bodies."

"Calm yourself, child," Madame Gilbert said sadly. "They did not find the bodies, but they found the boat; it had capsized off Le Hourdel. It was washed up on the shore there."

"Oh, my God." I experienced a feeling of doom. Le Hourdel was notorious for its currents; there were notices all over the place telling people not to swim, not to sail or fish at certain times.

"And Fabrice? He knows?"

"Madame, I know no more than I have told you."

"I must go up to the house."

"Yes, go. They will welcome you. I am too énervée to go just now."

I rushed across the street to my car, drove up the main street and into the road that led to the château. The sight of the bay, my beautiful bay, made me shudder. It had become a graveyard—something treacherous.

The château was dark when I got there, what lights there were must have been on in the front. I parked my car by the pavement and rang the bell, and the gates swung open immediately. Madame Barbou was looking down the drive as I drove up and rushed over to open the car door. Her eyes were swollen with tears and we silently embraced.

"Madame, it is a terrible thing."

"I've only just heard. Where is Fabrice? Does he know?"

"He knows that they are missing. We make out we are anxious, nothing more. He is watching television with Lisa. He has no comprehension."

She started weeping anew, and I held her in my arms patting her back.

140

"Where is Jeanne, Madame?" I said quietly. Jeanne . . . I thought of Rose, of Michelle's remark about the evil eye. No, it was too horrible.

"Jeanne had the day off, Madame. Monsieur took the children out for the whole day. Doctor Bourdin is here, the young doctor. She came to see if everyone was all right. No one has any idea what to do or whom to contact. They are waiting for the mayor."

Thank God for Michelle. I went into the house by the back entrance, into the salon, and found her standing by the window alone. From her face as she turned to me I could see how the tragedy had affected her.

"Michelle! Is there no hope at *all*?"

"There is no hope," she said. "The boat capsized off Le Hourdel. There was no trace of them. They are dead."

"It's too horrible."

"What I can't understand," Michelle said bitterly, "is how Laurent allowed himself to go to Le Hourdel at this time of year, especially with the strong autumn currents and the wind."

"He must have drifted."

"He is too good a sailor to do something like that. No, something else happened."

"But what?"

"Maybe he became ill or the boat went out of control. Both the children are used to sailing, but they are not good enough to take charge of the boat in a stormy sea. No, he should never have gone. It was an error of judgement."

"Let's have a drink," I said. It was after six o'clock.

"I won't drink," Michelle said, "or I won't stop." Michelle had taken it very badly. I got my drink and motioned for her to sit down.

"Do you think there *is* a curse on the family? Do you believe in such things?"

141

"Now I don't know. I almost do. And you?"

"I know it's fanciful, but remember what you said about Jeanne?"

"What did I say?"

"About the evil eye."

"Oh, that—that was a joke. Honestly, Clare, you don't believe in that sort of thing, do you?"

"Well, I wonder." I took a drink. It was difficult to know how to put it.

"You're not serious, are you? Are you still thinking about Rose's death? My brother said you even asked him. It's obsessing you."

"Yes, but Rose was right, wasn't she? She said she thought Jeanne would harm the children. She also said in a letter to her boyfriend in England that she thought Jeanne was a witch."

"How do you know that?"

"I read his reply. She'd left it in a book I found in my room."

"Jeanne wasn't even here today. Tell me, how could she have made a boat sink?"

I gestured helplessly. "Michelle, you're making it very hard for me, but that *is* what it means, isn't it? The evil eye means that you only have to look at a thing to cause harm. You put a spell on something. I can't honestly believe that I'm saying this, but I have an awful feeling I'm right, or that something very sinister is going on. All these accidents, these mishaps . . ."

"The Burgundian curse," Michelle said softly.

"Of course," I echoed.

"I told you how the place was deserted and we used to play here pretending to see ghosts and things. It was kind of spooky and all children play these kinds of games. Our parents told us to be careful or the Burgundian curse would get us. You know the family is descended from the dukes of Burgundy?"

"Yes, of course."

"Well, that's all I know. Being of a scientific turn of mind even from childhood, I had no interest in such things, but a lot of the villagers still believe it."

"Madame Barbou does."

"I think my mother does too. Every time anything goes wrong for the de Frigecourts they all shake their heads and mutter about the curse."

She looked at me and tears came into her eyes. "I spoke about him in the present tense. I can't believe he's dead." She broke down and sobbed.

"Oh, Michelle. Did you care for Laurent very much?"

"Oh, I didn't *care* for him. I adored him. It was puppy love, but it lasted even when I was grown up. Whenever I used to see him, the occasional times he visited, I thought he was a real fairy-tale prince, so tall and handsome. The family has always been a legend in our town, and when he came with his wife and I met him again, he seemed to me to embody the hero of olden days. Everything about him was beautiful and perfect. And I was a rather plain country girl. He never looked at me, of course, in that way, but he was always very kind to me, as he was to us all. It is an adolescent craze that I've never outgrown."

I was rather suprised by what I was hearing. And here was I rejecting the fairy-tale prince. But that, after all, was what love was all about. Laurent was undeniably handsome, but for me he didn't have the kind of glamour he had for Michelle. Of course, the local lord, the Marquis, the great family home, the wealth. I could see how appealing it all must be to a young country girl, even though she had grown up and become a doctor—an achievement in itself, but nothing to compare with the charisma of the fairy prince.

"Did Laurent know how you felt?"

"Of course not! He hardly noticed me. I was the doctor's daughter; that's about all he knew, and he smiled at me as he did at everyone else. Why shouldn't he have? He would never have looked at me in any other way. Elizabeth was also from a wealthy family; they attract one another, those kinds of people."

She was wrong; but I couldn't tell her.

"I never hoped for anything from Monsieur Laurent, please don't misunderstand me. Even when his wife died it never crossed my mind. I just hero-worshipped him, that's all, and because of him I loved the children so much, and the place and everything to do with him."

Michelle blew hard on her handkerchief and made a visible effort to control herself. At last she managed a wan smile.

"Well, now you know."

"There's nothing wrong in what you tell me. You mustn't be ashamed of it. Listen, Michelle, Laurent would never have gone out without wearing life jackets, himself and the children, would he?"

"Of course not."

"Well, aren't they inflatable?"

"Yes."

"So how can they drown?"

"Clare, in that water they would die of cold. It's nearly November."

"I'd forgotten about that," I said. "And their bodies will be . . ."

"Washed up on the tide," she said. "Here or somewhere else."

## CHAPTER 12

Jeanne was standing in the doorway. How long she'd been there I didn't know. Had she heard any of our conversation concerning her? I didn't think so because it was a slight movement that alerted me to her presence, and I thought that must have been when she'd arrived. She had just come in, looking like a nineteenth-century schoolmistress in a curious little black straw boater and a drab green coat that reached to her calves; she carried a small black handbag and wore black gloves. She was staring at us, her face white, petrified.

"What bodies?"

"Oh, Jeanne!" Michelle and I went up to her together. The sight of her looking so striken made me inwardly reproach myself for what I'd said about her.

"What bodies?" she repeated monotonously.

"Jeanne." Michelle took her arm, obviously feeling as I

did. "The family, there's been a horrible accident. We're afraid they're dead, all except Fabrice and Lisa."

"In the boat," she said, staring at us. "I told them they shouldn't go in the boat. The Marquis laughed at me, only this morning at breakfast. I pleaded with him. I said it was too windy, the wrong time of the year. I had some awful foreboding; I knew something would happen. I know these things."

Jeanne sat down, staring straight in front of her, her lips quivering.

"She's in shock," Michelle said. "Give her a small brandy."

It frightened me, the way Jeanne sat there, clutching her handbag on her lap, her hands still gloved, staring, muttering. I held the brandy glass to her lips, but she refused to take it.

"I never touch alcohol."

"It's medicine," Michelle insisted. "I'm telling you to take it." She opened her lips obediently and I poured the liquid between them. The colour slowly came back to her face.

"I knew all day that something was wrong. I couldn't place it, it was such a lovely day. I saw them in the bay on the boat, and I waved to them from my window; then I saw them turn back into the bay and, thinking they were on their way home to safety, I went to Boulogne with a happy heart, but when I got there I was unhappy, restless. I went into the church for a long time and prayed, the lovely church on the hill. I prayed very hard to St Jeanne d' Arc, but I always do."

Just then Fabrice came running in, followed by Lisa, and we all tried to assume cheerful expressions, all except Jeanne, who maintained that awful staring straight in front of her.

146

"Papa is lost!" he said to me with excitement. "And Noelle, *and* Philippe. Lisa told them it was too cold; she warned them and got out of the boat. But we thought it was fun! Now they're lost."

He said it with a self-satisfied little smile and my heart went out to the baby so unaware of what tragedy can bring. Madame Barbou came in with a tray and laid the table for his tea.

"Fabrice will take his tea in the kitchen," Lisa said. Madame Barbou looked at her with dislike and marched out again. I couldn't help feeling sorry for Lisa; her poor command of French was a disadvantage, so that what was a simple request seemed like an order. Lisa was about to follow Madame Barbou, taking Fabrice by the hand, when Jeanne interrupted her fixed stare to look sharply at Lisa.

"You!" Lisa stopped, looking surprised. "Why did you get out of the boat?"

At first, Lisa didn't understand, and we all went over Jeanne's question very carefully. "It was too cold," she answered. "We have not enough clothes on."

"Then Papa said take me," Fabrice chimed in. "But I had my big sweater on and I wanted to stay."

"You should have known," Jeanne said and turned her head away in a gesture of disgust.

Lisa shrugged her shoulders, gave a sign to indicate she thought Jeanne was crackers, and took Fabrice into the kitchen.

"Jeanne, why don't you go upstairs and have a rest," Michelle suggested. "It's been a very great shock for you. We have had time to absorb it." But Jeanne went on staring into the distance, her face gradually brightening. Then she looked at us, smiling.

"They're not dead," she said. "I can see them. They

**147**

will return. Now I think I will rest"—and gathering up her things, she went slowly out of the room. Michelle and I stared after her.

"I think she *is* mad," I said. "If that isn't mad I don't know what is."

"That's an oversimplification," Michelle said, still frowning. "She is in shock, that's certain; her pupils were quite dilated. As for the knowing . . ." She shook her head."We shall see. Let us hope she's right. Thank God Nicolas comes back on the tide tonight. He may be able to tell us something. On the other hand, maybe they won't be back until tomorrow. He said they were going into the North Sea in search of herring. It will depend on the size of the catch. I wish he were here; he's a great source of strength."

"I can see that," I said. "He's like a rock."

Michelle smiled, the first time I'd seen her smiling like that since I'd arrived. "Be very careful," she said. "He always likes older women; he may be after you."

"That will be a nice change," I said. "It will make me feel wanted again. I must go now, Michelle. We must try to keep things normal for the sake of Fabrice."

"I'll stay here for a bit and then I'll go," Michelle said. "I can't believe it's happened. I just can't believe it."

I could hear Fabrice chattering away in the kitchen as I crept out the back way. The sound of his voice made tears come to my eyes. It was the first time I'd cried in months, and I wept all the way home, great huge sobs that, thankfully, nobody could hear.

There was a letter from Tom waiting for me when I got home. It was very brief. He said he'd been in Edinburgh and had only just received mine, "which I am going into very carefully and will write to you." Well, that was something. No protestations of undying love. I wondered why he'd been to Edinburgh. I suddenly felt very far away from Tom, and I wondered if I'd lost him and if I really cared.

I cooked supper and ate it hunched over the stove. I even wondered if I could continue to live in Port St Pierre, to be reminded every time I passed the shuttered château of those splendid children and that handsome, tragic man, and of poor little Fabrice being brought up somewhere by a distant aunt.

And then, absurdly, I thought of the ghost. The ghost Noelle claimed to have seen before her mother's death. No one had reported seeing a ghost before the deaths of *three* of the family. A tiny flame of hope surged inside me. Could Jeanne be right after all? But I passed a troubled night. The wind was up, and I seemed to see the swirling seas of the bay and the flickering of the light at Le Hourdel. There seemed to be a woman with a lamp beckoning a ship onto the rocks, and I woke up in an awful sweat. It was the wind buffeting the door. I listened. No, it was calm, and dawn was streaking the sky. What had awakened me was an urgent knocking on the door downstairs. I lay there fearfully; I didn't want to leave my warm bed for—what, this time?

I dragged myself downstairs, fumbled with the key and then the outside shutters. It was Michelle. It was raining and she looked cold and wet, as though she'd just come out of the sea, but her face was transformed. It was shining and she hugged me excitedly.

"They are safe! They are safe! Nicolas brought them in on the night tide. Oh, they are safe!"

I dragged her in, half-laughing and weeping as she was, and drew her to the stove. "Let me make coffee, let's put brandy in it. Oh, Michelle, *tell* me."

She followed me into the kitchen as I found the matches and lit the stove.

"He did see them. Nicolas did see them, and they set out together. He told Laurent he shouldn't go too far because the wind was strong on the other side of the bay. Nicolas passed them and saw them turn round, just before Le Hourdel, and when he was in the Channel he turned again to look at the bay, to see which ship was following him, when he saw the boat with Laurent and the children listing heavily out of control and drifting beyond Le Hourdel, where it was caught in the cross currents. The wind was rising and the sea was rough; they were all leaning heavily trying to right the boat, but the sail was almost in the water. Nicolas changed course and got to them, throwing a rope just as they were flung into the sea and the boat went under. Laurent caught the rope and the children held on to him. Nicolas said it was a miracle they survived."

"But why didn't they come back?"

"It was too late. The tide had turned and the boat would have foundered on the sand in the middle of the bay."

"But they could have made for a nearby port!"

"You don't know Nicolas when he goes fishing. It is his living and he takes it seriously. They were safe, and he wouldn't dream of missing a day's catch."

"He can have no imagination," I said bitterly.

"He hasn't," Michelle said, warming her hands on the hot cup of coffee. "He *is* a peasant, you know. Laurent apparently protested that people would worry, but Nicolas said he should have been more careful and they could help with the catch. That was that. At least he came back last night instead of going up towards Holland as he'd intended."

"Decent of him," I said, wondering if he'd realised how upset his sister had been, to say nothing of anybody else.

"You could have told me earlier," I said. "I've had an

awful night. I dreamt Jeanne was beckoning a ship onto the rocks with a lamp, like the Cornish wreckers."

"But Jeanne knew they were safe; it's extraordinary, isn't it? She was so happy when she saw them that she wept. I think we have been awful about Jeanne."

"Awful?"

"The evil eye."

"You're not telling me you think she's normal?" I replied incredulously.

"Well, what *is* normal? A lot of people have precognition, and she says she has. And as for not telling you earlier, I'm sorry. Nicolas at least brought them to our house before going back to unpack his catch; some of it has to be in Paris by morning. My mother gave them a meal and father made sure they were all right. I took them up to the château, and then we put the children to bed and sat about chatting. I haven't been to bed."

But she looked so blissfully happy, I knew she didn't care.

A sort of shyness overcomes one when people have survived a disaster. So it was with me when I went up to the château later and found a party in full swing, with everyone kissing and congratulating Laurent and his two children. All three of them looked remarkably well, I thought, hovering at the edge of the group when Laurent looked up and saw me. I'd seen his drowned face in my sleep, and there was such happiness to see it living and breathing that I gave a gasp, and the expression on my face made his eyes light up. The crowd seemed to part for me and I walked up to him and shook his hand.

"I'm so glad," I said. "So relieved." Then Noelle and Philippe surged up and had to be kissed, and Fabrice had to be consoled for not being a hero.

"It's not *fair*," he kept on saying to anyone who would listen. "Not *fair!*"

"I thought of you," Laurent whispered, "I knew how worried you'd be. That cretin Nicolas, I nearly threw him into the sea."

"I can't exactly picture it," I said laughing. "He's about twice your size. But Laurent, how did you lose control of the boat?"

"It was the tiller. It stuck, and the boat veered to starboard and we couldn't right it; then we were just swept out on the current. I'd just been turning at the point. It was pretty awful, I can tell you. Thank God the kids didn't seem to realise what danger we were in. Papa was there and that kind of thing; consequently they didn't panic. Ah, there is our rescuer."

Everyone stopped talking as Nicolas came into the room, looking grim and taciturn. He had a strange attraction, I thought. I'd certainly not like to cross him. He went straight up to Laurent, whispered something to him I couldn't hear, and the two of them left the room. It seemed to be a signal for the party to break up. The mayor and Dr Bourdin left together, Madame Gilbert and Martine waved to us and departed, and soon the room was empty except for Michelle, the children, Jeanne, and myself.

"I must go too," I said. "Leave you to try and get back to normal as soon as possible."

"Oh, stay for lunch," Jeanne pressed. "I know the Marquis would like you to."

"Do you know or did he tell you, Jeanne?" I asked.

"How do you mean, Clare?" Jeanne was very cool; she knew quite well what I meant.

"I'm talking about your second sight, your remarkable gift." I heard Michelle quickly draw in her breath, but I didn't care. If I needled Jeanne perhaps she'd be less withdrawn for a change.

"You're mocking me; you shouldn't, Clare."

152

"I'm not mocking you, Jeanne. I simply don't understand you. You said you had a premonition of disaster. You saw them go out to sea, turn to come home, and yet you didn't see the yacht founder. That I can't understand, because it must have happened almost simultaneously."

"What are you trying to say, Clare?"

"I'm wondering if you did see the accident, see them rescued, if you could have saved us all a lot of worry. I'm just wondering how much about you, Jeanne, is pretence!"

"Clare!" This time it was Michelle, the tone of her voice reproving me. But something had got me worked up; this awful calm of Jeanne's, this terrible air of *knowing*. Rose was right. Jeanne was weird, she was sinister, and, for all I knew, she was evil.

Jeanne and I were now glaring at each other; or rather Jeanne was looking at me in her infuriatingly calm way and I was snorting back like a young heifer.

"You're mistaken, Clare." Michelle had begun to sound very annoyed with me. "Jeanne couldn't possibly have seen the detail of the accident from here. Le Hourdel is just a dim point."

"You can see the lighthouse very clearly," I said stubbornly.

"Come up and see," Jeanne invited, cloyingly sweet now, leading the way to the door.

Her room was a long climb up. I had never been to the turret, and I was intrigued. After the second landing, where the children's playroom and Laurent's room were, there was a door and the staircase became narrow and circular. On the first floor Jeanne stopped outside her room and opened the door.

The room was small, with a single bed, very little furniture, and few personal objects about. It looked neat and austere—like a nun's cell, I thought, seeing the crucifix

153

over the bed and the rosary and prayerbook on the small table by her bedside. Jeanne swept to the window and we all looked out.

It was quite true. Had I stopped to think I would have realised it before I made the accusation. Whereas Port Guillaume was very clear, Le Hourdel was right at the extremity of the bay and the boats that were coming in on the tide, even quite big fishing boats, were minute specks.

"I'm sorry," I said. "I'm too emotionally overwrought."

Jeanne was looking at me earnestly. "I'm your friend, but you don't realise it, Clare. You're resisting me. Why?"

I didn't reply, and Michelle was looking uncomfortable, her friendly face creased with embarrassment.

"It's because of Rose, isn't it?" Jeanne went on. "Of what she said about me? You haven't got Rose's death out of your mind, have you, Clare?"

"No. Rose haunts me."

"That's because she was evil," Jeanne said, turning back to the window and looking seawards, "and evil lives on, even after death." She saw us to the door and closed it after us with a sweet, forgiving smile.

"That woman gets my goat," I said when we were safely down in the hall.

"You make it obvious. I think she's teasing you half the time and you know, Clare, she is very religious. How can she be that religious and still have the evil eye?"

"That's what they said about Joan of Arc," I said, "and I'm beginning to think that that Jeanne and this one are rather alike."

We halted at the door of the salon, where Nicolas and Laurent were engaged in serious conversation that ceased as soon as they saw us. They didn't smile, and I knew that something was wrong.

154

"What is it?"

They looked at each other and Nicolas shrugged.

"It's the boat," Laurent said at last. "Nicolas examined it when it was brought round from Le Hourdel this morning. He's pretty sure someone or something tampered with the tiller. The bolts had all been loosened, which was why it stuck."

"But the boat must have had an awful buffeting," Michelle quickly intervened. "How could you possibly tell?"

"I am a sailor." Nicolas gave his sister a withering look. "I can tell when a boat has been interfered with. I simply examined the wreck to see if it was seaworthy again and I tell you what I saw. The bolts are very heavy ones and they had been loosened."

"We've decided not to say anything," Laurent said.

"Because you don't want a fuss," I said.

"Exactly."

"And you didn't want a fuss about Rose because you are the de Frigecourt family and you have had enough trouble."

"It isn't that, Clare, don't sound so harsh."

"I feel harsh," I said. "I feel unhappy and frightened and harsh. Everyone's talking about ghosts and curses and things that go bump in the night, but I feel that something out of the ordinary is going on here. I may be wrong, but I feel it in my bones, and I think you should do more than just pray for peace."

At that moment Madame Barbou opened the door and swept to one side, and my husband, Tom, walked in.

## CHAPTER 13

I shall never forget the look on Tom's face as we all stood there gaping at him. For one thing, I was the only person who knew who he was, and shock had momentarily rendered me speechless. Laurent took a step forward, looked at me, then stopped. Michelle and Nicolas, looking puzzled, said nothing.

"Tom!" I said at last, in a squeaky falsetto, then more normally, "hello, Tom, you gave us a surprise."

"More of a shock," Tom said. "I should have told you I was coming."

"Haven't you a bag?"

"I left it with Madame Gilbert, who told me you were here. There's been an accident, it seems."

"Laurent, this is Tom; Tom . . ."

I performed the introductions in a zombie-like trance. Why was it that the last person I'd expected to see was Tom? And did I want Tom here at all?

Madame Barbou interrupted us to ask if we wanted any lunch and that if we did a cold buffet was ready in the dining room.

"A drink," Laurent said after telling Madame Barbou we'd be ten minutes. "We all need a good strong drink."

"It's nothing to do with you," I whispered to Tom. "He's just heard something disturbing. I'll tell you later."

"High time I came, I can see," Tom said without smiling, but I couldn't decide whether he meant because of the situation or because of Laurent, whose face had worn a furious frown ever since Tom's arrival.

At least we'd decide a number of things in the next few days, I told myself philosophically.

Jeanne slipped into the room, and after being introduced to Tom, whom she appraised impassively, she stood there sipping Perrier water and doing her best to look mysterious. Tom and I moved to the window.

"This is the bay," I explained.

"Your bay," Tom smiled. "I can see why you love it."

"It was a horrible bay yesterday. Laurent and two of the children nearly drowned." As I told him the story, his eyes never left my face. "And then, just before you came in," I concluded, "which was what made your entry so dramatic, Laurent told us that Nicolas thought the boat had been tampered with and that it wasn't an accident at all."

"It doesn't sound very psychic, does it?" Tom said grimly. "I'm glad I came."

"To protect me?" I said.

"I thought you didn't need that kind of thing. No, to help sort out this business."

"Did you find out anything?"

"A little. I'll tell you after lunch when we get out of here."

Where did Tom think we were getting *to*, I wondered, as the children joined us and we filled our plates, seating

**157**

ourselves around the large table. I hoped he didn't think we were simply going to shack up in 33 Rue du Château together. Oh, no. Laurent poured the wine. Tom only listened; he couldn't speak French with any fluency, but I noticed him paying a good deal of attention to Jeanne, who as usual ate little, as though she was on a permanent fast.

Laurent called for silence and held up his glass. "A toast," he said, "to providence and to Nicolas Bourdin, who saved us from the sea."

A lump came into my throat and I bowed my head.

"Thank God," Jeanne whispered, and we all drank silently.

The children were in high spirits. Thank heaven they had never realised what real danger they'd been in. Only Fabrice was sullen, having missed the big adventure, and he tried his best to gain the maximum attention for himself by being naughty until his father threatened to send him to his room.

Lisa, who spoke very little French, took no part in the conversation. I thought she looked pale, too. The fact that she had not been in the boat and had taken Fabrice had undoubtedly saved all their lives; five people in heavy seas would have been almost impossible to haul aboard. This factor must have weighed on her mind; no wonder she looked pale.

Noelle was chatting on. "This time yesterday." She giggled and pretended to shiver.

"It's nearly two," Laurent said. "This time yesterday we were safely aboard Nicolas' boat. Don't forget the tide is nearly an hour later today."

I was curious. "Noelle, were you frightened at all? Did you ever realise the danger you were in?"

"But Papa was there," she said with some surprise. "We knew Papa would not let anything happen to us. Besides, as we passed the château we saw Mademoiselle standing at her window looking at us through her glasses, and we knew she would send help if anything went wrong. But it all happened so quickly . . ."

Noelle went on talking, but I was looking at Jeanne, and so was Michelle. Then Michelle and I exchanged glances. Between the three of us a silent communication was taking place. Of course, Jeanne had been looking at them through binoculars. She could have seen everything as clearly as if it were an arm's length away, and if she had, then presumably she had gone off to Boulogne, leaving hours of agony to the rest of us.

I was determined to have this out with her after lunch and to speak to Laurent about her. I would not have any peace of mind so long as Jeanne was with the children.

"I have to go to Paris this afternoon," Laurent announced suddenly. "I have business that really can't wait. Jeanne, is that all right with you?"

"Of course, Monsieur."

"And no sailing." He smiled.

"Or climbing trees, Papa," chimed in Philippe. "Fabrice fell down a tree the other day."

"Ah, yes, I heard about that. You must be very good." Laurent glanced around. "Will you take them up for lessons, Mademoiselle? I want things to continue as normally as possible, and they seem to be perfectly all right."

"Oh, Papa!" Cries of protest, but Jeanne got up pursing her lips firmly.

"You heard your father! To the schoolroom. Vitez!"

Nicolas and Lisa, who had been sitting together, were deep in conversation.

"The power of love," Michelle murmured to me as we got up from the table, "overcomes language barriers."

I looked at her in amazement.

"I noticed he was attracted to her immediately. I told you he always likes older women, and she is not only ten

159

years older than he, but she has that big buxom peasant quality that he likes."

"I must say they're getting on well. I don't think they've even noticed the table is empty except for them!"

Tom was standing with Laurent, who was pointing out spots of interest in the bay and telling him where the accident happened. Tom was nodding and commenting, and I thought the two men were getting on well. Michelle started pouring the coffee and I joined them.

"I was just showing Tom Le Hourdel." Laurent turned to me, smiling.

"I thought you might be. Thanks, Michelle." I took the coffee cup from her. "Tom has his black, please."

Laurent suddenly looked at me and I saw an expression of surprise on his face. Did he care so much for *me*, I wondered. Was that why he'd gone all stern when Tom appeared? Did he sense, and perhaps resent, my proprietary air about Tom? Those familiar little things that husbands and wives know about each other—black or white coffee, milk or sugar, the right or left side of the bed. The trivia that make up a shared life together, that can cement it into a firm relationship or cause it to break up. The trivia had upset the relationship between Tom and me; our personal lives had been disorganised because neither of us had been willing to give in to the other. Yet, after two months away from Tom I could appraise him afresh and, as he stood beside Laurent, I compared them.

Tom was about two inches taller than Laurent, standing well over six feet. He was always aware of his height and seemed to walk with a permanent stoop which grew even more pronounced when he was depressed. Tom was not conventionally handsome as Laurent was. He had a naturally pale complexion, permanent dark rings under his eyes and a great beak of a nose which dominated a face which, in my tender moments, I used to call craggy.

160

His hair—ash-blond, not golden like Fabrice's—was generally badly cut and fell about his ears like the proverbial mop. It was his eyes that made Tom—great luminous blue eyes that registered deep emotion and often made me think he should have been on the stage.

Despite his lack of obvious sex appeal, Tom had an indefinable quality that made him very attractive to women. He always had several female students in love with him who wrote him long love letters in the guise of psychological essays. As far as I knew, Tom, though flattered, hardly noticed, and was impervious to it all. His work came first, then his ideal wife, then me, the imperfect wife. Tom wanted everything perfect, and no amount of psychological training had ever convinced him that it couldn't be.

I suddenly realised that Michelle was staring at me, and I smiled at her.

"Are you pleased to see him?"

"What do you think?"

"I think you don't know."

"You're right."

"Laurent," I called lightly. "Do both of you come and talk to us. Tell us more about the Burgundian curse, Laurent."

"Ah, you think we're in the middle of it, don't you?" Laurent laughed and sat opposite us on one of the deep sofas.

"Something like that."

"It is the legend that one of our ancestors, maybe Jehan de Frigecourt, whom I described to you and who made a lot of enemies, had a curse put on his line. When things are bad, we call it the Burgundian curse, and when they're good we conveniently forget about it. I don't think we'd have lasted so long if the line were really cursed. It's a sort of family joke."

"And you don't know who put the curse on Jehan?"

"No, some old necromancer of medieval times, I imagine."

"When did the curse begin this time?" Tom asked quietly.

"Well, we've had a run of bad luck. My wife had an automobile accident and has died, our nanny had an accident and died; Fabrice fell out of a tree; we nearly got drowned. Add them up, and I don't know if it amounts to anything."

Tom was looking at him gravely.

"Clare thinks it does."

"I do think Jeanne is bad for the children," I said. "I am convinced Rose was right. She told a whopping lie about yesterday. She went to great trouble to demonstrate to Michelle and me that she couldn't have seen the accident, and then Noelle said at lunch today that she was looking at you through binoculars and could have seen the whole thing."

"Yes, we did see her looking at us. She waved to us and we waved back. But why should she pretend not to have seen the accident if she did see it?"

I shrugged. "It isn't logical," I said.

"I mean she couldn't have caused it, could she?"

I didn't reply.

"Could she, Clare?"

"What about the screws?"

"How could Jeanne have got near the yacht? I only decided to sail in the morning. I was the only one with a key to the boathouse. I don't think Jeanne even knows where the boathouse is. What's more, she said she didn't think we should go; so there."

"Tell us what did happen," Tom said. "If someone tampered with the bolts who could it have been?"

"I don't think it was anyone. I know Nicolas knows what he's doing, but that yacht got a very rough battering. I'm sure it could have worked loose at sea."

162

"If Nicolas says it couldn't have, I don't think it could have," Michelle said firmly. "I'm convinced about that."

"Go on," Tom persisted, "give us the sequence. You decided to sail when, at breakfast?"

"Yes, it was a nice day and I felt like it. I knew I was going back to Paris today and it would be a treat for the children. Jeanne agreed they should be released from school, but she didn't want to go herself and advised me not to. She said it looked calm, but it wasn't the right weather. I explained I knew the bay like the back of my hand, but I was relieved in a way because two adults and three children was a much better balance for the boat than three adults and three children.

"The kids got into their warm clothing and I went down and opened the boathouse, which is just by the jetty. Lisa and the children came down, and I went to get help from one of the sailors. I don't have a slip and you have to lift the boat into the water."

"I should have thought Lisa was as good as a sailor," I murmured.

"That's my girl, the perfect bitch." Tom smiled at me.

Laurent flushed but went on quietly. "No, I couldn't ask Lisa; the boat actually needs two other men. I got them in a couple of minutes and we lifted the boat onto the water. We saw Nicholas, who helped hoist the sails, and we passed the time of the day with him and that was it."

"It seems most unexceptional," Tom agreed.

"Are *you* disturbed about Jeanne, Michelle?" Laurent seemed to notice her almost for the first time that day.

She blushed and lowered her head. Yes, she was like a schoolgirl, flattered that she had been noticed. "I . . . er . . . not so much as Clare. Not at all, in fact, though it's true she did try to show us she couldn't have seen the accident, because she never mentioned binoculars and we never thought about them."

"But what have binoculars got to *do* with it?"

"She said she saw you turn, and it was just after you turned that your boat began to list, wasn't it?"

"Yes, but we turned twice; we did two complete tours of the bay, and it was the first time past we saw Jeanne."

Hell, I felt an idiot now. "You didn't see her the second time round?"

"I didn't look. But we all clearly waved the first time because we came very near the château, and I'm sure that if she had still been there the second time the kids would have noticed her and we'd all have waved again."

"You've lost your case, Clare." Tom got up. "Clare and I have a lot to talk about," he said to Laurent. "Would you excuse us?"

I thought for a moment Laurent was going to do nothing of the kind; his eyebrows knotted in a frown, but good breeding won out, as of course it would. I was irritated by the way Tom had taken the initiative. How did he know *I* wanted to go?

Lisa and Nicolas had disappeared and Madame Barbou was clearing the table.

"Lisa is going to be like Rose," she said to me darkly. "If she has a man, we shall not see much of her."

"Oh, I think Lisa is a very different kettle of fish," I replied. "I don't think she'd neglect her duties. Laurent, could I have a word with you before we go?"

"Certainly. Let's go into the library."

Now it was Tom's turn to scowl, but I ignored him and left the room with Laurent.

Laurent closed the library door and we stared awkwardly at each other.

"It's nothing personal," I said quickly. "Don't be afraid, but Laurent, I want to stay here if I may."

"Of course! Not with Tom?"

"No. If Tom thinks I'm going back to the house to sleep with him, I'm not. We are separated, and in England two years living apart is enough for a divorce, if the partners agree. I don't want to compromise my relationship with Tom."

"I'm glad."

Laurent came nearer to me. Looking into his eyes I knew the strength of his attraction for me, and I suddenly wondered about my own feelings. The arrival of Tom had thrown everything into confusion so far as emotions were concerned; he seemed to have precipitated something between Laurent and me that had been lying dormant until now. He was looking at me so intensely I thought he was going to kiss me, and I backed away.

"Don't get the wrong idea, Laurent. Tom could go to the hotel, but I know you won't be here so I shan't be compromised here either. Oh, it's all ridiculous, isn't it? I want time on my own to think. I'd also like to be near the children while you're away."

"Oh, Clare, now that . . ." He turned round and threw up his hands. I knew nothing annoyed him so much as this.

"I'm sorry, Laurent. Yes, I am worried about Jeanne. I am also worried about Lisa."

"Lisa! For God's sake, *Clare*."

"What do you know about Lisa?"

"*Know?* She came from an agency, highly recommended. You think Lisa wants to harm the children too?"

"Lisa got out of the boat, didn't she? Didn't you think that was odd?"

"No, I didn't. It was cold once the boat was on the water. I was glad she decided not to come because I was worried about Fabrice; the older children are hardier. You think Lisa sat there unscrewing the bolts?"

"Not in the boat," I said thoughtfully, "but couldn't she have done it while you went to fetch the men to help you?"

"No! I, I never thought of it. I mean, the children were with her."

"Running in and out, no doubt?"

"Oh, Clare, stop it. Nicolas Bourdin could have, if it comes to that. We all went and had a coffee while he helped put the sails up, and I saw Fabrice and Lisa back off home. Now I don't suppose you suspect Nicolas Bourdin?"

"Laurent, let me stay?"

"Of course you can stay! I want you to stay! I don't want you near your husband. I don't like him. I don't like his being here."

"Oh, Laurent, you can't say you don't like Tom. What did Tom do to you?"

"Yes, you're defending him immediately, don't you see, Clare?"

"But I don't think you're being fair. I'd say that about anyone, not only Tom. He's just arrived. You don't like him because he's my husband!"

Laurent seemed to swoop down upon me before I'd finished speaking and scoop me up in his arms. His kiss was savage and exciting, and I responded to it. The sexual tension we had created between ourselves made it unavoidable.

Or that's what I thought when I tried to rationalise it afterwards; but what actually stopped the embrace was the sound of the door opening and Michelle standing there, her cheeks flaming, staring at us.

## CHAPTER 14

I got Tom out of the château very quickly. I'd simply
brushed past Michelle without even trying to explain.
What could I say? How could I explain what even I did
not fully understand? Thank heaven Tom wasn't with
her, but was still in the salon standing by the window,
looking angrily out over the bay.

We picked up Tom's suitcase from Madame Gilbert
who was extremely intrigued by the whole thing and
tried to persuade us to stay longer. We said very little as
we walked through the town but Tom voiced his approv-
al of the house.

"It's better than that château," he said, throwing his
case carelessly on the floor. "That house gives me the
creeps."

"The château? But it's beautiful. I adore it."

Tom smiled. "One more example of our failure to
agree."

His words angered me. "Tom, why did you come?"

"Well, you wrote to me, didn't you? I did as you asked. I went to see Cliff and I wanted to see how you were. You may not remember it now, but your letter gave the impression of someone seriously alarmed. Unexplained deaths, witches, and God knows what."

"Are you going straight back?"

"That depends upon you."

"Tom, I'm not staying here with you."

"Oh?"

"I'm staying at the château."

"So you *are* involved with the handsome Marquis," he said softly. "I wondered about that as soon as I saw you together."

"On the contrary. I am not at all involved. Besides he won't be there. I want to keep an eye on the children. I really am worried about them, Tom, after yesterday."

"And is it your business?"

"Yes." I lit a cigarette and sat down by the stove, shivering slightly, whether from nerves or the cold I wasn't sure. "I've made it my business. Jeanne doesn't seem fit to be in charge of the children. At the very *least* she's mystical, and at the most, dangerous. And as for Lisa, she can hardly speak French and seems totally disinterested in their welfare."

"I was observing Jeanne," Tom's voice thawed and became chatty. "She is a very odd woman, I agree. She is withdrawn, almost schizophrenic."

"That would explain a lot," I said quickly. "A schizoid personality. Oh, Tom, I think you've got it! The only thing is, she is fairly consistently like that. They usually vary, don't they?"

"There are different degrees. Jeanne may be only mildly disturbed; I wouldn't know unless we had her properly observed and examined, which we can't."

168

This was Tom at his best. "I've missed you, Tom," I said. "I've missed this part of our relationship which is so good—the exchange of ideas."

"We should never have married," Tom said, "then we would have been lovers forever. Jacob Bronstein said that to me only a couple of days ago."

I was totally uninterested in the views of Tom's boss, who I felt exerted too great an influence over him.

"Let's talk about Rose," I said coolly. "What did you find out?"

"I didn't find out all that much. Cliff, her boyfriend, is away in Northern Ireland. He's a soldier and was sent there shortly before Rose died. I was able to see his mother, which was very interesting. She said Rose was always a strange girl and she wished her son had fallen for someone else. Oddly enough, she also used the word 'bewitched' to describe Rose and thought she exercised an undue amount of influence over Cliff."

"Mothers are like that, of course," I murmured, thinking of Tom's mother, who was overbearing enough to drive any self-respecting daughter-in-law to drink.

"She was sure Rose would never marry Cliff but entertained ideas above her station, as it were. Temperamentally, she said, they were unsuited, as Cliff is a very extroverted sort of boy, a real commando type, and Rose had a secretive quality about her."

"Attraction of opposites. Rose was also very pretty. According to local gossip, she had a gentleman friend here as well."

"Really? Well, Cliff's mother didn't like her, and I don't think she's sorry she's gone. However, she told me something else that was interesting. Before Cliff went to Ireland and until Rose's death, she began writing to him much more often than before."

"Had she any of the letters?" I asked eagerly.

"No. Cliff took them all with him, and the others she'd sent on. One was quite a bulky packet."

"That would be the pages," I said.

"Quite. She didn't know anything about that."

"So how have you left it?"

"Well, when I got home I wrote to Cliff. I said that we weren't quite happy about the circumstances of her death and could he add anything. I also asked about the missing pages. I had to send it to some mysterious army address; apparently he's near the border and in quite a lot of danger. All we can do is wait to hear from him."

"Mmmm." I was very thoughtful.

"There's just one other thing that will intrigue you," Tom said. "Rose's mother was a well-known medium."

"Was?" I said excitedly.

"She died a couple of years ago. That's what made Rose so restless and Cliff so protective of her."

"How very interesting," I said, and described something of the eerie atmosphere of Rose's room.

"You mean you actually *feel* a presence?" Tom said incredulously.

"Oh, no, no, nothing like that, but, yes, I do feel that something unexplained is there. It has a very curious effect on me. It's one of the reasons I want to go back to the château again, and your being here has given me an excuse."

"Besides decency," Tom said, smiling.

"Oh, decency, hell; but, Tom, our relationship *is* ambiguous. Let's try to sort that out first."

"The sex was never ambiguous."

I stood up quickly. "We've got to sort the *whole* thing out, Tom, and then we'll see. Either we come together for good or we part for good."

"And what do you think will happen?" Tom's voice was low.

"I don't know, Tom."

When I got back to the château with my case, Laurent had already gone; the children were still in the schoolroom, and except for Madame Barbou humming in the kitchen all was quiet. I had a curious feeling of excitement as I went up to Rose's room—my room.

It was very cold in the room. I shut the door and stood where I was, as though looking for something. The bed had been freshly made and the room cleaned. It was impersonal, like a room in a hotel. With my things I would make it my room, as Rose had made it hers. I unpacked and put my scents and cosmetics on the dressing table, my underclothes in the chest of drawers, my dresses in the wardrobe. When I'd finished I looked around again. That was better, but it was still very cold. I couldn't understand why it was so cold when the rest of the house was so warm.

Suddenly there was a soft breeze; the curtains stirred, though the window and door were closed. I felt chilled and apprehensive.

Rose.

"Rose," I whispered. "If you are there, will you . . . can you . . . tell me what I should do."

Nothing happened. The room grew imperceptibly warmer. I went over to the window and felt the central heating pipes. They were warm, but not hot. Perhaps for some reason they'd been turned off and the heat was just beginning to circulate again.

I looked out of the window. It was dusk and the lights of Port Guillaume were beginning to twinkle across the bay. There was one very bright light in particular that shone through the trees, higher up than the others. I opened the window and craned my head forward. Could that be Mr. Schroeder's light? I thought it was, and then suddenly something he'd said that day on the beach seemed to assume an enormous importance in my mind. I wondered why I hadn't remarked on it before; it must have been lurking in my subconscious.

When I'd asked him if he knew the de Frigecourt family, he'd replied, "Yes, before the children were born." Yet all the time he'd appeared to have assumed the children were mine. But he'd known *I* wasn't a de Frigecourt. He'd known then that the children weren't mine, that they were members of the family. This was also assumed when I'd seen him at his home. "How are the children?" "Their mother has died" and so on.

I shook myself and closed the window. "Clare Trafford, you are making mysteries," I told myself. "If you go on like this, Tom will have you put in the nut house, and not before time."

Jeanne greeted me coolly, I thought, at tea. The children appeared delighted to see me and plied me with questions about Tom. "But if he's your *husband*, why aren't you with him in your house?"

"Because we don't live together."

"Why not? Husbands and wives always live together."

"Are you divorced?" Noelle asked knowingly.

"Tish, be quiet," from Jeanne, looking at me disapprovingly. Jeanne would certainly not approve of divorce. I glanced at her before replying. One had to be honest.

"We are not divorced yet, but we may be."

"Is *that* what he's come to see you about?"

"In a way."

It was quite a neat answer, also a solution to these endless questions. It would stop everyone speculating as to why Tom was really here. Lisa was late to tea. She sat down, her face flushed, and was awarded a disapproving glance from Jeanne. She made no excuses, drank her tea quietly, and afterwards took the children into the television room.

Between Jeanne and me the air was heavy with things unsaid. We tinkered around with our teacups before Jeanne spoke. "About the binoculars," she said quietly. Her voice had a slight tremor in it.

"Yes, I wondered about those."

"I really didn't see the accident."

Now that I knew the yacht had gone twice round the bay I was more ready to believe her, but I said nothing. She seemed to think that my silence was an accusation.

"I thought they were coming round the bay again. I put the binoculars down and prepared to go out. I didn't look out of the window again."

"Does it much matter what I think, Jeanne?"

Jeanne flushed. "Yes. I know you don't like me and I want you to."

"Why?"

"I still have this strange feeling that you will bring me harm. That is why I am uneasy with you."

"Can't you be more specific, Jeanne? This does intrigue me, as I wish you no harm at all."

"You will be the instrument of it."

I pulled my chair nearer to hers and lowered my voice. "Jeanne, if you are so close to the Maid that her spirit lives within you, as you say it does, can you tell me more about her? So much of her life is a mystery. If you could perhaps help me with my book?"

Jeanne, I saw, was looking at me nervously.

"I mean, there are so many unexplained things. For instance, why did she refuse to say the *paternoster* when asked at her trial?"

"If you have studied the *procès* you will know that Jeanne d'Arc maintained her independence throughout."

"Yes, but this was considered proof that she was a witch. Witches were supposed to be unable to recite the pater without stumbling."

"Oh, she knew that, but she wasn't a witch. So it didn't matter to her what people thought. Besides, she knew she was going to die, so when and how death came didn't much matter. It was the will of God. Maybe when you've finished your book, Clare, we can talk about it again and you can raise the points that worry you."

"But it won't be finished for ages."

"In that case, I may not be here to help you." She drew back her chair and got up, but her words chilled me.

"Why, Jeanne, are you leaving?"

"It is up to God," she said. "Only He knows."

I sat smoking furiously for awhile after she'd gone. Jeanne was obviously some kind of religious nut, but there was nothing consoling in that. Like her namesake, she was so utterly certain about what she was doing. She'd told me nothing new about the *paternoster*, but it was consistent with the Maid's character and with hers.

I drained my last cup of tea and was about to go up to my room when Michelle Bourdin walked in, unannounced. She looked surprised to see me, then embarrassed.

"Oh, Clare, I didn't expect to see you here. I'd heard Laurent had gone and I looked in to see how things were."

"Are you worried, too, Michelle? Come have some tea. It's a bit cold. Shall I send for some fresh?"

"Oh, no. Are you staying on here, Clare?"

"Yes, for the time being. I can't set up house with Tom, you see."

"Yes, I do see," Michelle said in a sarcastic tone of voice I'd never heard from her before.

"There is nothing between Laurent and me, Michelle. A kiss isn't anything much, you know."

"So Laurent said."

"Oh, he did explain?"

"Not really. I don't think he thought it any of my business, which it isn't, of course. He simply said it wasn't what I thought and walked out of the room."

"I'm sorry, Michelle. That's all I can say."

"You've got two men," Michelle said bitterly, "and you can't make up your mind! I haven't even one. I've spent my whole life working hard and studying, and where does it get me?"

"That's a silly thing to say, Michelle. I've spent all my life studying, too. I can't help it if I've left my husband and if Laurent and I are partly attracted to each other."

"Partly? What does *partly* mean?" Her voice was shrill.

"It means partly. It's a flirtation; nothing will come of it."

How could I tell her that if Laurent wasn't for me, I didn't think he was for her either? But any further conversation on this subject was suspended for the time being as the door opened and Jeanne came in, looking angry.

"Have you seen Philippe?"

"He's in the television room with Lisa."

"No, he is not. He said he wanted to work on his French verbs."

"Well, he's working on his French verbs then."

"He is not. He is not in his room or in the schoolroom. I said I would give him extra coaching this evening for which he had to come up to my room."

I was apprehensive but nothing more. Even a clock striking in this house scared me these days; I seemed to have developed an extra sensibility that was permanently tuned in to the possibility of disaster.

We all went into the television room, where Lisa and the other two children were watching the set. Lisa dragged herself reluctantly to her feet and managed to tell us that Philippe had never gone into the room with them but had gone upstairs saying he had to work.

"Let's divide the house among us," I said, "and let's get on with it."

By eight o'clock that evening, everyone in Port St Pierre knew that Philippe de Frigecourt was missing. After we'd searched the house, and there was plenty of area to cover, I went down for Tom, who had happily settled in as if for a long stay.

"You do have an exciting time," Tom said, striding in front of me towards the château. "Maybe you should become a policewoman when the faculty chucks you out because you haven't finished your book."

"It's not funny," I said grimly. "He's only eight."

Michelle's father was also at the château when we got back, and the first thing we did was to call Laurent in Paris.

Laurent was not in. No one knew what to do. The policeman who'd been alerted scratched his head saying nothing could be done in the way of an outside search until dawn. Jeanne, ashen-faced, sat staring in front of her, and Lisa did what she could to keep the other two children occupied. Madame Barbou kept us supplied with food, but no one was hungry except for Tom, who ate several large chunks of bread with meat. I watched Tom with loathing as he ate.

"Only you," I said accusingly "could eat at a time like this."

"Oh, that's not fair," from Michelle. "He hardly knows Philippe."

"It's not that I'm insensitive," Tom said, biting on his bread and smiling at Michelle. "It's that I'm hungry. Now"—he finished his food and wiped his hands on his napkin—"we are clear there is nothing more we can do. I suggest we all have a good night's sleep and start again at

176

dawn. You will be at the house if anything happens, Clare, and we shall all be nearby."

"But . . ." I began.

Tom held up his hand. "There are no buts, Clare, if you will forgive me. There is absolutely nothing more we can do, and to lose sleep will not help Philippe. If he is not found by tomorrow, his father must decide what action to take. Have you thought," he said, dropping his voice, "that he may have been kidnapped."

"Kidnapped!" Jeanne cried, holding her face in terror. "Mon Dieu! I shall pray all night."

"There may be a note. It is a possibility. This is a large house and anyone could easily get in or out. You say a number of sinister things have been happening . . . well."

Tom was right, of course, but I wanted him to stay. "If you were here," I said, "maybe it would be better. I mean, to be on hand."

"There is plenty of space," Jeanne said eagerly. Jeanne wanted him too.

"Then I'll stay," said Tom. "As long as I don't compromise Clare. You must make sure we're not even on the same floor."

"If you're going to be childish about this you might as well go back," I said, furious that he was making us feel so helplessly feminine and foolish. "I just feel that to have a strong man about the place might be a good thing. If you can't stay, Nicolas Bourdin might."

"He's at sea," Michelle said shortly. "I think you should stay, Tom. You can sleep in Laurent's bed. He won't mind, and it will save fuss at this time of night."

Tom glanced gratefully at Michelle. "You have a very level head, my dear. Thank God for you."

It was such a typical Tom-like thing to say, chauvinistic and patronising. This little woman was being level-

**177**

headed, as opposed to all the other little women, like me, who were not so reasonable.

"Oh, Christ!" I said. "For heaven's sake, go back to the Rue du Château, and I mean it. I'm going to bed. Come, Jeanne, we can look after ourselves."

Tom gaped at me, but I was too exhausted, too worried, and too angry with Tom, myself, and everyone else to care.

"I could stay," he began.

"No, go home. Take Michelle home first. We'll see you all in the morning."

With that, I swept out of the room, their voices echoing after me. Tom would be saying how difficult Clare was and they would all be agreeing, presumably.

Once inside my room, I leaned against the door without putting on the light. I'd left my curtains open; the moon was not full, but there was enough light for me to discern the outline of the furniture once I'd grown used to the darkened room. I closed my eyes and tried to evoke her presence.

"Rose, Rose, where are you?" I whispered, my body taut with anticipation.

But there was nothing, no little stir of air, no incipient presence.

Rose wasn't there.

## CHAPTER 15

Half-dreams came from half-sleeping. I'd wake up and sit upright, listening, but the sounds only told me the tide was coming in and then the steady chug of the boats returning with the catch. I drifted off to sleep again, but the voices in my dreams offered no help, no reassurance.

Then, something called me insistently. Rose!

I propped myself on my elbows, wide awake and alert. I had heard a voice, a very clear voice calling my name. "Yes, Rose, yes?" I breathed into the night. Yet it wasn't night. It was almost dawn.

I was positive I'd heard a voice. I put on my gown and opened the door.

"Claaaarrreee . . ." I heard it again, as though from a long way off. It was a child's voice! *Philippe!*

I rushed along the corridor, but it was quiet and dark. The sound seemed to have come from above. I went up to the next floor, quickly opened all the doors—the children's playroom, the schoolroom, Laurent's room (Tom wasn't there!). I opened the door to the turret and tiptoed up until I stood outside Jeanne's room. Silence. Should I call her? I knocked on the door. Silence.

"Jeanne, Jeanne!"

She fumbled with the catches; the door opened a slit.

"Clare! What is it?"

"Someone called my name. I'm sure it was Philippe. Listen!"

"Claaaarrrrrrre . . . Jeannnnnnnne . . ."

"It's you, too. Oh, Jeanne, it's Philippe!"

"It's outside," she said, and we both rushed to the window, flinging it open wide.

"Philippe!"

"I'm here. I'm here."

"He's on the roof," Jeanne breathed. "Oh, merciful God!"

"Philippe!" I shouted. "Where are you?"

"I'm over your head, on the roof. I tried to get down, but I'm stuck. If you come onto the balcony—oh, help me."

"How do we get to the balcony? The roof balcony?" I asked urgently.

"The room above this. There is a window."

"Come on."

We rushed up the next flight of stairs and opened the door into an empty room roughly the size of Jeanne's. The balcony with its delicate balustrade was before us, empty, and opposite the twin turret with an open window.

"He was in the other turret. He must have got out."

"Philippe, we are here but we can't see you."

"I got over the balcony. I'm stuck on the roof below."

"Mother of Christ," breathed Jeanne.

"Why did we let Tom go?" I wondered, climbing out the window onto the flat surface and crossing to the balustrade. And there, straddled across the sloping roof, which was part of the earlier medieval structure, was Philippe. Like Fabrice in the tree that other day, he seemed unable to go forward or backwards.

I hadn't the slightest idea how to get to him. "Stay there, Philippe. Don't move. We'll get a ladder." There was a movement beside me and Jeanne stood gazing down at Philippe, her hands to her face.

"Oh, mon Dieu," she sighed, and at that instant Philippe looked up at her and, losing his grip, fell down the sloping roof and plunged to the ground below.

Time seemed to have stopped. I flew downstairs, out to the terrace, and down the steps to the garden, leaving Jeanne a long way behind. Philippe was lying on the ground, but incredibly, marvellously he was alive and conscious. He raised his head as I ran up to him.

"Oh, Philippe, Philippe . . ." I knew one must be careful with someone who'd fallen, but still I touched his head and his face.

"Are you all right?"

"I can't move my leg."

I looked and it was tucked grotesquely under him. "I think it's broken, but if that's all, Philippe, it's a miracle; but you mustn't move. Stay there. I'll call Michelle."

Now Jeanne ran towards us, her hands still clutching her face.

"Oh, my God. He's all right? He breathes?"

"I think he's broken his leg; but don't move him. Oh, Jeanne, it's a miracle! Did you ever see such a fall? From a roof, three floors up?"

In the dawn light I saw her face, and the look on it took my breath away. It was exultant; and, as I looked she raised her eyes to the sky, which was now flushed with

181

the pink of morning. Suddenly I remembered how Joan of Arc had fallen sixty or seventy feet to the ground from the top of the tower in Beaurevoir, where she had been imprisoned. She'd been found completely without injury. Then Jeanne looked into my eyes, and I knew she knew what I was thinking.

When I got back from phoning Michelle, Jeanne was sitting on the ground, Philippe's head in her lap, talking gently to him.

"Is he all right?"

"Perfectly. He is quite rational and nothing hurts, not even the leg, probably because it is broken. He's telling me that he felt something holding him up as he fell, and I was telling him the story of Jeanne d'Arc, my namesake, and how she fell from the tower at Beaurevoir, and how God saved her."

"And she told me that as she saw me fall she said a quick prayer to St Joan, so it is a miracle," Philippe finished, his little voice puffed with pride.

I felt my eyes welling with tears. "It's very remarkable," I said. "Ah, here is Michelle."

Michelle pronounced him unhurt except for a broken leg, and he was moved inside to the couch in the salon. I think she was more amazed than either of us and couldn't stop measuring with her eyes the distance between the top of the roof and the ground.

"Of course, a child's body is very much more elastic than ours, the bones aren't as brittle. But I can't explain it. How did he come to be *there?*"

In the confusion, none of us had thought to ask, and we all now stared at Philippe.

"Yes, how did you get on the roof? We were frantic."

"I got locked in the room in the back turret."

"But Philippe, what were you doing in the room in the back turret?"

Philippe hung his head. I could see he was afraid that here his heroism would end.

"I didn't feel like doing my Latin verbs. I'd heard Madame Barbou talking about the tower and how it had been closed because the house was too big. I'd never seen inside it; the door was always locked. But this morning as I was eating my apple in the kitchen and Madame Barbou was talking to Pierre the gardener about the turret I noticed that the door was open, and I shut it so everyone would think it was locked.

"I was on my way upstairs last night when I remembered the tower and thought I must see inside it. I don't know why. I waited until Madame Barbou went into the larder for something and then I shot past her up the stairs of the turret."

His eyes were gleaming and I could sense the thrill of his adventure. I took his hand and pressed it.

"The turret was very disappointing. It was just like the front turret where Jeanne's room is, and I've seen that lots of times. But when I came down and tried to get out, the door into the kitchen was locked. I was too scared to make a noise and thought I would get out when everyone was in bed."

"But Philippe, you must have known how frightened we would all be."

Philippe looked uncomfortable. It was too easy, of course, to see how it had all happened. The child doing something he shouldn't; the door accidentally locked; his fear of being found out; his total unawareness of the effect it would have on the rest of the house. Did he really think everyone would just go to sleep and hope for the best?"

Well, in a sense he'd been right. We had gone to sleep, and then he'd tried to get out over the balcony and down the roof. My eyes closed as I pictured him there again, straddled across the roof, and then another picture came into my mind. Philippe had been perfectly all right until Jeanne had come and stood beside me; he'd been panicky but not desperate. After Jeanne had come he'd looked at her and suddenly lost his grip and fallen, just like Fabrice, I thought.

The evil eye. I stared at Jeanne sitting in the chair opposite Philippe, looking so pale, so anxious about him. Yes, it was genuine, I was sure and, if Tom was right, and she did have some kind of psychotic disorder, did she perhaps not *know* what she was doing?

Before we knew it, it was morning. The children came tumbling downstairs, released Goofy from his shed in the back garden where he spent the night, and fell on their brother. In no time Fabrice was in tears at having missed all the fun, but Noelle, my dear little sensitive Noelle, was shaken and cried for a different reason. Then Madame Barbou came, and the elder Bourdin and the policeman and finally Tom, who looked as though he'd fallen straight out of bed into his clothes.

"My hero," I said when I saw him.

"How the hell did I know. Was I just *supposed* to stay the night even though you were so bloody rude?"

"I thought you were a psychologist," I said, "and that you would understand the delicate mechanism of the female psyche."

"Like hell I do," Tom said. "That is exactly what I don't understand."

Michelle was watching us with what I took to be amusement.

"You two," she said, "one would think you were still in love."

"In *love!*" Tom and I spoke together.

The tremendous scorn and indignation in our voices didn't seem to reassure her otherwise, because she went on smiling as she prepared Philippe for the ambulance which would take him to Abbeville for X-rays and to have his leg set.

The rest of the morning was chaotic. The ambulance came and went, taking Philippe and Michelle with it. The children were sent up to the classroom with Jeanne, work being considered the best thing to take their minds off the accident. Lisa went away to do whatever it was she had to do, and by about twelve Tom and I were on our own, sipping coffee served by Madame Barbou. She looked harassed.

"You have too much to do, Madame."

"I have, Madame. Thank God my daughter Agnes, the one with the large family, is coming to help me from tomorrow on, and she will do the cleaning."

"Oh, that's good. Thank you." I took the coffee and sipped it. "Madame Barbou, was the back turret not searched yesterday?"

"I don't know, Madame. I don't think so. That door is always locked. Monsieur never opened that turret after the restoration. He said the house was big enough."

"And the door from the kitchen is always locked?"

"Oh, bien sur, Madame. I have never known it to be open."

"It's never cleaned?"

"No. I was saying only that morning to Pierre that he should go up one day and make sure there are no rats."

"But he didn't go up yesterday?"

"I am sure not, Madame. It is his half-day off."

"Then why was the door open?"

"The door was *open?*"

"It must have been when you were talking to Pierre that Philippe was in the kitchen eating an apple?"

Madame Barbou thought for a long moment, finally agreeing with me. "I think it was, Madame, yes."

"He saw the door open and shut it so that he could go up later without anyone knowing."

"The monkey!"

"But who opened it?"

"I never saw it open, Madame."

I looked at Tom. "Yet another mystery."

"It is very strange," Tom agreed, drinking his coffee. "But it isn't sinister, is it?" I thought I saw the trace of a smile on his lips.

"*That* isn't sinister, but how about *this?*" And I gave him a full account of the fall and Jeanne's curious behaviour. "She looked as though she was seeing a vision. She seemed to be staring up to the heavens and saying 'thank you.'"

"But first you think she made him fall? I don't get it, Clare."

"I can't say what made him fall, except that it happened just as she appeared and stood beside me. He seemed to catch her eye and then, wham!"

"But your appearance might have unsettled him, too."

"Yes. What worries me more right now is how he ever got up there—the open door."

Just then we were interrupted by the telephone. It was Laurent. It appeared he'd stopped overnight somewhere and had only now received our message from the concierge. I was pleased I could tell him all was well; he sounded overwrought and anxious.

"I have had further bad news," he said.

"What?"

"It can wait until I see you. I won't be here long, just a few days. Is that husband of yours with you?"

"Yes, he came early because of Philippe."

"Philippe needs a good smack. I'm thinking of taking all the children back to Paris so I can keep my eyes on them. Something very funny is going on, Clare."

"We think so, too."

"*We?*"

"Tom and I."

"I think I've lost you, Clare. It's the conjugal 'we' already."

"Don't be silly, Laurent. Hurry back. We'll see you soon. That is, the *family* and I."

Laurent laughed and rang off.

When I returned to the salon, Michelle was there with Philippe, who looked very happy and important, with his leg in plaster. Michelle was drinking coffee and talking animatedly to Tom. Tom liked intelligent women, and he was responding, smiling back at her and telling her to slow down because his French was not so good as mine.

"Ah," she greeted me. "Philippe has no broken bones other than a nasty fracture of the femur, no internal injuries, and is quite fit. The hospital staff were amazed."

"You were very quick."

"They took us immediately. I knew the doctor and it was over in an hour. He must rest for two or three days but may attend lessons."

Philippe's face fell.

"And pay particular attention to your French verbs," I said as severely as I could. "Your papa will soon be back."

"That was Laurent?" Tom asked.

"Yes. He'll be back in a few days."

"Then you'll have to find somewhere *else* to go."

"I shall go back to my house," I said spiritedly, "and you can move into a hotel. And Tom, I'm here to write a book, and for the rest of today and all of tomorrow I'm going to do nothing but work."

"What a good idea. Michelle, may I escort you home on my way back? No doubt we shall have a few hours before the alarm rings on the next emergency."

Michelle's eyes shone as she looked at Tom. He took her arm and helped her to her feet. Blast Tom, I thought; he was actually *flirting* with the girl before my very eyes. And she had a nerve, too. I felt irrationally annoyed.

"But Philippe!" Michelle turned. "Who will look after him?"

"Don't worry," I said sweetly. "I'll go and find Lisa this instant, and then I'm going to immerse myself in my work. Have fun, you two."

I was glad that Michelle had the grace to blush, while Tom smiled and gave me a broad wink.

For the next two days I did nothing but work. I saw no one outside the château and little of anyone in it other than at mealtimes. Something in my system was badly in need of a rest. The regular life of the house suited us all. Meals at the same time each day, seen to by Madame Barbou with the assistance of her daughter Agnès, who also did the cleaning. School, the long hours supervised by Jeanne, and play taken care of by Lisa.

I trailed around the house wrapped in my research, and everyone left me pretty much alone.

But the more I studied the personality of Joan, the more I was reminded of our very own Jeanne. They could even have looked alike. Although a great deal was known of the Maid, there were no extant likenesses of her, and one had to rely on the many descriptions history had provided in order to assemble a composite picture. She seems to have been a plain, sturdy country girl with dark hair and brown eyes, and so totally devoid of any sexuality that the handsome Duc d'Alençon remarked he was able to watch her undress without feeling a twinge of desire; in fact, they slept side by side during their campaigns.

This really was our Jeanne; she was plain, dark, and

asexual. She was pious, superstitious, devious, and
. . . witch-like?

As a seventeenth-century English divine wrote:

Here lies Joan of Arc, the which
Some count saint and some count witch;
Some count man, and something more;
Some count maid, and some a whore:
Her life's in question, wrong, or right . . .

and it concludes that at the judgement day:

Then shalt thou know, and not before.
Whether Saint, Witch, Man, Maid or Whore.

I was confident we could disregard the question of
man or whore, as far as our Jeanne was concerned anyway, but saint or witch? Yet I couldn't believe that Joan
of Arc was wandering around under our roof teaching
three children the rudiments of learning. But Jeanne
didn't claim to be Joan; she claimed only *possession* by
the spirit, or oneness with the saint, and certain supernatural gifts, such as she had.

Philippe's fall and miraculous survival had shaken me
profoundly, and much as I wanted to dismiss it, I found
myself thinking about it a lot. Yes, I thought it would be
better if Laurent took his brood back to Paris, sent them
to day schools, and kept the château for holidays—and,
of course, got rid of Jeanne.

Laurent was due back by the weekend, and on Friday,
having completed three good days' work I packed my
things and prepared for the move back to my house the
following day. Tom would have to go to a hotel or some
other digs. Why didn't he go back to England anyway?

Fabrice had been out of sorts ever since Philippe's accident—jealousy had made him fractious and naughty.

But Lisa managed the children well. I approved of Lisa; her monumental calm was good for them and made up a lot for the language barrier.

Every day we all had a big lunch together, and then the children had tea. To make it easier for Madame Barbou, they sat with the three of us while we had a light supper, and then they went up to bed. That Friday I told them it was my last night. "Your papa comes back tomorrow."

I was flattered at the sight of their sad faces.

"But Clare, we'll miss your reading us stories at night."

"Your papa will read to you."

"He is always too busy."

"I will tell him, and I'll come to see you often."

"Are you going back to your *husband*?" giggled Noelle.

"No, not yet; now eat up."

Yes, I would miss them, I thought, as one by one they emerged from the bath and I rubbed them with warm towels and helped them into their pyjamas. With what big eyes they listened to the story of Red Riding Hood, so deathly quiet you could hear their excited breathing.

Noelle clung to me as she always did, and I kissed her and wished not for the first time she was mine.

"I wish you were my mummy," she said again.

"So do I."

"Can't you marry my daddy?"

"I'm married already."

"But you don't love your husband, do you?"

"I don't know."

"I don't think he loves you." Noelle stopped abruptly and I sensed something in her manner.

"Why do you say that, Noelle?" I asked casually, tucking her in.

"No reason."

"Please tell me."

"Promise not to tell?"

"*Promise.*"

"Madame Barbou saw him with Michelle; she told Agnès and Philippe heard."

I laughed. "Oh, I know that. He took her home the other day."

"No, they were eating at the Hotel du Port. Madame Barbou saw them in the restaurant when she went home the other night."

"I don't mind, Noelle. One nice thing about us is that we let each other do as we like."

Nevertheless, despite these noble sentiments, I felt a peculiar constriction in my throat as I put out the light and returned to my own room.

I couldn't blame him if Tom was attracted to Michelle. In many ways they were well suited, and she would make the admirable French bourgeois wife that Tom wanted so much. There would be no question that she'd put him first and have warm slippers and a good meal ready on the dot every evening, *and* she'd run a clinic and have dozens of babies as well.

Good luck to them. I should probably go to America. That way I'd get a professorship *well* before Tom.

Despite my emotional unease, I read for a long time and then put out the light, gazing into the darkness until I grew accustomed to it and could make out the shapes of the furniture and the pile of books on my table.

Rose's room; my room. I'd miss it. I hadn't thought of Rose for days. Did it really matter how she died? She'd seemed an unpleasant girl in many ways; but she had come to me, and she'd warned me. In a way, she'd been right.

A breeze stirred my face and I sat up in bed. "Rose?"

I put out my hand to touch her. I felt a breath on my cheek as though she were bending over me; it was warm and alive. I looked, and there she was dressed in white;

191

she took my hand. I couldn't utter a sound; I felt as though I were going to choke.

"It's only me, Noelle."

I sank back on the bed, my heart fluttering like some old duck with the vapours.

"Noelle, you gave me the most ghastly fright."

"I didn't know if you were asleep or not. Why did you call me Rose?"

"I was thinking of her; now get back to bed."

"I can't sleep. I'm frightened."

"There's nothing to be frightened of."

"There's someone in the library."

"That's nothing to be frightened of. It's probably Jeanne looking for something to read."

"Jeanne and Lisa went up to bed; they looked in on me to say goodnight."

I looked at my watch. It was after midnight. I'd read for much longer than I'd thought.

"How do you know it's the library?"

"I went halfway down the stairs. I was too frightened to go further. My room is over the library. I heard a kind of tapping."

"Wait here and I'll go and see."

I remembered the valuable library of the dukes of Burgundy, displayed in a glass case. Maybe someone *did* know about them. I felt far from brave as I crept down the stairs, but when I saw a light coming from the library something reassured me. Surely a burglar wouldn't have left the light on!

I breathed more easily and walked across the hall to the door. At first I could see nothing and then a sound came from the far alcove.

"Jeanne?" I whispered.

Nothing. I felt a prickle of fear, but now I'd come too

far to go back. I put on more lights and called out more loudly.

"Jeanne!"

But it wasn't Jeanne. It was Lisa. I gaped at her in astonishment.

"Lisa? What are you doing?"

She looked at a loss for words. "I . . . I fetch something to read."

"Oh. That's all right. Couldn't you sleep?"

She shook her head. I gazed with interest at the shelves she had been exploring. Either she was extremely stupid, or I had underrated her intelligence. The shelves were full of books on the geography of Western Europe in the eighteenth and nineteenth centuries.

However, who was I to question Lisa's taste in reading matter, or the fact that she could read French at all? Maybe she wanted to look at the pictures. I turned to go.

"Don't leave the lights on, will you, Lisa?"

"No. I go now to bed too."

I put out the lights and we went quietly upstairs. Lisa obviously didn't want to take any of the books to bed with her. I thought that a bit odd, but I said a cheerful goodnight and went to my room. I'd forgotten about Noelle, who was sitting up in bed, her eyes bright.

"Was it a burglar?"

"No, it was Lisa. She wanted something to read."

"But she can't read French!"

"Well, maybe she wanted to look at a book. I don't know. Are you going back to bed?"

"I shall imagine things."

I sighed.

"All right. Move over, and not a sound all night."

I smiled as her little body wriggled up to me. "Were you cross about Michelle and your husband?"

"Of course not. Go to sleep."

Silence. I felt myself dozing.

"Clare, are you awake?"

"What is it now?"

"It's about Lisa."

"What about Lisa?"

"She has a whole set of keys in one of her drawers."

"What?" I turned over and faced her in the dark. "What on earth were you doing looking in Lisa's drawers?"

Silence.

"You were snooping, weren't you, Noelle?"

Silence.

"That's a horrible thing to do. How do I know you don't do it to me?"

"I love you; I don't like Lisa."

"Still, that's no reason to look in her drawers. What sort of keys?"

"I think they're the keys to the house. Why would she want those?"

"I don't know. Go to sleep."

Eventually I heard regular breathing. Noelle was asleep, but I was wide awake.

Lisa had seemed so much part of the house that I had never given her much thought, certainly nothing like the attention I'd paid to Jeanne. Yet what did we know about Lisa? She had come into the family under peculiar circumstances; she spoke no English and very little French. How odd to look for a job as a nanny in a country where you could hardly speak the language, an *au pair*, perhaps, because that would be the object, to learn the language. But a full-time, proper *nanny*?

To me, Lisa was so amorphous and unappealing a character that I'd never really taken her into consideration, certainly not in the role of villainess. That I had as-

194

signed firmly and in full prejudice to Jeanne. Yet Lisa had been in the boat and had got *out*. Had her conscience been appeased by trying to save the youngest child? More than anyone, Lisa had had a chance to loosen the screws. And now we knew that Lisa had a full bunch of keys. I kept on thinking of the open door to the turret— the turret that hadn't been opened for years.

## CHAPTER 16

The idea of Lisa as a creature of mystery was hard to believe. One always saw her as a competent and unimaginative person. Withdrawn, yes, but cunning, no. The following day I learned something even more extraordinary about Lisa. She regularly saw Michelle's brother Nicolas, who spent his time taking her out in his boat.

"He's absolutely crazy about her," Michelle reported, obviously distressed. She had called round in the morning to see how we were. If there was a reserve in my greeting, she didn't notice it. She wanted to tell me about her brother's latest affair and I, deciding for once in my life to be discreet, thought it unwise to tell her what I felt about Lisa or what I already knew—all intangibles, like everything else in this house. She was in the boat before it sank; she had a full set of keys for the house; and she

196

was snooping round in the library at a very odd time and among a curious set of books.

"You told me he liked older women," I smiled, "though I must say she's a lulu. Maybe she's sexy. To change the subject, Laurent is due back today. He's talking about taking the children back to Paris. I think it's a good idea."

"Before Christmas?"

"My goodness. How the time has flown. It's nearly Christmas. I've no idea, Michelle. Tell me, how was your dinner with Tom?"

Poor Michelle; I wasn't being fair. She couldn't even begin to cover her confusion, so I got up and walked to the window. The bay looked blustery and cold, and the trees were almost bare. It was early December—a bleak, cold month. Imagine anyone yachting in the bay now.

"That was mean of me," I said, my back still to her. "I just heard about it—village gossip."

"It was nothing at all—he talked all the time about you. I think he wanted someone to talk to. Tom is a very lonely man, Clare."

"Oh, he gave you that line, did he? It's really quite effective. Michelle, Tom has *hundreds* of friends, acquaintances, and colleagues, to say nothing of students. He is the least lonely man I know."

"Oh, I know that, Clare. But he feels it in his relationship with you, this loneliness; he has missed you terribly. That's why he came over, not because of Rose. He just can't seem to say it to you, so he had to say it to me. I'm a doctor, after all. I'd like to help you if I can."

I felt chastened.

"You honestly think I don't give Tom enough warmth and understanding, don't you?"

"I'm not saying that. I think you don't understand each other enough; you're both strong personalities, both too defensive. This makes you seem more aggressive toward each other than you really are. Tom says inwardly you think that he wants to lock you in the house with a large kitchen and half a dozen babies."

"*And* write books as well," I said caustically. "Tom wants me to be all things. Clever and cuddly . . ."

"Well? Can't you be clever *and* cuddly? Can't you see Tom is as insecure as you are? There is a deep well of affection there, Clare. The way you bicker at each other, the way you look at each other, shows all that. But you simply haven't come to terms with giving to each other as well."

I was beginning to weaken. I was touched that Tom cared enough about me to unburden himself to Michelle. Maybe he'd asked her to talk to me; I wouldn't inquire. Anyway, most of it was true. I did care very deeply about Tom, yet half the time he made me want to scream.

"There's a lot of truth in what you say," I said casually. "Maybe we should try and sort something out. I still think we should give it the full year, and Tom should go back to England."

"Then, if you want my opinion, I don't think you'll ever come together again, if you leave it that long."

We were both, I noticed, very careful to make no mention of Laurent de Frigecourt.

As it was a Saturday, the children had school only in the morning. In the afternoon Jeanne would be off and Lisa in charge.

I'd started the day badly, waking from a heavy, disturbed sleep with Noelle turning and muttering beside me. As the day progressed, I felt restless and depressed, unable to find any real cause. I knew that as long as so many questions remained unresolved, I would have no peace. Just before lunch I went up to my room to tidy myself and looked at the packed suitcase, the stripped bed.

*This* was why I was depressed. I didn't want to leave. I knew then that I had to stay at the château either until the family went to Paris or something else happened. But what did I expect to happen? I went to the window and gazed at the bay. The tide was in and the water was brown; the bay could be very muddy at times. Low clouds and a December mist obscured the skyline and Le Hourdel was invisible.

Then I noticed a small rowboat coming towards the château, the kind that fishermen used for getting ashore when they left their boats anchored in mid-Channel. In the bow a sturdy man, his back to me, was pulling steadily for shore. We had a small anchorage just at the walls of the château—a large ring which could be attached to the painter — and some steps like a stile to get over the wall.

As it came nearer, I saw that the woman in the stern was Lisa, and the man in the bow Nicolas. What a day for a morning row, I thought, amused, as Nicolas stood up, steadied the boat, helped Lisa onto the tiny stone jetty, and kissed her. She stood poised on the wall waving to him, then climbed over and down the steps on our side. Nicolas cast off and pulled round toward the port.

I watched, fascinated. Lisa had a full shopping bag and she looked happy as she came trotting up to the house, almost under me, then round to the back. She would be just in time for lunch.

At one the children came thundering down the stairs, Goofy leaping to greet them from his waiting place in the hall. Philippe, with Jeanne holding his arm, came down more slowly. He now had a stick, of which he was very proud.

I looked closely at Lisa during lunch; her face was pink and her eyes sparkled. I decided to tell her I'd seen her in the boat. At first she pretended not to understand, and then she went even more pink.

"It is to shop in Port Guillaume."

"You go shopping in Port Guillaume?"

"It is Nicolas—he take me there."

Jeanne glanced at her with raised brows, and the children chaffed her about Nicolas. Most of it went over her head, however.

"This afternoon Nicolas take us hunting—me and the children."

Oh no, not hunting! "Philippe can't go hunting," I said quickly, "and Fabrice is too small."

Fabrice let out a terrific wail and all three spoke at once.

"They will come to no harm," Lisa assured us. "Nicolas, he very careful. Philippe can sit in the car, and I will hold Fabrice carefully by the hand."

Despite Nicolas' strange taste in women, I did think he would be careful. I trusted Nicolas that the children would be safe with him. Jeanne looked unhappy.

"You must not stay out long. It gets dark very early."

"Not long. Nicolas, he is here."

In through the back door came Nicolas, already clad in stout jacket, high boots, and a cap. The children jumped from the table into the hall, except Philippe, who leaned theatrically on his stick and had to have his boots and jacket brought to him.

"Can Goofy come too?"

"Of course."

Nicolas and Lisa looked happy and the children were ecstatic. Only Jeanne and I appeared unmoved by all the excitement, and when they'd gone we stood on the terrace watching them jump over the wall by the jetty, the way Lisa had come back from her curious shopping spree in Port Guillaume.

"Don't stay out late," I called. "Your papa is coming back today." But I don't think they heard me.

"I think I'll go sit in the summer house," Jeanne said. "After the bad weather we've had, it's very mild today."

"Yes, it is. The mist has gone and it's quite warm. Summer house? I didn't know there was one."

Jeanne pointed to where the formal garden ended and a thicket of trees obscured our view of the bay, from ground level, not from the windows of the house. "See that pointed roof, like a little pagoda? I love it there in the summer. I feel very close to *her* there."

My scalp prickled. The vague apprehension I'd had all day became a certain, riveting fear. My mouth dried up, and my tongue stuck to my palate as I tried to speak.

"Her?"

"Jeanne d'Arc. Would you like to come with me and see if you can feel it too?"

No, no, I didn't want to go. I wanted to go upstairs, to run away. I should have gone with the children. Instead, I was alone with Jeanne. Even Madame Barbou had gone off for the afternoon and Agnes wasn't due to prepare supper until about five.

"Come," Jeanne said, taking my arm and propelling me gently down the stairs. "You're shivering, Clare. You'll find it very warm in the summer house."

I felt as though I were in a dream as I walked with her along the path, through the thicket, until we stood at the door of a perfect little pavilion, with a balcony all round and ornate turrets, as though someone had tried to imitate the château.

"It's perfect!" I breathed. "Why have I never seen it before?"

"I am the only one who uses it. It's too small for the children. They play here at the beginning of the summer,

**201**

but they tire of things so easily. It's only in the winter that you can see the roof, but during the spring and summer it's entirely obscured. Through a gap in the trees you can have a marvellous view of the sea. Come."

Of course, everything was normal. It was a lovely day and my imagination was making me neurotic; but as I went into the pavilion I felt like a small fly in the grip of a great web. Inside it was dark. The shutters were fastened against the windows, and only glimmers of light came in through the slats. I could hardly see anything. Why had she brought me here?

"Isn't it lovely? Isn't it peaceful?"

Jeanne moved around and began touching things, some chairs, two small tables. She seemed unaware of my presence and hummed a little song to herself.

Suddenly a gentle breeze wafted through the room. I recognised it. It was like no ordinary breeze. I lifted my head to listen. So did Jeanne. She was listening too.

"You can feel it too, can't you?" she said.

"What?" I was whispering.

"The presence. I know you can feel it. I saw your body stiffen. This site is part of the château, the old château, where Jeanne was imprisoned. The modern château is much smaller than the old one, you know. And next to the tower, *her* tower, there was a windmill—you can still see it in the old prints—and she used to stand at her window in the tower and watch the windmill turning, turning.

"When I first came to the château that's why I asked for a room in the tower, but her tower was here, and the windmill just over there."

She took my arm and led me to one of the shutters, which she unfastened. I saw along the promontory as far as the distant wall and beyond, across the bay.

"Can you see it?"

"What?"

"The windmill."

"Of course I can't. There isn't a windmill. There's just the wall and the sea."

"You can see the windmill if you try very hard. Like this. Watch."

Jeanne's body stiffened and she closed her eyes tightly. "There, I can see it. Turning, turning. That makes the breeze. Can't you feel it?"

The breeze stirred again. I felt an uncanny chill. I closed my eyes tightly, very tightly. "I can't see any windmill," I said, opening my eyes and looking at Jeanne.

*"There is the windmill and there is the bay,"* she said. *"The ships have sails. I had never seen the sea before because I was born inland, in the tiny village of Domremy. As a child I was very happy, helping my father and mother, playing with my friends. But all during my childhood we were harrassed by the hated Burgundian soldiers who swept from their lands in Burgundy to the ones they owned in the low countries. The Burgundians pillaged, raped, and looted. I made a vow to drive them from our country, and St. Catherine and St. Michael helped me."*

"Jeanne . . ."

*"Yes, my name is Jeanne d'Arc. I never sought glory, only for God, and through my death He brought liberation to France. The rightful King was crowned, my poor Dauphin, never much of a man, but the real King; he didn't even try to save me when I was captured. They brought me here and left me for a month. It was the only place I was ever happy in since I'd left Domremy, and here I had my first sight of the sea. God brought me contentment here and peace, and He told me that I would die but that I would live forever in glory with Him and the saints.*

*"How I loved the sea and the sight of the bay. I used to*

203

*ask my gaolers to let me walk on the cliff, and I stood under the windmill which towered over me, and felt such peace. But I never forgave the Burgundians, and I cursed them. The son of Philippe the Good, Charles, was killed ignominiously in battle thirty-six years after my own death, and that was the end of the royal Burgundian line.*

*"I could forgive the English for what they did; after all, they were foreigners and our countries were at war. The French I could forgive, for they were my own people; they killed me as the Jews killed Christ by preferring Barabbas, a common thief, to Him. They acted out of stupidity rather than malice, for the English were their enemy. No, it was the special treachery of the Burgundians that I could never forgive—Frenchmen who allied with the English to cause the defeat of France. So I cursed the Burgundians, even to this day."*

Jeanne stopped talking, but her trance-like state continued for some moments. I hadn't moved all the time she was speaking, and my flesh was like marble, cold and hard to the touch.

Nothing could ever blot out that moment from my mind. I believed we were in the fifteenth century, that Jeanne was in her tower, and that the windmill turned and turned on the promontory overlooking the bay. And I, who was I? One of the many people who looked on and did nothing to help. But Joan was preordained to die; she wanted to, and because of it for centuries her name and ideals had been an inspiration to millions of people. Maybe it had helped them to die well too.

Jeanne gave a deep sigh and opened her eyes; she seemed to have difficulty in focussing at first and then she looked at me. "Did you see it," she said excitedly. "Did you see it?"

"No," I breathed, "but I heard it. You talked to me as Joan."

"And you believed it?"

"Yes."

"Oh, good. Good. Now you will tell everyone that she was a holy person, a saint, not a witch."

"Yes. Joan was not important in herself, but for what she did."

"As an instrument of God. Yes, yes."

"Then you have helped me with my book."

We smiled at each other, and the atmosphere grew warmer. What time it was I had no idea; an hour could have passed, or five. But the sun was still high and I guessed we had not been in the summer house more than half an hour.

"Let's sit down," Jeanne said. "I want you to understand something."

I felt so easy with her now, so relaxed.

"I am not evil," Jeanne said. "You thought I was, didn't you?"

I didn't reply.

"Rose thought I was?"

"Yes."

"She told you I was, but she was the evil one. There is a force here that threatens the family. I know you feel this and that is why you stay in the château."

"Yes. Is it a supernatural force?"

"No. But Rose was involved in it, and her death was evil, an evil act. That's all I know."

"But you thought I was going to harm you."

She looked at me solemnly and nodded. "Yes, I know, but now I'm not sure. A visitor to the château will harm me, but maybe it is not you."

"Could it be Lisa?" I asked.

"Lisa?"

"I found Lisa in the library last night. She has a set of keys to the house. I don't think she is all that she says she is."

Jeanne appeared to consider this very gravely. "I sense something bad in Lisa, but there is someone behind her." Jeanne looked at me sharply. "Could it be your husband?"

"Tom? Of *course* not. He's never seen Lisa in his life before."

"No, I'm sorry. The person is not a stranger, not to this house."

"Nicolas Bourdin?" I said.

Jeanne jerked her head. "Maybe—the person is certainly not a stranger."

My hands flew to my face. "Oh, my God, and we have let the children go out alone with Nicolas and Lisa!"

## CHAPTER 17

Of course, that had been the cause of my apprehension, the reason for my fear. Not Jeanne, not the summer house, not Rose—not that day anyway. Something was going to happen to the children. I of all people should have known better than to let them go off to those dunes where danger lurked.

Jeanne and I hurried up to the house to get our coats, and as we put them on and ran out, Laurent came up the drive in his car, braking sharply when he saw us.

"What is it?"

"The children are out hunting."

"What's wrong with that?"

"We have a feeling they're in danger." Laurent looked angry. His face was already pale and unshaven. "Oh, my God, not that. Clare, you should see a psychiatrist—seriously."

"Please," I begged. "Let's just be sure."

"Are they alone?"

"No. They're with Lisa and Nicolas."

"Then they're perfectly safe."

"Please, Laurent. It will soon be dark."

"All right, hop in, but Clare, about the psychiatrist . . ."

"Yes, I promise, after today."

I got in with him, and Jeanne got into the back. The sun had set by now and it was getting very dark. As Laurent sped through the lanes too angry to say anything, I began to have misgivings. Maybe they were driving home this very moment.

He parked the car in the wasteland by the side of the dunes; there were still a few others there.

"Now what do we do?"

I looked at Jeanne, who shrugged.

"I mean, where do we start?" Laurent said caustically. "You had this premonition; you should know."

"Look, the car! There's your Fiat. Nicolas must have taken it for Philippe."

But Philippe wasn't in the car. A strong wind had blown up and the dark clouds were racing in from the Channel. Laurent began to frown.

"Well, that's funny, if the car's still here."

"And there's Mr. Schroeder's car. That white Mercedes."

"Who?"

"He's a writer. We met him here one day." A twinge of fear ran through me, seeing the German's car, and I recalled the day I had seen him watching the children.

"Papa, Papa . . ."

Oh, heaven! Little Fabrice emerged over one of the dunes and ran to his father's outstretched arms. My heart bounded with relief until I saw his face. He flung himself at his father, crying like someone whose tears would never stop.

"Fabrice! What is it?"

"Oh, Papa! Noelle is lost, and it is so dark, and Philippe has hurt his foot again, and we are alone. Oh, Papa."

"Where, where is he?"

"Over there. We were sheltering from the cold behind that dune."

Laurent was already over the shoulder of the mound, still hugging Fabrice, I following quickly after him. Philippe looked at us stoically, smiling but close to tears. We crouched by his side.

"Where are Lisa and Nicolas? What happened?"

"It was Goofy, Papa; the gun frightened him."

"But Goofy is used to guns."

"I think it went off too near him. He flew away and Noelle, who loves him best—you remember you gave him to her as a puppy for her birthday, Papa—went after him. Then she disappeared. We couldn't see her because of the dunes. First Nicolas went to look, then Lisa. They told us not to move."

"They should have put Fabrice and Philippe back in the car," I said angrily. "A boy who can't walk and one who is still only a baby. They're blue with cold."

"Let's do that now," Jeanne suggested.

We went back to the car and I took Fabrice on my lap, rubbing his frozen hands. Now that the danger was upon us, I felt calm—frightened, but composed. Yes, I'd known it was going to happen, and it had, but at least two of them were safe. Then I thought of the little angel, the sensitive one, who had snuggled up to me in my bed only the night before. I looked at Jeanne; her face was ashen.

"I'm going to look," Laurent said. "Take the children back to the château."

"Can't we help?"

"You can help best that way. It's nearly dark."

It was. The row of lights in the distance were from Port St Pierre, and we could no longer see across the bay. Thank heaven the tide was out. It was the only consolation I had.

Jeanne drove while I comforted Fabrice. When we got back, the lights were on and the place looked cheerful. Dear Madame Barbou and Agnès were busy with the evening meal, and the succulent smells of a French kitchen greeted us with a familiar sense of homecoming.

Tom had just arrived and was looking cheerful. His expression changed when he heard our news.

"Let me get you drinks."

"No. I want to change Fabrice. Give him a warm bath. Jeanne will see to Philippe. I think he fell over and hurt his shoulder. Maybe you'd call Michelle."

Philippe was looking horribly pale. Fabrice started whimpering again, but I half-carried him upstairs and murmured soothing things to him. By the time he was in the bath and had started a complicated game with his bath toys, he was laughing again.

Afterwards I took him downstairs, where Philippe was also resting in his dressing gown and Michelle was rubbing his shoulder which she said was sore but not sprained.

"This is incredible," she said. "I cannot believe so many bad things can happen. Maybe there is evil in this house."

I looked at Jeanne and gave her a comforting smile. "Jeanne and I think somebody *is* trying to harm the family."

Tom was staring at me.

"We had a long talk this afternoon," I continued, "and without saying too much, I can say we reached this conclusion for a number of reasons."

"May we know what they are?"

210

"Not yet." I looked meaningfully at the children.

The evening passed and we grew more fretful. For the sake of politeness we sat down to the meal Madame Barbou had prepared with such love and care. Jeanne, Michelle, and I toyed with our food, while Tom ate a hearty four-course dinner washed down with plenty of wine. He was a brute, I thought, looking at him with disgust. Yet, I was glad Tom was there, the comforting, clumsy bulk of him. I knew he cared and that he was concerned but, like the rest of us, he didn't know what to do.

We were on the cheese course when Laurent, Lisa, and Nicolas came in. They dropped into chairs, looking cold, pale, and exhausted. For an awful, seemingly endless moment, no one said anything. Then Laurent shook his head.

"No sign. We've called the police. I'm asking for someone from Abbeville."

"But it was an accident . . ." Nicolas began to protest. From the atmosphere I guessed there had already been words among the three of them. Laurent held up his hand.

"There have been too many accidents. My children keep on getting lost or falling down things; my nanny is found dead; my wife is killed in a crash—there are too many, too many. If we go back to Paris, how do we know it will end there?"

"The curse." Michelle said softly.

Laurent looked at her. "Do I hear you right? A doctor of medicine? A scientist? You're telling me a fifteenth-century curse is what's afflicting my family? Why now?"

I thought of Jeanne and the afternoon, but I said nothing. I wondered if Laurent knew that the original curse had come from Joan of Arc?

Laurent had poured himself a strong whisky and gave one to Nicolas. Lisa refused anything.

"It's very late," Laurent said.

Tom stood up. "You can always call me. Michelle?"

"You don't want us, Laurent?"

He shook his head.

"I'm staying ," I said, and when Laurent looked at me I shook my head. "Don't you see I can't possibly leave? I'm too involved."

There was pain in Tom's eyes; once again he didn't understand. I avoided his gaze.

After they'd gone, Lisa and Jeanne excused themselves, and Laurent and I were left alone.

"Not tired?"

I shook my head. "Anxious. Very anxious."

"I'm glad you stayed." He came and sat beside me, putting his hand lightly on mine. "You don't mind?"

"Of course not."

"Something always stops our being romantic, doesn't it?"

"It seems to."

"We can't do anything, Clare, until this problem is solved. I'm going to get a very high-up Parisian policeman on the job, someone from the Sûreté."

"You're as convinced as all that?"

"I want to know, dammit. Burgundian curse, bullshit. My wife's car was tampered with."

"Laurent!"

"I found out only by chance. You know the car was a write-off after the accident and was towed away by a local garage, which kept it for scrap. Yesterday morning I called at this garage for petrol. It is on the way into Paris from the north, near where Elizabeth had the crash. The owner recognised me and he said he'd wanted to talk to me. They'd stripped the car, as they do with wrecks, to salvage any valuable parts, and he thought the brakes could have been tampered with. It was hard to prove and, under the circumstances, didn't seem likely. But he said

212

he couldn't get it out of his mind and was glad he'd told me. I said thank you and that was it. The wreck was disposed of ages ago."

"You think someone wanted to kill Elizabeth?"

"Or me. We both drove the car. In fact, *I* usually drove it; except that when she had the accident I was out of Paris. Anyway, as soon as we know what has happened to Noelle I'm calling the Sûreté. Oh, Clare, you don't think she . . ." He pressed my hand and we stared at each other.

"What can I say, Laurent?"

"You had a premonition about all this, didn't you?"

"Something like that. Only I don't think Jeanne is involved. I think she's strange, but she's not bad. Let's say that, in the old days, she might have been burned or canonised. She is not of this century. Now, Lisa . . ."

Suddenly there was a banging at the back door and we both jumped up. The kitchen was closed and dark, but Laurent raced through it and flung open the back door. Two figures stood outside, one tall and one small. The tall one stepped forward.

"Pardon, Monsieur, for the disturbance, but I bring you your daughter."

Noelle, weeping and dishevelled, fell into her father's arms.

The deliverer was Gustav Schroeder. As he stepped into the light, a sort of mental cogwheel slid into place. I should have known it would be Schroeder. We'd seen his car.

But before the introductions were made, Laurent took Noelle inside, hugging and kissing her, weeping too. I followed them, close to tears myself. We led them through the dark kitchen into the salon, where Laurent forced some brandy between Noelle's cold lips.

"How? Where?" I began. "It's so late."

"It is a long walk back," Schroeder said, frowning. "I am very tired too. The girl had gone way beyond the bird reserve and it was difficult to persuade her to stop looking for her dog."

"Goofy is lost," Noelle sniffed.

"Goofy will turn up," Laurent said gently. "Didn't you think about us? Weren't you frightened?"

"No. I was only frightened of this man when I realised he was following me, and then I ran even faster."

"She didn't know who I was," Schroeder said apologetically. "I must have frightened her badly, I'm afraid."

"We've met Mr. Schroeder before," I explained to Laurent. "He's a writer." I looked at him suspiciously.

Jeanne, having heard the commotion, appeared in the doorway in her gown and took Noelle into her arms, sobbing over her.

"Jeanne, take her upstairs," Laurent said. "Make her warm. We'll bring up some hot milk. Clare, is there any food left? I suddenly realise I'm starving. Sir, Monsieur Schroeder, may I tempt you to food?"

"There's plenty," I said. "Nobody could eat a thing at dinner."

"I'll fetch some wine," Laurent said. I went into the kitchen and put game pie, cold meats, salad and cheeses onto a tray.

Schroeder was standing by the fireplace when I went in and Laurent was uncorking a bottle of Burgundy from its basket. I noticed Schroeder staring at Laurent, and an extraordinary feeling came over me, so that I almost anticipated what Schroeder next said.

"Laurent."

Laurent turned round in surprise at his name, which was said without any intonation, merely as a statement.

"Laurent," Schroeder repeated.

Laurent stopped uncorking the wine and as though summoned by a power outside himself went over to Schroeder and looked at him.

"Yes?"

"I am your brother, Laurent. I am your eldest brother, Jean."

Laurent stared at Schroeder, his face registering a variety of emotions, none of them pleasurable, and stepped back.

"My brother Jean is dead."

"I am Jean. I did not die. I was captured and tortured so badly that I lost all memory of who I was. But I did not die."

"Then why"—Laurent's voice was a mixture of disbelief and hostility—"why did you wait until now?"

"I didn't know for sure until recently. The trauma of my sufferings in the war completely changed my personality, and I was brought up as a German boy, yet speaking perfect French. All the years of my childhood were blotted out for me. I was smuggled out of the camp by a good man who adopted me with his wife, and I became a sort of artisan, a furniture maker. But always I wanted to know who I was. I became good at my trade and made money. Then I studied and began specialising in antiques, writing books. I married and had two children, got divorced. Then, three years ago, I started treatment with a psychiatrist who specialised in hypnosis. Gradually the truth, all the awful things became clear to me. When I knew I was a de Frigecourt I came to live near here, to explore my surroundings. Yes, I remembered. I saw your children. I saw you once or twice, but I couldn't approach you; I didn't know how. Then today God brought my little niece to me, and thus to you."

God had indeed been very busy today, I thought, listening to this incredible story. Laurent listened too, pale

**215**

and, I sensed, incredulous. When it was finished I got up, shaking with fatigue.

"Laurent, would you mind?"

"I'd be glad if you would leave us alone," Laurent said tersely. "I have a lot to ask this man. Would you kiss Noelle for me and make sure she's all right?"

Closing the door I left the two . . . brothers?

I woke up late; the sun was streaming into my room through the unshuttered windows. I lay for a long time listening to the sounds of the house, knowing that it was very late.

It was after ten. The door opened and Noelle tiptoed in; she was still in her dressing gown. I opened the bed-clothes and she snuggled in beside me.

"Something so exciting . . ." she began.

"I know," I said. "When did Papa tell you?"

"At breakfast. He didn't go to bed all night and had just come from a walk. He was still looking for Goofy. Monsieur Schroeder is our uncle Jean. Papa said he wasn't sure at first, but now he is convinced. Oh, isn't it *exciting*?"

"Very," I said, squeezing her. "Is he still here?"

"No, he went home; he's coming later, maybe for lunch. He didn't sleep all night either but stayed up with Papa, talking."

"Come on, let's get up. I want to hear it from Papa."

Laurent was in the garden when I finally found him, clearing the dead flowers of summer.

"I had to do some work," he said when he saw me. "I can't concentrate on anything else except hard physical labour."

"I know. Do you really think he's your brother?"

"I am convinced; the things he said, what he knew that only we knew."

"Don't you think it's funny he remembers so much if he'd lost his memory for all those years?"

"Oh, no. He explained it all. Once he began to remember, it was like a floodgate, and he had total recall."

I felt the need to talk to Tom. Tom would know about amnesia and total recall. "It's very odd, isn't it, Laurent? He has a wife, children. He will be the Marquis de Frigecourt."

"Oh, but *that* doesn't matter! Clare, don't you realise what it's like to find my brother again, after thirty-two years? He can have *everything*, just to have him *alive!* But you liked him, didn't you, Clare? He said you went to his house. He wanted to tell you then."

"I can't understand why he waited until now. You'd think once his memory was restored he'd have come straight to see you, not hovered around the place for a year."

I'd begun to displease Laurent again. One could always tell. He didn't really want to know anything but good about his brother. But I was far from satisfied. I wanted to know a lot more. I wanted to know why someone with a clear conscience and so much to gain had held back so long.

And that was the point. If his conscience was clear— why had he?

## CHAPTER 18

The ears of my dear Tom were willingly bent to my story. Yes—dear Tom—so robust and sturdy after those volatile de Frigecourts. Back at the house in the Rue du Château I found Tom working in my study, puffing away at his pipe, oblivious to the goings on in the outside world.

"I'd heard about the brother," Tom said. "It's most remarkable. I was on my way up to the château when I stopped for the paper. When I heard about the brother I decided to come home. You don't think it is his brother?"

"How do I know? I suppose after thirty-two years it's difficult to recognise anyone, especially with a beard. On the other hand, is it a *likely* story? Think what he has to inherit. Can one be an amnesiac for all those years?"

Tom screwed up his eyes, exhaling clouds of smoke. "I would have thought the older you got the less likely you

218

were to experience amnesia. It's a neurologist you want, not a psychologist. No, I'd find it hard to believe that all this time elapsed."

"Then why does Laurent believe it?"

"Because he wants to. He wants a brother. We know how affected he was by what happened to his family. Maybe he feels guilty that he alone was saved."

"Yes, that's it," I said, "that's Laurent." I looked around. It was cosy here with both of us talking in the civilised way we liked so much, surrounded by books.

"Coffee, Tom?"

"Why, darling, shouldn't I . . . ?"

I smiled and went into the kitchen. When I returned with the tray, I noticed the contented look on Tom's face as he puffed away at his pipe, making notes—or pretending to make them. I couldn't believe he was oblivious to the highly charged atmosphere between us.

"You can make the coffee next time," I said.

Tom put the cup on his desk and put a hand round my waist. "Next time?"

"We're going to try to understand each other, aren't we, Tom? That's what you wanted Michelle to tell me. We're going to give more, share things more."

Tom pulled me onto his lap and put both arms around me. He was trembling. "I've been awfully thick."

"But Tom, I shall never change completely. Warm the slippers, that bit."

"I don't want you to. I'd be bored to death."

"Michelle would make an awfully good wife, and she can cook something lovely."

"And Laurent de Frigecourt could give you everything you ever wanted."

"Like jewels and big houses," I said. "All the things that, in fact, I've never wanted. Laurent is like a gorgeous butterfly, a prince—he's not for me."

"Just prosaic old Tom?"

"Clever, dear old Tom," I said kissing the top of his head.

"Shall we go to bed?" he said.

"But, darling, it's noon."

"Whatever's wrong with noon? You can do it any time, you know."

"So you can."

"And we *are* married."

"Better and better," I said.

Tom kissed my neck. "For such a trendy thing, you're horribly square."

"Try me," I said.

Tom and I spent the rest of the day in bed. I'll pass over the bit where the waves crash in from the sea, or the sun is seen glinting through the leaves, as they do so delicately in the cinema, because this story is only incidentally about love or whatever you call that peculiarly complex emotion.

"I'm very hungry," Tom said. "We had no lunch."

"Oh, I'm so sorry. It's all my fault."

Tom sat on the edge of the bed and smiled at me. "I'm too befuddled to smack you. Let's go and get something to eat."

I hope no one saw us in the dining room of the Hôtel du Port. We sat close together like a pair of adolescent lovers, and although Tom, naturally, did justice to his meal, we did a lot of gazing into each other's eyes and murmuring sweet nothings, while I pecked at my food.

"We must go up to the château to get my things," I said.

"Do we have to?"

"They'll wonder what's happened."

"They'll guess. Laurent's got his brother, and I've got you. Get the things tomorrow."

I didn't need very much persuading. One has so few

220

idylls in one's life, and this rediscovery of our love was one of them.

When we went up to the château at noon the next day, a party was in progress, or rather the town had called to pay its respects to the new Marquis. I can't say it seemed like a festive occasion; everyone stared mutely, as stunned by the whole thing as we were. Laurent and Jean stood next to each other, and as people came up Laurent introduced them to his brother. From the way Jean seemed to recognise them and chatted, there was no doubt he was who he said he was. Dr Bourdin wandered amiably over to talk to us.

"It's miraculous," he said.

"Did you talk to him, Doctor?"

"Yes, for a long time."

"And you're sure he is who he says he is?"

"Oh, no doubt. I deliberately talked a lot about his boyhood, when he broke his nose, that sort of thing. He fell out of a tree once. Those boys were always climbing trees. Ah, Madame Gilbert . . ."

Madame Gilbert came through the door accompanied by Martine and looked bewilderedly into the crowded salon. We waved to her and, relieved to see us, she came up to us.

"Oh, la, la, la, la, I never hoped to see this day. Where is he, the beautiful Jean?"

"There, Madame, next to Laurent. He's not quite so beautiful now and a lot older."

Madame Gilbert frowned. "Mais non, my eyes are poor. Voilà!" She put on her pince-nez and studied the man whom Laurent was bringing towards her.

"Now who is this, Jean? You remember."

"Bien sur." Jean held out his arms. "Madame Gilbert."

But Madame Gilbert was studying him through her pince-nez; she stepped back looking up at him, small and frail compared to him. I felt my heart quicken and I seized Tom's hand beside mine. Jean looked at her quizzically, but smiling, still confident; after all, he had recognised her.

"Mais qu'est-ce que c'est?" cried Madame Gilbert. "It is not Jean, it is your brother Henri! Mais oui." She turned to the flustered Dr Bourdin, who was also gazing at the brother. "Don't you remember, Claude, it was *Henri* who fell down the tree and broke his nose. Not Jean."

Now the brother's smile had vanished. Laurent looked concerned and, sensing something, everyone in the room seemed to stop talking.

"Yes," Dr Bourdin said slowly. "It was Henri who broke his nose; it was the middle boy, Henri, not Jean."

I looked at the brother, who had a large nose that bent sideways and had at one time been broken. I remembered that at the lunch at Dr Bourdin's house they'd discussed Henri's nose. This was unmistakeably Henri, with a lot of other disagreeable characteristics besides.

"I am Henri?" he said incredulously. "Then this completes my treatment, don't you see, dear brother, now I know who I am!" And he clasped Laurent in his arms.

Now even I wasn't sure whether or not he was acting. I looked at Tom, but it was impossible to read his face.

"But why should you have thought you were Jean?" Tom asked quietly. "Wouldn't your analysis have revealed your identity?"

"I didn't know my name for a long time," Henri explained. "I wasn't sure. Oh, thank you, dear Madame Gilbert." He tried to embrace her, but the old lady backed away. She looked confused and suspicious, and her hands were fluttering at her sides.

"Viens, Martine," she said nervously.

"We'll come with you," Tom said, adding when Laurent protested, "no, no, it really is time we were going."

222

Laurent smiled sadly at me. His eyes told me that he knew.

"I'll be back later, for my things," I murmured, "when the crowd has gone. We can have a word then."

He pressed my arm and kissed my cheek. "I'm so happy about my brother," he said.

"I know," I whispered back. "I'm happy for you too."

Dr Bourdin joined us and we all walked back in silence to Madame Gilbert's, deeply preoccupied with our thoughts.

Without being invited, we went inside with her and Martine produced a bottle of vermouth while we made ourselves comfortable in chairs, the doctor as well. Madame Gilbert sat at her desk, looking formidable.

"C'est un conseil de guerre, n'est-ce pas?" she said.

"I think we know what you're going to suggest, Madame," Tom said quietly in his halting French. "Council of war it is."

"Henri was the traitor," I said. "He betrayed his brother and father."

"And friends," Madame added menacingly. "One of whom was my cousin Auguste."

"We have no proof at all," Dr Bourdin insisted.

"This is the sort of thing Henri would do, not Jean; that is why he wanted to pretend he was the elder brother."

"He couldn't bear the personality of Henri," Tom explained, "Henri the cheat, the betrayer, the coward."

"What shall we do?"

Everyone looked at me, as though this was the last question they had expected.

"Well, we must do something."

"Why? We know. We can't prove it, as you said, but it is quite in keeping with the greedy, sneaky character of Henri as a young man. He would have done it for money

**223**

and to save his skin. Maybe the Gestapo found out and used his weakness to their advantage. After all, he was very young," Tom said. "Surely he has suffered enough from his memories."

"But he did have a memory," I insisted. "He never lost it."

"I don't think so, no." Tom got out his pipe and puffed on it unlit. "But then we never thought so, did we?"

I got up and walked about the room. "I don't like any of this," I said. "It's too, too unfinished."

"Things arrange themselves," Madame said to me, her old eyes bright with wisdom. "You will see."

Against Tom's wishes, I went up to the château alone later that day. I did want to talk to Laurent; in a way I wanted to say goodbye. Tom and I had had a long talk that afternoon and decided that after Christmas we should go back to England and then complete the sabbatical year in the States. Sad as I would be to say goodbye to Port St Pierre, I was convinced that I would never get any work done here.

Laurent was alone when I found him, standing by the summer house. He'd felled a tree and was stacking logs.

"I've only just discovered this place," I said. "Jeanne showed it to me."

"We loved it as children. Mine don't seem so keen on it."

"Did your father build it?"

"No. Some say it was the original hunting lodge, but my grandmother rebuilt it during that period of Victorian mania for the Gothic. We just added a coat of paint when we restored the château."

"Where's Henri?"

"He's in the library. It's a treasure chest for him. He's writing a book, you know."

"Yes, he told me. Is he going to live here?"

"We don't know what we're going to do yet. There's a lot of legal business to see to. He may finish his book in the house across the bay." Laurent looked at me and took my arm.

"Clare, everyone seemed troubled when Madame Gilbert discovered he is Henri and not Jean. You don't find it disturbing, do you?"

Gazing at Laurent I realised the simplicity of ignorance. He seemed to have complete trust in his older brother.

"I don't understand much about it, Laurent. You must trust in your own good sense. The only thing that puzzles me is the nose. Didn't you remember that Henri was the one with the broken nose?"

"No, I was too young. We are talking about my childhood. I don't recall the broken nose at all. However, that proves more than anything that he *is* my brother. Madame Gilbert recognised him at once. Besides, he knows many intimate things that only a member of the family could know. He is my brother; there's no doubt about that!"

Laurent went on sawing his logs, stacking them in a pile by the hut. "Did you ever see inside this place?"

"Yes, Jeanne showed me. She's very fond of it."

"You seem happier about Jeanne," Laurent said, unlocking the door.

"Yes, I am. I don't think I understood her before. She is a visionary."

We now stood inside the summer house and, as Jeanne had, Laurent undid one of the shutters. The sun streamed in, dazzling me.

"It's really beautiful," I said. "Look at the little staircase into the tiny turret. It's bigger than I thought."

"Yes, there's another landing. It was built to look like a miniature château."

I went up the narrow stairs and stood looking out of the

225

window. Yes, I could see the wall and the bay. The setting sun was like a ball of fire, dazzling in its brilliance as it sank towards the horizon beyond Le Hourdel.

I blinked my eyes and when I opened them again I saw the huge windmill standing there silhouetted against the sun, its giant sails turning, turning; there was a rush of air, and I heard a faint cry, as though for help, then the sound of the turning sails grew deafening.

"Clare, are you all right?" Laurent was by my side, his hand on my arm. ". . . called and called you. Clare, your hand is so cold. Are you ill?"

I shook my head. All I saw now was the wall and the bay beyond.

"I'm perfectly fine," I said, trying to make my voice sound normal. "I think I had a rush of blood to the brain. Let's get out of here."

"Come and have a drink. You haven't really met Henri."

The drink stilled my agitation, but it did not explain my vision. For I was sure it had been a vision. I did not have that kind of hallucinatory power, or did I? I had to get to Jeanne and ask her.

When we'd looked in at the library, Henri had his head in a huge pile of books and seemed reluctant to be disturbed. He looked perfectly at home to me.

"Do you mind if I just pop up and get my things?" I asked Laurent. "I won't be long."

"You're not staying?"

"No, I'm afraid it's goodbye. I mean not finally goodbye, but Tom and I are reconciled."

"I thought you were. I saw the writing on the wall the day he breezed in here."

"Well." I smiled. "I said we should know one way or the other. It was fate, I guess."

"Go and see the kids. I think they're with Jeanne in her room. The central heating has failed upstairs. It won't be

226

repaired until after Christmas. Just as well you're not staying. It's awfully cold up there."

I smiled to myself as I climbed the stairs. So many little things could suddenly be logically explained. The cold, the central heating . . .

I knocked on Jeanne's door and popped my head round. The children were seated near her being read to. How could I ever have thought she was evil?

"Hello!" I said. "I just came to get my things."

"Oh, Clare! You're not *going?*"

"Yes, and I'm going back to my *husband*, now aren't you pleased?"

"I'm not pleased," Noelle said. "I wanted you to marry Papa."

"Ssshhh!" Jeanne chided, but smiled at me.

"I'm so glad for you; you seem very happy."

"Maybe you'll have children now," Fabrice said.

"I hope so. Three, all like you."

The children squealed with laughter, and my heart contracted. I would miss them very much. I blew them kisses.

"See you soon, Jeanne."

Jeanne waved and I closed the door. I felt I was leaving a chapter of my life behind me, in many ways not a very pleasant chapter, but an important and vital one. I opened the door of my room. The sun I'd seen from the pavilion was now low on the horizon, sending beams of red and gold into the room—Rose's room.

I'd forgotten Rose. Had I failed her? We would never know how she died. There were a lot of things we would never know, now that I was leaving. Well, Laurent was alert now to any danger, and it was his duty to protect his family, not mine.

I quickly packed my things and stripped the bed. Yes, there were still many things unsolved—the missing pages, the loose bolts in the yacht. I shrugged, and then I paused and listened. I thought I heard a whisper. I listened again and opened the door. There was no one outside. I closed the door again. It was very cold. The pipes were icy to the touch.

I heard the whisper again, and then I felt that sense of another presence, of not being alone. Only I was less certain now that it had been Rose trying to contact me. I'd recognised the breeze I'd felt in this room and the breeze that swirled about us in the summer house as one and the same. Yes, this was Rose's room, but had I mistaken the spirit, if there was a spirit. Was it Joan after all?

"Rose," I whispered, less certain than I had been before. "Joan? Whoever it is, are you there?"

The sun had gone down abruptly and the room had lost its colour. I strained forward in the gloom.

"Rose, Rose, are you there?"

The door opened silently and I let out a small cry. "Jeanne!"

"Did I frighten you? I'm sorry. I thought I heard you talking to someone."

"Only Rose," I smiled. "I've always felt her presence in this room, or I thought I had. Now I wonder if it was St Joan. The summer house has made me doubt."

"Only the good come back," Jeanne said with certainty. "Rose was not good; her spirit would not be benign. It is St Joan of Arc whose spirit you feel."

"I'm not sure," I said. "Someone who was wrongfully killed might come back, however good or bad."

Jeanne glanced round, less certain now herself. She shrugged. "Maybe," she acknowledged. "After all, this was her room."

"Yes." I went to the window and looked out. Now that the trees were almost bare it was quite easy to see the outline of the summer house. "Jeanne, I saw your windmill. I was in the summer house just now with Laurent."

"And you *saw* it?" Jeanne looked ecstatic.

228

"I saw it and I heard it. What does it mean, Jeanne?"

"It means you can see into the past as I can. The windmill was destroyed at the end of the fifteenth century at about the same time as the château."

"But I've never had an experience like this before."

Jeanne smiled. "Don't worry about it; you might never have another. But as an historian isn't it nice to be able to say you've seen into the past?"

"I don't think I'd dare tell anybody, except perhaps Tom. And what of the future, Jeanne, can you see that too?"

Jeanne looked puzzled. "Sometimes I think I can, but now I can't see very far into the future; I don't know why."

She was standing near me now looking out of the window, and I felt a sudden depression of the spirit and a sense of foreboding.

"Jeanne, did you know Rose's mother was a medium?"

"Yes, she once did tell me; she said she thought it was rubbish. I felt sorry for her because she didn't have much insight into that kind of thing."

"So you think my sensing her presence here is a trick of my imagination?"

Jeanne looked at me gravely. "Who can say what mysterious happenings come from beyond? Clare, I must run back to the children. We shall see you again soon?"

"Oh, yes, we'll be here over Christmas. Jeanne . . ."

"Yes?"

"I'm sorry for the misunderstandings."

"There was a lot to misunderstand," Jeanne said.

"And there's a lot I still don't understand about Lisa and so on; but I feel now that Laurent knows it's his problem and that it must be resolved."

"He will know what to do." Jeanne smiled at me reassuringly. "Au revoir."

She closed the door. The room was now quite dark. I

looked out of the window once more, with a sense of finality. I knew I would never sleep here again. My room, Rose's room.

I stood at the door and listened. "Goodbye Rose," I said.

But Rose had gone.

Downstairs Tom had joined Laurent and Henri who had come in from the library.

"You were an age," Tom said. "I thought I'd better come and fetch you."

"She doesn't want to say goodbye," Laurent smiled. "She is in love with this house, Tom, you should take care."

"Clare is always in love with the past," Tom said. "This is where one has so much competition, being married to an historian."

Tom was at it again, re-establishing that I was his. Oh, well, for the time being I certainly was.

Lisa put her head round the door. "I go get the children, Monsieur?"

"Please, Lisa. They're with Jeanne. Lisa, come and meet my brother properly."

But Lisa shut the door, and Henri smiled.

"No offence," Laurent said. "She is shy and doesn't understand the language well. Tom, Clare, will you stay to dinner?"

"No thanks," I answered quickly. "I'm actually going to do the little woman act and make Tom a lovely meal."

"It won't last," Tom said. "But it's nice for now."

"We'll go out the back, Laurent. I want to say thanks to Madame Barbou."

But Madame Barbou wasn't in the kitchen. Agnès, her face very hot from the oven, looked up as we went through and explained that her mother had gone home with a headache.

230

"I'm sorry, Agnès. Please wish her well."

Agnès came over and gave Tom and me a conspiratorial look. She jerked her head in the direction of the salon. "The brother! Eh!" she said, tossing her head disdainfully.

"Why, Agnès, why ever should you say that? He really is Monsieur Laurent's brother. There is no doubt about that."

"I'm not saying there *is*," Agnès replied defensively, wiping the perspiration from her face. "It is simply that *he* is the one who was Rose's boyfriend. It is *I* who saw them together when I went to the market in Port Guillaume!"

I stared at her. "Are you sure, Agnès?"

"Quite sure, Madame."

"You told your mother?"

"Yes. She said not to tell anybody."

"But you told us."

Agnès hung her head. "I knew you'd be interested, Madame, because of Rose's death."

"Agnès, I'm sure Monsieur Henri had nothing to do with Rose's death, and if I were you I would take your mother's advice and tell no one else."

Tom took a fifty-franc note out of his wallet and gave it to her. "Monsieur Laurent has had enough trouble," he said.

## CHAPTER 19

For the next few days Tom and I stayed away from the château. When we weren't working, we talked incessantly about the family and the brother, and Jeanne's vision and my hallucination, as Tom insisted on referring to it. Apparently it was all right for Jeanne to have visions but not for me.

"I refuse to be married to a visionary," Tom insisted. "It was a trick of the light coupled with your overripe imagination. You *wanted* to see the windmill."

"Perhaps I did. Darling, you did say you'd get the coffee this morning, didn't you?"

I took off my glasses and gazed severely at him from across the desk we'd decided to share.

Tom returned my stare, and I thought he was going to be rude, but he was trying—we were both trying—so without a word he put down his pen, got up, and went into the salon. In a second he was back.

"Clare, there's a letter. Look at the size of it." He waved a bulky envelope at me. "It's from Northern Ireland."

"Cliff!" I cried excitedly. "Gimme."

As Tom tore open the envelope, the jaggedly torn pages fluttered to the floor. There were also two letters; one was from Cliff.

Dear Mr. Trafford,

I'm sorry I couldn't see you when you called on my Mum. There's a lot I'd have liked to talk to you about in connection with the death of my late fiancée, Rose.

I got her last letter, plus the pages which I am enclosing, after her death. They were held up by the military authorities here in Northern Ireland who are very strict about censorship. They couldn't make head or tail of them, nor can I. I hope they are of some use to you, as I loved Rose, although my Mum thought she was no good.

Being on active service here there's nothing I can do. I hope you can.

Yours sincerely,

Clifford Brown.

Tom then read Rose's last letter out loud to me. Listening to it was like hearing a voice from the dead—the familiar Rose whom I knew and whose room I had lived in these three short months.

Dear Cliff,

Be an angel and keep these pages for me. I think I'm onto something quite big and could make myself a lot of money. There's a man here who is ever so interested in the château and the family. He's offered

233

me money to let him in when no one's about. I think it's ever so fishy.

Then the other day, that Jeanne, whom as you know I can't abide—she's so *weird*, Cliff! honest—lent me this book on Joan of Arc. I could hardly believe my eyes when I read these pages. But I don't want *anyone* to know. Keep them for me, Cliff angel; they are safe with you. I hope you don't go to Northern Ireland. May see you *very* soon?

Rose.

I listened with my head on my hands, my arms propped on the desk. There was a sudden movement behind us, and I looked up.

"Sorry, did I startle you? The door was open."

"Michelle, we're just in the middle of a drama. Sit, listen. Tom, show Michelle the letters while I skim through these pages. I may get on to what is important more quickly than you."

My hands were trembling as I took the torn pages from *The Last Journey of the Maid*. I had to control myself and start reading from the beginning, not skip. The author continued the narrative of Joan of Arc's last journey until she came to Port St Pierre. Then the name Jehan de Frigecourt appeared and I read quickly on:

The good people of Port St Pierre believed in the saintliness of the Maid, whom many considered to be a witch, and entreated the governor not to hand her over to the English, offering to ferry her down the river and out of Burgundian hands.

It is said that the governor was a man of like mind and would have weakened, save that the squire Jehan Sire de Frigecourt, the bastard son of my lord John, the late Duke of Burgundy, hated the Maid with his whole evil heart and threatened the governor with an awful death if he set her free. It is said that the Maid, hearing of this, cursed the whole family of Burgundy . . . and there were many who remembered this and told the story long after Charles Duke of Burgundy was savagely done to death on the battlefield at Nancy and all with him perished.

There was a legend, however, that the son of Jehan de Frigecourt, who served with Charles the Bold in his efforts to conquer the Swiss, saved much of the *Burgunderbeute*, the famous booty or treasure of the dukes, and took it safely back with him to Picardy.

I finished reading it aloud for the second time, and when I'd finished no one spoke until Michelle breathed: "It's like a voice from the past."

"It is a voice from the past. It is Rose telling us all we want to know. Shall I tell you how I see it? It's like this." I stood up, as though I were giving a lecture, and paced back and forth.

"Henri de Frigecourt, at the tender age of fifteen—and who are we to judge?—for some reason betrays his family. In exchange, he is allowed to live and goes free. Maybe he does blot out the bits and pieces he doesn't like from his mind. He certainly doesn't try to see his family again—he is too ashamed—until he studies, becomes an antique dealer, makes money. He becomes an authority on jewels and in his researches, which, incidentally, are about French royal jewels . . ."

"How do you know that?" Tom interrupted sharply.

"He told me. I'm sure that was quite accidental. However, in these researches he discovers that part of the *Burgunderbeute*—the fabulous Burgundian treasure that Duke Charles, who was a very vain man, carried with him wherever he went, even onto the field of battle—was stolen for *sure* by one of his kinsmen and taken back to Picardy. What had only been a rumor now became a cer-

**235**

tainty. And where did the treasure eventually end up, but in the family home in Picardy, the de Frigecourt château, which stood on the site of the old prison. As far as anyone knew, the jewels had never been dispersed; perhaps he found out for certain they had not.

"He then felt compelled to probe deeper, to discover more. Maybe he actually found evidence that the *Burgunderbeute is* hidden in the château at Port St Pierre. But he still felt he couldn't reveal himself to his brother, who might guess his treachery—the only thing he was really ashamed of. He meets Rose and uses her, but she dies too soon. Perhaps she tries to blackmail him and he kills her. I don't know. He then hits on the idea of 'returning' as Jean, who would never have betrayed anybody. Henri must have known he was a nasty, sneaky kid, and . . ."

There was a furious pounding at the door. Tom rushed out and came back with Nicolas Bourdin, whose face was ashen.

"Michelle, Michelle, come quickly, the château is on fire!"

The sequence of events then, even as I think about it now, is too disordered to remember. I know that we left the house and ran up towards the château. We could see great clouds of smoke billowing from the trees that surrounded it. But when we got there, we saw it wasn't the château; it was the little summer house that was ablaze, setting fire to the trees surrounding it.

As we got there, the top window in one of the little turrets was pushed open and Jeanne's head appeared.

"Jump, Jeanne, jump . . ."

But she stood back, and Fabrice came out onto the sill, where he stood looking fearfully down.

"Why don't they break the door down?" I screamed.

"It's too stout, and it's locked."

236

"The windows."

"The shutters are made of iron. They are locked too. Look . . ."

Fabrice jumped. I shut my eyes, but he landed in the arms of Nicolas, who hugged him and rushed him over to Michelle. I was amazed there were so few people there. It must have happened within minutes, and Nicolas had come immediately for his sister. We could hear the sound of the fire engine now in the distance.

Then Tom took Nicolas' place and Noelle jumped. Tom caught her and staggered. And then Philippe was clinging to the sill, wavering, too frightened to let go. Jeanne leaned out and gave him her hand. He clutched it and then dropped.

Thank God the children were safe. I rushed as near as I could go to the blazing hut and stood below the window.

"Jeanne, *jump!*

Jeanne stared down at me, her face blackened with smoke. She seemed to try and climb out onto the sill and then suddenly she disappeared.

"Jeanne, Jeanne!" I screamed. Then Tom appeared and dragged me back.

"It'll be going up like a torch in a minute."

"But Jeanne's in there! Oh, Tom, do something!"

"Darling, I can't. I wish I could."

The fire engine swept round the drive and in seconds three men were battering at the door with a stout pole. The door gave easily, and they rushed in as smoke came billowing out.

One of them held Jeanne over his shoulder. He laid her tenderly on the ground and put his mouth to hers. Michelle ran up and massaged Jeanne's chest, then she too put her mouth to hers.

I couldn't believe it. A minute ago I'd seen her . . . I left the children who were huddled together covered with blankets and went up to her inert body lying on the ground. Her eyes were closed.

"Is she dead?" I whispered to Michelle.

"She's still breathing, but listen!"

Jeanne opened her eyes wide and seemed to be looking for something. Her dim gaze rested on me. She seemed to be trying to speak. I bent close to her.

"Jeanne, you'll be all right."

She gave a cough and shook her head. I put my ear to her mouth.

"I said the harm would come from someone who knew the house. Look to it, Clare, look to it." She started breathing very rapidly and her body jerked in a sudden spasm. Her eyes opened wide and looked upwards. Then she died.

The cause of death was asphyxiation, or so the autopsy later said. I thought that what Jeanne had known would come—her death—had come, and at the appointed time. Her body was taken into the house and put in the library. The children were rushed upstairs, bathed, dressed in warm clothes, and given hot drinks.

People seemed to be streaming in and out of the château all the time, but once the fire engine arrived, the fire was quickly extinguished. Nicolas had noticed it start when his boat came in on the tide; he'd rushed home immediately and then to Michelle—that's why he'd thought the château itself was on fire. It began as a wisp of smoke, he said, coming from the trees.

I can't remember when it was that somebody asked, "Where is Laurent?" And we realised that neither Laurent nor his brother were anywhere about. Lisa, it appeared, was out too. It was puzzling to me that Jeanne had decided to hold afternoon lessons in the summer house until Philippe explained, his teeth still chattering with shock.

"It was very cold in the château. One could make a fire in the summer house. Lisa suggested it and laid the fire for us."

"And was it a spark from the fire that started the big fire?"

"Oh, no. That came from outside. There was a sudden big crackle."

I thought of the logs that Laurent had piled up against the summer house that day. "And where is your papa?"

"He went hunting with Uncle Henri. It was such a lovely day. They left this morning, before we were up."

I looked at Tom, who was already getting on his coat.

Michelle caught our glance and nodded. "I'll stay with the children," she said. "Go, go quickly."

"And don't let Nicolas leave you, for a *minute*."

"The Fiat," I said to Tom. "In the garage. I'll drive because I know the way."

As we sped through the countryside, I found it incredible that we were doing this yet again. "Those dunes always spelt danger," I said. "It was bound to end here."

"You think he'll kill his brother?"

"He'll try. If he thinks the children are dead, the brother is the only one in his way."

"But he could have had anything he wanted."

"He was always afraid someone would get on to the truth, now that they know he's not Jean. He'd never feel safe."

Laurent's car was in the park, but there was no sign of the men. It was a good day for the hunt and quite a few cars were there. Tom and I looked despairingly out over the flats.

"I don't know where to begin," Tom said, and I thought of Laurent and the day Noelle was lost.

"Let's go north towards the bird sanctuary. There's not much shooting there, and if Henri wants to take a pot shot at Laurent, that's where he'll do it. If he hasn't done it already."

Suddenly, in front of me, I saw a figure running. It was far off, but my eyes were good. At first I thought it was a man.

"Tom, quick, look over there!"

Tom followed my pointing finger. "It's Lisa."

"*Lisa!* She must have seen them."

We set off at a pace after Lisa, dodging among the dunes so that if she turned round she wouldn't see us. Soon we came to the signs marking the limit of the hunt, but still Lisa ran on.

"She's running towards that house," I said. "She seems to know where she's going."

And sure enough, among the trees we could see a small hut, just a rough shooting box. Now it dawned on me that of course Henri would have had a hiding place near the château, and that . . .

Lisa got to the hut, pushed open the door and went inside. Tom stopped.

"*Quickly!*" I urged him. "But quietly. Do your best pathfinder act."

We crept up to the hut and listened at the door. There was no sound. My heart lurched.

"There's no one there," Tom said.

"We know Lisa's there."

Before I knew what he was doing, Tom pushed on the door. It opened into an empty room, but we could hear voices coming from the adjoining room. As we stood in the doorway, we heard Lisa say, "Come quickly. There is a fire at the château."

We heard the sound of chairs being pushed back. Laurent's voice said sharply, "Henri, I told you I saw smoke."

"Oh, relax," Henri said.

Then to my astonishment, Lisa started speaking rapidly to Henri in German. The scales, as they say, fell from my eyes. Tom, who speaks German, was listening intently.

"She's telling him the fire is a disaster, that everyone is alive. He's trying to tell her to shut up."

Not only could Tom speak German, but Laurent was listening too.

It was then that we announced our presence by walking into the room. Lisa and Henri stopped arguing with each other and stared at us. I was happy to see the guns resting in a far corner.

"What *is* this?" Laurent began, but I could tell by the look of horror on his face that he was beginning to understand.

"Your brother wanted to kill you," Tom said, and he rapidly outlined all I'd said at the house. Distraught as I was, I was proud to see how right my deductions had been, if Henri and Lisa's faces were any measure.

"The only thing I didn't realise," I said, "was that Lisa was your girlfriend."

"She's my wife," Henri admitted. "She wanted it all for our two sons."

"You would *kill* your whole family for that!" I felt too weak to go on.

"*He* always had the weakness for money," Lisa said, "which was why he betrayed his father and brother. You only have to offer Henri money and he will do anything. The *Burgunderbeute* was too much for him."

"So it *was* the *Burgunderbeute*," Tom said with satisfaction.

"What?" Laurent cried. "Whatever can that have to do with all this?"

"Your brother is greedy, very greedy. You don't remember this from your childhood, as you don't recall the

241

broken nose. Obviously you were too young, and time has made you honour his memory and forget the bad things, if ever you knew them. Your brother didn't dare return home because of what he had done. He became a writer, and in his researches he came across references to the famous *Burgunderbeute* of Charles the Bold and saw how it was linked with his own family. Supposing it did still exist? What fabulous wealth—something worth finding beyond an ancient title and a few mortgaged estates. Something worth risking exposure for. And that is what happened."

As Tom related the story, it sounded like a fairy tale. The whole thing appeared incredible to the normal mind.

"But you would never have got away with it," I said.

"Oh, yes, we would have. We covered our tracks in everything we did. We would have sold the château and gone back to Germany. But it is not true that I wanted to kill my family. I wanted to frighten them away."

"And me," I said. "The pot shot was from you, wasn't it?"

"I missed you, didn't I? I knew you were sniffing around the château. I used to see you on the beach looking at it. I wondered what you knew."

"You were lucky he missed you," Lisa said derisively. "Poor Elizabeth wasn't so fortunate." Then, seeing the pain on Laurent's face, Lisa faltered before hurrying on. "He's been planning this for years. It was an obsession. He thought you would recognise him if he came back, so he tried to cause an 'accident' in Paris. I think he thought it wouldn't be murder if you were killed because it was just a chance. He was very timid then. He was shocked when Elizabeth was so badly injured, and his plans lay dormant for a while. After all, he *was* a de Frigecourt," she said mockingly.

"It is not true, it is not true," Henri hissed savagely.

"The plan to terrorize you came from the German here, brought up by her Nazi father. Frighten them to *death*, she urged me. She relished it, staging little accidents—the boat, the disappearance of Philippe. She shut him up in that room and wanted to push him out of the window. In time she was persuaded he'd panic and jump. I was horrified when I heard."

Lisa lunged at him, and I was appalled by the savagery and hatred engendered between two people who had perhaps once loved each other.

"*Nothing* you say is true," Lisa shouted. "Everything was done at your suggestion. You *did* want to be rid of them; you simply lacked the will. I tried to give you *guts*."

"Lisa just set fire to the pavilion," Henri screamed, "and Lisa wanted to kill Rose. She was jealous of her because she thought we were having an affair."

Henri had gripped Lisa's arms and she struggled to try and free herself.

"That is *not* true. I could see at once, as soon as I came to visit Henri, that Rose was attracted to him—always hanging around, pretending to be interested in his work. He had deliberately sought her out once he came to the district, knowing she was employed at the château. He pretended to be interested in her in order to use her; she would look in the library for him, let him in when everyone was in bed. It was he who discovered the treasure, and then sent for me to remove it, but first he had to get rid of Rose. She knew far too much and had threatened to blackmail him, to expose him to the de Frigecourt family."

I released a loud sigh and Lisa stopped talking. For now I knew why Rose had died. Silly, stupid girl—neither wicked nor bad, just silly.

"Of course, Rose didn't know Henri was one of the

243

missing brothers," Lisa continued, curling her lips venomously. "She didn't realise what sort of person she was dealing with—someone who had suffered remorse for many many years and then been overcome by greed. She should have taken more care. Well, one afternoon there was a scene at Henri's house in Port St Pierre. Rose realised she was late and ran from the house. Henri followed her and offered to row her across the canal, explaining that she could easily walk across the bay. He didn't tell her the tide was due soon and that she had very little chance of getting to the other side."

Tom was quietly translating for me as Lisa spoke, hastily, casting hateful looks at her husband.

"It was an accident," Henri insisted. "She was across the canal in plenty of time."

"How can one believe anything you say?" Tom said. "Your life has been dominated by greed and deceit."

Now I knew *how* she'd died. Poor Rose. I thought of her embarking on that lonely walk across the sand; it was beginning to get dark, but she thought she had plenty of time. Her lover—was he her lover? I suppose we'd never know, but somehow I didn't think so—would have assured her there was plenty of time, hours maybe. Certainly he'd sent her to her death. He had murdered her as surely as if he'd held her head under while she drowned. Then the tide began rushing in, the way it does; she couldn't swim. She was stranded on a sandbank. The water rose higher. Maybe she could walk—it would be better than death. But death came anyway, as the wet exhausted girl, struggling up to her neck in the swift current, lay down on the bank and was exposed to the cold night air.

What I still didn't know, and probably would never know, was why Rose came to see me. Was she trying to tell me she was in danger? Did she suspect that Henri would try and kill her because of what she knew? But she was greedy, too; she was going to stay and blackmail him when she should have run for her life. That was it! She wanted to try and get rid of Jeanne, to spread poison around so that Laurent would hear and tell her to go. Then Rose would have the château to herself, to search for the booty alone. She was going to implicate me in her web. But Rose hadn't left enough time . . .

"Lisa, how did you get the job with Laurent?" I asked suddenly.

"We knew he'd want a nanny now that Rose was gone. I simply turned up at the house and said I'd come from the agency. The poor man never troubled to check; he was too trusting."

"It all seems so *futile!*" I protested. "All this plotting and killing when it was so unnecessary. Laurent loved you; you were the real Marquis. You could have had everything—jewels and all."

"He still had a conscience," Tom said. "He is, after all, a de Frigecourt, one of a noble line. To have betrayed his father and brother was a crime even he couldn't live with. Everything he did had to be done by stealth."

"You don't know what it was like," Henri whispered, looking at his brother. "It wasn't for money. It was from fear. They knew my father was the leader of the group, but they could never catch him at it. One day they took me after school and threatened to torture me and kill all my family if I didn't tell them the next assignment. They promised no harm would come to me or to my family; they would just be warned. I was only fifteen."

Laurent turned away from his brother, his eyes filled with tears. It was a terrible tale we were listening to, more terrible because we had no idea what was true and what wasn't.

"Go, brother," Laurent said. "Go now, right out of our

lives. Don't ever communicate with me again. As my brother, I love you, I remember our childhood together, but how can I ever forgive you? What you did in your youth is one thing; but what you have done just recently is something else. You could have come to me and asked me for the jewels; I would have *given* them to you."

"He didn't know you hadn't become as twisted and warped as he had," Tom said bitterly. "You'd grown up in different worlds—his tainted by his past and the guilt of what he must have known he'd done."

Slowly Henri made for the door. Lisa rushed up to him. "I'm coming too," she said. "Don't leave me with them."

"I don't want you," Henri said. "You've brought all this upon me, insinuating yourself into the household, to kill my family. If I'd have known . . ."

Lisa threw herself at him striking his chest. "You knew, of course you knew, but once you found out about the jewels you got so greedy you didn't care what became of anyone."

Lisa seized her husband by his neck. The story and the spectacle had so affected me I thought I was going to be sick. Suddenly Henri, in a superhuman effort, threw Lisa to the floor, where she lay sobbing. He went over to the door and stood on the threshold, looking at Laurent.

"Forgive me, brother? Try. I am just a weak man, not a wicked one. She"—he cast contemptuous eyes at the woman sobbing on the floor—"is the one for the guillotine. She has no pity."

Neither, I thought bitterly, had he, if he let Rose cross the bay on foot in the dark knowing quite well the tide was due in. No one tried to stop him going.

After Henri left we stood in silence for a while, in the tired, dejected way of people who have been through a great drama.

246

"What shall we do with her?" Tom pointed to Lisa.

"Leave her," Laurent said. "They have got nothing."

Lisa stopped sobbing and looked up. Again she spoke in German, Tom translating for me. "He has got everything," she said smiling wickedly. "Piece by piece I took what there was of the *Burgunderbeute* over to him; it is all in Henri's house now. Yes, it did exist. He found that out. He traced it through old family archives in the Bibliothèque Nationale. He spent months in Paris, Bruges, and Ghent, doing research. He traced it to the library, the oldest part of the house, and then it was all quite easy. You will find a panel behind the geography section, quite empty now. And he needn't think he will get away with it. Wherever he goes, I will seek him out."

"That should be enough punishment for anyone," Tom murmured.

"Poor Nicolas," I said. "No wonder she was so interested in his boat."

"Let's go," Laurent said. He stood by the door. "Leave her to find her own way."

Henri was no longer in sight as we stumbled out of the house and across the dunes, but as we got to the car park Laurent's Citroën suddenly leapt forward, Henri driving, and went straight out onto the beach.

"He's going to drive across," Tom cried. "Is it possible?"

"There's the canal," Laurent said. "But he may have a boat there. Let him go, let him go."

He turned to the Fiat and sank into the back seat.

"You drive, Tom," I said. "I've about had it."

Tom drove on to the coast road, skirting the trees at the edge of the dunes. As we came round we saw the bay again and in the distance the tiny shape of Laurent's car heading in the direction of Port Guillaume. Suddenly a Land-Rover started to race towards it, flag flying. We heard from the distance the sound of whistles being blown.

"Stop!" Laurent cried. "The sluice!"

"The what?" asked Tom.

"The gates; they open every day to let the water out, after the tide has receded. Henri will be caught by the water. They are trying to tell him."

Tom stopped the car and we jumped out; we were about a mile from the town. But Henri sped on, and the Land-Rover suddenly stopped and two men got out and watched. Laurent put his hands to his face.

"My brother," he said.

The first jet of water, which rolled away from the gates at a terrific pace, turned the speeding car over like a matchbox. If one can imagine a dam that suddenly bursts open taking all in front of it, this had the same kind of effect. Henri never had a chance, and as the water rolled on we saw the car first bobbing like a cork, and then it disappeared out of sight beneath the torrent that swept it out to sea.

# . . . A YEAR AFTER

The tide was out and the newly washed bay gleamed in the late August sunshine. The sand squelched under our toes, and the little creatures left by the sea rushed away from under our bare feet. Tom and I were taking what we called my constitutional, because the doctor said I should have plenty of exercise. But the way Tom and I ambled along one would hardly call it exercise. My enormous paunch protruded in front of me, and I rested my arms comfortably on it as I waddled along.

The pink brickwork of the château sparkled with colour and the shutters had been freshly painted white. All the woodwork was white, too, though the grey conical roofs of the twin turrets still dominated the town.

The doors of the château opened, and Tom and I stopped and watched as the children tumbled down the grand staircase, a young red setter pup frolicking in front of them, a replacement for poor Goofy, who had never been found. After we'd discovered Henri's hideout, it was not hard to guess he'd tried to lure Noelle there, as a means of gaining entry to the family, and probably done away with the dog.

When they saw us, the children came leaping over the wall, and Tom stood in front of me to prevent my being overwhelmed by their enthusiasm.

"Be careful of our heir," Tom said to the excited Philippe.

"The what?"

"Well, you're an heir, and Clare's baby will be our heir. The de Trafford heir."

The children laughed and scampered after the puppy. They looked sturdy, well, and happy—just as I'd seen them a year ago, before the awful tragedies that had cast deep shadows on their lives. As I looked at them, Tom seemed to know what I was thinking and took my arm.

"It's all over," he whispered. "They've forgotten."

Their father had forgotten too. Our gorgeous butterfly, the fairy prince, was honeymooning in the Caribbean with his new wife Alice—a charming socialite from Boston, to whom the children had taken immediately. She was just like their mother, everyone said.

Tom and I had come over to Port St Pierre on our way back from the States, where we'd spent six months, and we'd slept in the room where I thought I'd never sleep again. But the ghosts had gone—they'd been vindicated. The children had returned to Paris with their father at the same time we'd left Port St Pierre, and the château had been closed for the winter until the arrival of Alice had made Laurent want to open it up again, to banish the sadness.

The summer house had been levelled and made into an ornate garden with a fountain, and I'd been told that as the workmen had dug into the ruins they came across stones of such antiquity that there was no doubt they were part of the original château, just as Jeanne had said. The first thing we'd done on our return was to go to Jeanne's grave in the quiet little cemetery outside the town. How vivid were our memories of all that had gone before!

During the months away, we'd discussed Jeanne time and time again; we'd spoken to colleagues about her, but we had not come up with any real explanation, any final solution to the mystery. In my heart I felt that she had an extraordinary sympathy with Joan of Arc that gave her the powers she'd undoubtedly possessed. To some extent I felt she had foreknowledge of her early death but, like Joan, she didn't know how it would be. As it was, she had died in the noblest manner, saving the family; like her namesake, her courage was an example and an inspiration.

I thought of Jeanne with a great deal of veneration. My feelings about Rose were more complicated, as her motives were much more abstruse and difficult to define. One suspects that Jeanne knew Rose was up to no good and that Rose was either trying to get rid of Jeanne by spreading stories that would lead to her dismissal or by trying to cast some part of the blame on her.

I privately felt, in the light of my experiences, that the dead Rose had tried to avenge herself on those responsible and, through me, bring them to justice. Tom, of course, thought otherwise, and who could say which of us was right?

And my book? That had been difficult to write, and was still unfinished. I had excuses, of course—America and pregnancy, but the real reason was that I couldn't yet separate the two identities of Jeanne and Joan, and as I wrote about one I kept on seeing the other.

"You're day dreaming," Tom said. "Tired?"

"No, just thinking. We must get back, Tom. Michelle is coming to dinner. She's bringing a nice young doctor from her faculty in Amiens, and I'm hoping for big things."

"She's never got over Laurent," Tom said, as we turned towards the house.

"Oh, yes, she has; she's much too practical a girl. That was just fantasy. Laurent wasn't for her, or for me," I added slyly. "I'd never have made a marquise. Alice has the style and the inclination. She's also got money to enable the de Frigecourt family to continue their ducal kind of life."

"I should think the jewels would take care of that." Tom picked up a stick and threw it for the dog; the children were way down the bay now paddling in the warm pools.

"Oh, but they're heirlooms; you can't sell those, darling. I think Laurent's going to lend them permanently to the nation." The discovery of so much of the missing *Burgunderbeute*, though veiled in mystery as far as the public was concerned, had been one of the stories of the year. A fortune in jewels, uncut stones, rings, clasps and even some of the famous hats of Duke Charles, the last of the Valois dukes, encrusted with gems. The story was that they'd been hidden for centuries in the library, the oldest part of the house, and photographers came and took pictures of the panel in the alcove where the jewels had allegedly been found.

In fact, they'd been found in Henri's house, together with an amazing selection of old maps and documents that he'd amassed over the years in his quest for the missing fortune, as he'd gone from country to country, museum to museum, in search of the missing clue to the Valois dukes of Burgundy and their wealth.

252

Henri's body was yielded up by the sea near Dieppe, and a quiet ceremony preceded burial in the family vault in the church opposite the château. Laurent was grieved about his brother, but his feelings were undoubtedly mixed, and I imagine he put it all out of his mind as quickly as he could and went in search of a bride. Dear Laurent, ephemeral but charming, and always a friend.

Lisa vanished without a trace, and as for the rest of the business, as in any real life story , some things can be explained and some can't. Some events were obviously accidents—the boys' falls, for example—and some were clearly an attempt by Henri or his wife to destroy his family.

We who were closely involved knew this, but others could only guess. Everyone had said how ridiculous it was to have made a fire in the summer house in winter, when the chimney must have been clogged up with leaves and old birds' nests. But if the town and the citizens of Port St Pierre knew the truth, and I suspected they did, they stuck loyally to their premier citizen, their lord. The de Frigecourts, they reasoned, had had enough trouble already. Why should they have more?

"Tom, go after the children. I'll sit here for a while and wait for you." The exertion of the walk up the slight sandy hill had me puffing, and I sank onto the keel of an upturned boat, while Tom went off towards the shoreline. They had a new nanny now, a sensible girl from Harrogate with impeccable references, carefully chosen by me before we left for Chicago. She'd be helping to get their tea, and dear Madame Barbou would be doing her usual magical things in the kitchen.

I sniffed the air, utterly content. Yes, it was a heavenly day, hot, breezy, my beautiful bay at its shimmering best, just like this time last year. I glanced up at the château and the child in my womb seemed to jump in tune with the shock I had. By the window in Jeanne's old room, the turret room, now unused, I saw a movement; then a woman dressed in black appeared and stared out fixedly, first down at me and then over at the children splashing in the water. Despite the day, I felt my flesh grow so cold that goose pimples stood out on my bare brown arms.

I shielded my eyes from the sun and looked again, just to be sure, but there was no one there.